Consumed

Teri Bayus

Published by Siafu Productions, 2015.

CONSUMED

First edition. September 28, 2015.

Copyright © 2015 Teri Bayus.

ISBN: 979-8989800704

Written by Teri Bayus.

Table of Contents

Table of Contents 1

The Tao of Food 3

Nadailia 8

Chef Dylan 10

The Plain Master 13

The Five Elements 15

His Brother's Keeper 19

Recipes of Priceless Gold 21

The Donkey of Early Spring 26

Heart Sharing Swallows 30

Informing the Body 34

Pedro 37

Lauren 40

One Snake Head 43

Bamboos Converging on the Alter 47

Dipping Pelicans 54

Burning Entrée 58

The Soufflé Fell 66

Maman 75

Confusion 78

The Rescue 80

The Back of The Tiger 90

Returning to America 93

Seaside Resort 94

Fish Eye to Eye 98

Girl Talk 101

Joined Mandarin Ducks 106

Chopping 111

Silkworm Reeling 117

Shifting Turning Dragons 122

The Butterfly Opens 139

The Beast With Two Backs 145
Rear Flying Wild Duck 153
Kingfishers Intertwined 160
CTS 163
The Seagull Soars 165
The Paired Dance...168
The Wild Horse Leaps..175
The Pampered..184
Mean to Me...186
Rhythm of The Sea 191
Declarations...195
Monkey Springs 199
The Reveal..204
The Board 208
The Horses Shaking Hooves...209
Cicada Affixed 212
Dark Cicada Affixed 219
Mountain Goat Facing a Tree 222
The Tortoise Mounts 225
What Lies Beneath...230
The Phoenix Flutters..234
The Best of The Best...239
Fast Stepping Steed 244
Recumbent Covered Pine...249
The Greeks Have It...252
The Boy..257
The Monkey with Six Legs 260
Gamecock and Fowl Approach 266
A Great Bird Soars Over 273
A Phoenix Frolics 276
Wailing Monkey Embracing a Tree..................................278
The Dog of Early Autumn 282
The Master of the Cave...288

Strengthening the Bones..291
Blending the Conduits 296
Guess Who's Here for Dinner...................................299
The Stone Room 301
The Dragon Turns Over..304
The Tigers Tread 306
The Jade Stock 309
Fish with Scales Joined 311
Unicorn Horn 314
Exposed Fish Gills 317
The Buffet..319
Entanglement Revealed..325
Under The Cherry Tree..327
New Plateaus 330
The Climax...335
The Fight 337
Epilogue...342
Acknowledgements...343
About The Author..344
Connect With Teri..346
The Greatest Of Ease 347

Consumed

Teri Bayus

Dedication

To my muse, my inspiration and the love of my life. Thank you for sharing with me your passions. First there is truth, truth leads to trust, trust leads to love. There is no other way.

Prologue

Nadailia worked at the message, carefully making sure each word resonated with the passion from which she suffered.

To: Dylan

From: Nadailia

Regarding: Consumed

Dear Dylan,

I go to bed each night longing for you. I want to stumble into bed with you and make your body a road map that I learn by Braille. Every curve. Every edge. Every place that makes you tremble. I want your mouth to fill mine. I want your strong hands to touch me and squelch my desire, if only for a few hours.

The longing for my body to entwine with yours is dominated only by my mind's relentless need to meld with yours. Your food and your words inspired my lust. Now they are craved.

Like a starving beast, I return to our well of words to find a taste of you. I rake over the words, hoping for a seed of your desire for me.

It's been three months since we first shared food, words, passions, trust. We've built an empire of reasons to be together. To create. This seems to be the common thread: creation without conception.

I love all that we do and are. My body craves you. It's been torture from the start, as I would have taken you that first night. I felt the soul connection. I knew our bodies would heal and elevate each other.

I'm inappropriately drawn to you. There are times when the world falls away and I don't care about the ramifications; I want our bodies to join.

I can't sleep, and I needed you to know that you invade my every thought. Awake or in sleep, you are always there: the touches, the words, the kisses, and the food. The moments when we can be deliciously consumed. I hunger for you.

I am yours forever,

1

Nadailia

Alone with her thoughts, knowing she couldn't be with him, so she resolved herself to the fact that this was a permanent reminder of a temporary feeling. The sensation remained in her heart, in her loins and – most poignantly – in her brain. She knew a love affair that leaked from her brain to her heart was dangerous. She didn't want to damage or destroy the status quo. Her thoughts, her feelings, her pure desire for him was real. She had suffered for days without his touch. This passion suffering was a polite term for the torture her body and mind were experiencing. She tried to alleviate the tension with toys and multiple shower episodes, but the relief was not there. Each mental episode was not enough; her body craved him. She knew that whatever this was had entered a magical realm.

She had found the holy grail of a sexual muse, in a young chef.

This was the treasure of a lifetime. Something to be honored and revered.

Even if they never physically joined, this would be her sexual summit.

The Tao of Food

It was the best thing she ever put in her mouth. The taste and texture touched a long hidden pleasure center. She took it slowly, letting the experience lay bare and lock into her memory. The richness of the savory flavors, the sweet finish and the silky fervor was a sensation she cherished. It resembled an emotional awakening. She felt her cheeks flush and her toes curl in her Chanel stilettos.

She was seduced by this meal. It was an unusual combination of essences. She had to acknowledge that the erotic play going on underneath the table added to the experience. Her current "boy toy" was ascending up her bare thigh grazing the inside with the back of his hand. She let him climb higher lost in erotic eating.

An idea began to form. Sex and food was a formidable combination. Could she harness this in her new eatery?

Chef Dylan started the affair by sending out an amuse-bouche. It was meant to both cleanse and wake the palate and give the diner a glimpse into the soul of the chef. The raw Speciales Gillardeau oyster was rinsed in champagne and speckled with lime caviar. The taste of the sea soaked up the effervescence of the cava and married with tart orbs of citrus. The dish accomplished its goal of making Nadailia lust for more.

Then came the Foie Gras made from voluntary geese living freely in Spain. It rocked her culinary world. It was the essence of umami. Served braised with Panache tiger figs, sliced mangos, and a pomegranate infused balsamic vinegar on wilted spinach. It tasted of care and dexterity, like a skilled lover's touch. It caressed with sensuality the way it melted and carried the flavor.

The chef had not come out of the kitchen, so she imagined what he might look like. A schoolgirl fantasy formed as her amour dutifully kept her aroused by clandestine touches.

Nadailia's trance was broken as her date spoke.

"Good stuff?"

She blinked wanting to erase his words out of her reality. No small talk was allowed during this kind of gastronomic expedition.

"It's delectable."

"I guess. If you like weird food."

Nadailia started to defend the food, but refrained knowing with utter certainty that this would be the last time she laid eyes upon this embryonic eater. She flicked his hand off her thigh.

"What? You don't want me touching you? I thought you loved me?"

She sneered looking directly at him. "I hate all the men I love."

Chef Dylan peeked out from the kitchen. He wanted to witness this celebrity customer enjoying his meal. He aspired to cook in Nadailia's new restaurant and had prepared a feast guaranteed to impress even her developed palate.

"She's not smiling." Dylan worried.

His best friend Pedro peered out to watch Nadalia's reaction.

"Maybe she's a quiet lover?"

"What?"

"Chef, she's making love to your food. Look at the blush on her cheeks and how she's breathing shallow? She's aroused!"

"Are you sure it's not the boy toy?"

"Yes, he has nothing to do with that hidden smile she's wearing. Go introduce yourself."

"No, I'll meet her at the interview."

Pedro felt sad for his shy, young friend. As a man of passion, he headed toward her table. "I'm going in, I want to bask in that aura."

Chef Dylan returned to the stove to assemble the Trio of Causitas for his ovation. With the skill of an artist and the ache of a paramour, he assembled this impeccable dish.

He walked into the dry storage and grumbled at the rows of giant cans and coffins of chemically made comestibles. "Food should not come from a box." He mumbled. "My next kitchen will be filled with only fresh, real ingredients."

The waitress that had been actively pursuing Dylan joined him in the large closet.

"Are you talking to the food? Trying to seduce some flavor out of it?" She pined him against the wall wrapping a leg around his waist. "I can help."

He pushed her off.

"I don't have time for this. My future is riding on this meal tonight. Don't distract me!"

"I wasn't a distraction last night!"

"Yes, that's all you were." Dylan said stronger than was kind.

"I was hoping we could become more."

"It's the hope that causes pain."

Chef Dylan left the dry storage as the door closed behind him he heard her scream, "Asshole."

Pedro placed the Trio of Causitas in front of Nadailia and explained that this was a distinctly Peruvian dish. "Seasoned whipped cold potatoes are stacked with organic microgreens and then crowned with wild shrimp, king crab and ahi tuna tartar. Bon appetite, belle."

The dish featured three flavorful Peruvian potatoes; the famed papa amarilla, the huamantanga, considered to be the most delicious; and the huayro grown in the cold heights of the Andes. Three sauces were liberally drizzled on the potatoes, including rocoto[1] sauce, botija olives cream sauce, and huacatay sauce. It was a work of art to both the eye and the appetite.

Dessert was a Chocolate Torte; a cake so moist inside it was like pudding. Topped with candied pecans and served with jammed market figs floating in an anglaise sauce. If there was a dessert that seraph's make, this was it. Nadailia moaned with each bite. She no longer thought to share a scrap with her companion.

The key to success for her new restaurant was the right chef. After this meal she was certain that Chef Dylan had to be her executive chef. She had to possess him, to own him and discover this connection of nourishment and sensuality. He clearly knew that his food enticed the libido to join in the meal. She was disappointed that he had not come to the table, because that gesture would be required at her restaurant.

She took it upon herself after paying the bill to walk into the kitchen. As she threw the doors open, all activity stopped. The staff gazed on this brazen creature breaking the third wall of the restaurant.

"Chef Dylan?"

Pedro approached with a dazzling smile and bowed.

"Sorry my lady, chef has left the building."

"Tell him that meal was a fucking symphony. I want him."

Pedro grinned, "I will. He comes as a package with me. You want me?"

Smiling, she kissed Pedro straight on the mouth, "But of course, you are charming."

Pedro blushed surprised by the blatant act, "Senorita! My wife thinks so too."

"You get Chef Dylan to work for me and I will hire your entire family."

She turned on her Coco heels and left.

In the parking lot, her discarded escort leaned on her Jaguar with an impatient look. "Can we do In and Out on the way home? I'm hungry."

"Fuck you. Find your own way home."

She jumped in the car and drove away leaving him on the sidewalk.

Nadailia

"The passion of our imagination is only outdone when desire is matched with exquisite food. A great restaurant can be as wonderful an experience as sex," she preached with conviction to the board of directors. That one statement garnered their full, undivided attention. She followed it with; "I intend to create the most sensual, passionate and delicious experience for our clients. Every square inch of this restaurant will be designed for maximum pleasure and taste. We will call the restaurant: Consumed."

Nadalia's board was always impressed with her appetite for new projects. Her track record was flawless. She had never failed to fulfill her commitments to her company. Because of that, it was an easy and unanimous decision for the board. They enthusiastically agreed to support her idea for a new garden-to-table bistro called Consumed.

She had started the company with one small diner, using her husband's money. From those humble beginnings, she and the staff she drove relentlessly built an empire of four well known, five-star restaurants.

Now she was looking to test her creativity and passion in ways she had never before explored. Her goal was to hire an extraordinary new chef for her garden-to-table bistro and plant a fabulous garden, to be tended 365 days a year, adjacent to the restaurant. The organic garden and the new chef would be the secrets to yet another success.

Nadailia had a tall, lean, runner's body, which was strong but curvaceous. Her long, dark red hair had a curl to it that haloed around her face when she worked out. Her daily runs on the beach strengthened her body and cleared the clutter from her mind. She worked 18-hour days and then took more work home to complete at night while her husband slept. She was completely dedicated to her restaurants.

Her husband started off kind, but distant. Cold war was an apt description of their loveless marriage. Thirty years her senior, infirm and deteriorating mentally, he no longer even recognized her. He had been a cad with the ladies in the past. She always knew she was an appliance in his life. Before he turned ill, she played the dutiful wife role to maintain status quo. Now she paid nurses to do it and keep him comfortable.

Her mission was to get a young man and "teach" him the proper techniques involved in the act of sex. She had a dark side that simmered under the surface. She wanted to move on with her life; still being married to a Gollum of sorts was morally conflicting.

She had developed a self-protective habit of pushing potential friends and love interests away so that she would never feel abandoned. Only her best friend, Lauren, knew her secrets. Big secrets.

She had never had an orgasm.

She was determined to change that.

Chef Dylan

Nadailia sighed as she closed *Chez Pannise Café Cookbook,* by Alice Waters. After so many years on the business end, she had recently discovered cooking as a creative outlet. She was beginning to understand the sensuality of food and was fascinated to learn more. Her new restaurant would offer this kind of cuisine. Everything she served would be fresh and wonderful, grown in the chef's garden out back. To accomplish this she would need an impeccable executive chef. She thought she might have found one. Chef Dylan was all the rage in town, although she heard he could be high strung. Possibly, she thought, he was still young enough to be controlled. After the first meal of his she tasted, she didn't care what kind of trouble he made for her. He didn't know it yet, he was going to help her secure her future.

In the interview Chef Dylan talked too much. He was clearly nervous. He rambled on about Maman, his French mother, and about his dad, an American industrial chemist, and how they brought him up on a farm. He believed that because of his Maman's cultural taste for food and wine and his dad's knowledge of chemical compounds, he had been destined to be a chef. His dad died when he was a teenager. Dylan had taken on responsibility for Stu, his younger brother, who was now in law school. Dylan was paying Stu's tuition and expenses. Dylan had never been free to pursue his own dreams. He had always been someone else's support system. This job, he believed, would offer him freedom.

He rambled on while Nadailia scribbled notes and noticed his hunky frame, his blue eyes and the passion in his nervousness. She liked what she saw.

After his father died, his mother moved back to France, where she lived on a pittance. He went on about his Maman living in Marseille and behaving like an artist, although never making any money from her art. He was momentarily lost in thought, and then he continued, "She spends the small amount of money she receives from Dad's Social Security within the first two weeks of each month. Mostly on expensive wines. Then she hits me up for money."

"So, your mother knows wine. How is *your* palate?"

"Outstanding! I have been drinking wine we could not afford since I was a toddler. I find one of my gifts in the kitchen is wine pairing."

"Your Maman served you well." Nadailia smiled and noted to take him wine tasting to test this palate.

"She taught me to cook, the French way. For that I am grateful, but feel responsible for her. My brother appreciates me financing his schooling and wants to make it on his own, but he can't. Stu and I meet twice a month for dinner. He gets a great meal, and it gives me the opportunity to try out new recipes."

Dylan was as handsome as he was talented. He nervously kept talking about his love of soccer, which he still played. Nadailia's figured that was how he maintained that 6'1", chiseled hard body. She noticed his natural grace. It must be the French genes, she thought. She caught herself staring at his piercing blue eyes and dark, wavy hair. She imagined he never had any difficulty bedding any lady he wanted.

He continued, talking fast, "For now, I only want to create in your kitchen. I'd love to cook for you again; I mean cook for your new garden-to-table bistro.

'Cook for me?' She hoped she was reading the right amount of innuendo into that comment.

The Plain Master

After their meeting, Dylan did some research on his potential new boss. Restaurants are notorious gossip centers, and he discovered much about Ms. Nadailia.

Nadailia was the owner of four of the biggest and best restaurants in the area. The word on the street was that she was looking for not only a new restaurant but also a new distraction. The rumors were that she had had flings with many on her staff, but dumped them immediately after the situation became intimate. The gossipers relished sharing with Dylan their analysis. She believed it was impossible for anyone to love her. She believed they only wanted her money and power. Her beliefs might be rooted in the fact that her father left when she was only four years old. The bastard up and disappeared.

Her mom died two years later, possibly of a broken heart. She was raised in the foster care system and never found a truly loving family. Her mom had been a professional dancer, her father a writer. She saw them as saints and wanted to be as gifted as her parents. She possibly overcompensated by building businesses to hide her self-perceived lack of artistic talent. She had dabbled in writing and enjoyed it but was afraid to allow anyone to read what she wrote. She was terrified that she might not be good at it and others would ridicule her.

Dylan was disappointed to hear she had a husband. He caught himself wondering what her lips would taste like, but stopped that thought before it developed into a full-blown fantasy. She was married. Her husband was much older than her and rumored to be suffering from dementia and was not an active participant in her life. Yet, the fact remained that she was married. Dylan loved and protected his family. He wouldn't break up a family, no matter what the circumstances.

The Five Elements

The restaurant open date had been set, the garden planted only thing missing was the chef. Nadailia's anticipation of the coming meal was palpable. She eagerly awaited meeting him and discussing the food, its origins and its preparation. She also wanted to size him up. This new chef came with great references, and she was interested in seeing how he would utilize the fresh produce from the prolific garden behind the restaurant. Auditioning a new chef was always like a first date for her. She was excited to sample his culinary mastery using her garden.

He seemed a bit intimidated by her. Within the first two minutes of meeting him, she knew she wanted to fuck him, but a serious affair would be impossible. Maybe one thrilling night she thought. She was okay with that, as most chefs were so high strung that what started out as a fuck became an overly dramatic affair and always ended in flames.

She had called him back after the interview and asked him to cook for her as the second part of the interview process. He would be able to use the cook's garden. Dylan was confident he could secure the job with a classic Italian meal. He cooked all day, lit the candles and arranged everything flawlessly in preparation for her arrival.

Nadailia was wrapped up tight in her navy Theory business suit. Dylan thought the suit jacket looked binding, so he offered her a kimono to wear while she dined. She thought the suggestion was ludicrous, halfway through the meal, she wished she had obliged him.

"Welcome to your restaurant," he said as he pulled out her chair. The chivalry instantly stirred something in her.

"I am excited to try you out," she replied.

He laughed at the innuendo, and she blushed. It was the first time she had blushed in years, and it threw her slightly off balance.

Dylan opened the meal with a bottle of Terrabianca 2009 Campaccio Toscana. This Italian varietal was nice and bold, with the forward taste of Cabernet. It paired perfectly with the first course, a Caprese salad constructed of his homemade fresh mozzarella, garden cherry tomatoes and freshly picked basil, drizzled with Robbins Family Farm extra virgin olive oil and a bit of balsamic vinegar. He knew that the secret of a great Caprese is the proportions, and his were impeccable.

Next, he served Involtini di Melanzane, a brilliant, thinly sliced eggplant rolled with Gruyère cheese and prosciutto. It was surprising and delightful; she was beginning to fall in love with this chef's food.

Next was Spaghettini Carbonara, which was her favorite Italian dish. After two weeks of traveling in Italy, she rarely experienced it prepared correctly stateside. His was. Thin, hand-cut, freshly made spaghettini noodles tossed with raw eggs, then tossed with prosciutto pieces fried in garlic and olive oil. Sprinkled with Parmigiano-Reggiano cheese, and magic was made. She knew that heaven would taste like this. Simple, delicious and elegant.

She saw him watching her eat. She figured he was visualizing the scene from *Lady and the Tramp;* all she wanted to do was put her foot in his lap. The Risotto con Funghi di Stagione came next, with savory seasonal mushrooms nestled in perfectly done Arborio rice. His fresh focaccia bread was perfect for dipping and savoring. Next he served a homemade tiramisu that was a work of art. It was made of ladyfingers dipped in coffee, layered with a whipped mixture of eggs, sugar and mascarpone. The final dish was a Pera al Vino Rosso, thinly sliced pears with wine. The sweetness tingled on her lips.

After the meal, he offered her a glass of Italian Prosecco and a moonlit tour of the chef's garden. She hadn't been in the garden since it was planted. Strolling and talking about his plans and plants, she tripped in a gopher hole. He moved gracefully and caught her in a tango-like grip. She felt his strong arms and rock-hard torso. He loved the feel of her body next to his. Her smell was intoxicating. Her hair brushed his face, and he found his lips inches from hers. Their eyes locked, and his smile resembled a cocky grin. Before she could regain her balance, Dylan, almost reflexively, kissed her neck. Nadailia was at first surprised, she did not resist. She loved the tenderness and appetite his lips imparted to her bare décolletage.

In her mind she blamed it on the wine, her body was leading this expedition into desire. With each moment, their passion grew. She knew that if she didn't put a stop to this, they would be tearing each other's clothes off with no regard to work or consequences. Part of her wanted this. Part of her feared this. For unexplainable reasons, she stopped and told him, "I can't; I am married." The door shut on his passion like a bank vault. He took her hand and walked to her town car and bid Nadailia adieu.

At home she took a shower with her trusty dildo and played to the many thoughts and images of him. She stood under the water of the shower and changed it from hot to cold. The raw sense of feeling on her skin was inspired by these differing degrees of temperature. She felt scalded, healed and purified. She slowly took the water from the coldest setting to the hottest. Afterward she lay on her bed, wet and dripping, breathing hard and praying for the longing to subside. It did not.

Her phone sounded the text tone, and she was sure it was her best friend, Lauren, looking for a report on the evening. She looked and was stunned to see it was Dylan.

First Text:

Dylan: Hello dream boss.

Nadailia: Weird night.

D: Why? Because we are attracted to each other?

N: No, I want to relive tonight and move forward, it's dangerous.

D: Was it fun?

N: Yes, I have never been so affected by someone's touch. I felt like I was 16. You had me shaking when you kissed my neck.

D: I enjoyed our embrace. Been replaying it in my mind with a bottle of wine.

N: The meal was miraculous.

D: I liked holding you.

N: I was trembling.

D: You were great.

N: Your touch was so tender, yet strong. I was sure my driver could see and feel my heat.

D: You were very controlled.

N: I really want to hire you.

D: I liked your naked neck against my lips.

N: I felt you. But.......

D: But what?

N: I want to hire you. But no more hanky-panky.

D: I would fuck you stone cold sober.

N: OMG! Watch your dirty mouth.

D: Yes Ma'am. Did you like the food?

N: You are an inspiration. I am beyond impressed.

D: So I have the job?

N: Consider this my formal offer. But, no more kissing.

His Brother's Keeper

The next night he fixed his brother, Stu, a magnificent meal. First course was Chickpea Fries. To make these, Garbanzo beans are mushed down to a paste, formed into French-fry shape, breaded with a garlic-herb mixture and then deep-fried. Dylan's were served with a calabrian chile aioli that was hot and addictive. Next was Barbecued Pig Wings. Stu was told to imagine that if pigs could fly, this is where the wings would come from. That is what this dish is all about – a pig wanting to be a chicken. Under-the-rib meat, seared and cooked slowly on the barbecue, like a distinctive version of pork belly. It was served with a whimsical accompaniment of celery pieces and Bay Blue cheese with grilled nectarine, lima beans and micro greens.

Stu was once again sure his brother was a culinary genius.

Next came the Mushroom Toast. Stu was told to expect breakfast, lunch and dinner in this one dish. He remarked that it had a perfect presentation. A large piece of brioche toast stacked with mushrooms, Parmesan shavings and crème fraîche. It was topped with a poached egg that exploded like a little whale getting ready to breach out of the water, spilling forth its yellowy goodness. It was marvelous; all at once it was a savory breakfast, lunch and dinner.

For dessert they had Peach Sundae with Blondie (a white brownie), with fresh peach slices, butter pecan ice cream and a bourbon maple sauce, served in a parfait glass with real whipped heavy cream on the top. The presentation was as luscious as the indulgence.

After dinner, Stu could see his brother was preoccupied. Dylan kept picking up his phone and checking for messages.

"What has got you nervy?"

"I met a lady. She had me cook for her."

"I am sure you dazzled her. She take you home?"

"Actually it was a job interview, and I think I almost blew it."

Stu knew one thing was for sure about Dylan: He never blew a meal.

"Not even possible."

"She liked the food; it was my behavior that may have blown my chance."

Stu opened another bottle of wine and said, "Details, I want graphic details."

Recipes of Priceless Gold

The next two weeks flew by as Nadailia and Dylan created, tested and tried hundreds of dishes. The chemistry between them was palpable, and the kitchen staff was betting on when they would catch them fucking in the dry storage.

They were both ecstatic about the partnership and jumped out of bed each morning, excited to spend the day creating. Together, a real trust was being formed. Nadailia told him they were going to start going out together to taste the other chefs in town, to get ideas and inspiration. Dylan hoped it was another excuse to be together. They met at a new Cajun style restaurant for their first meal out. It was one of Nadailia's favorites, and she wanted to share the flavors with him.

She always started with the garlic soup. She dreamt about this dish and was afraid it would never pass her lips again every time she finished it. Dylan agreed it was fantastic, perfection in a bowl, as his foot found hers under the table. Even the slightest touch through the leather of their shoes sent tidal waves of energy exploding within them. The reduced garlic served in a cream sauce with Creole croutons and Parmesan sprinkled on top made them both moan with pleasure, or maybe it wasn't the soup. The chef, Rick, also made the best rolls in the world, and Nadailia tried like crazy not to fill up on them. Jalapeño-cheese rolls. Georgia sweet potato muffins. And Rick's hot buns were an unsurpassed yeasty surprise.

Dylan ordered Seafood and Smoked Sausage Gumbo. A New Orleans treat with shrimp, mussels, oysters and andouille sausage with Savannah red rice and pickled jalapeño remoulade, it tasted as good as meals Dylan had had in the South. He spoon fed her, and the intimacy of him touching her lips paralyzed her. They tried the Louisiana Blackened Sea Bass Salad with baby greens and red wine mustard vinaigrette. The fish was flawlessly cooked and seasoned with the right amount of heat.

Dessert was a Six Layer Sweet Potato Pecan Cake with cream cheese frosting. The pecan cake was a Southern delight with a combo of sweet, salty and creamy. They also shared the coconut cake, which was impeccable, made with Foxen Chenin Blanc wine in the cake mix, layered with a fresh coconut icing and sprinkled with fresh coconut shavings. Nadailia took a bite and grabbed Dylan's knee in a fervent outburst that surprised her.

The conversation was all about food and wine with a ton of lightly covered erotic inference. They would lock eyes and the world would fall away. Nadailia had to shake her head to regain composure. When Chef Rick came to the table, he instantly sensed their chemistry and teased Nadailia about her new boy toy.

"What is the name of your new enterprise?"

Nadailia stumbled at the irony of his question and answered, "Consumed. Erotic Eatery."

Chef Rick threw his head back with a loud laugh, "Perfect, you have always needed this."

This was not the impression she wanted the world to have. She needed to curb this energy with her new chef.

After the meal, Dylan was seated next to her in her town car. "Somehow I am relating cooking well to pleasing you. It is driving me. I am now trying to craft each sauce and dish as if I am giving you a personal, guided tour of my story line. I have the cooking skill set; now I am learning the passion from you.

Nadailia smiled and touched his thigh. "I like that. I am afraid people will see our desire for each other. Then I have to remember that only you and I are privy to this passion."

Dylan took her hand and kissed it, she pulled away.

He was undeterred. "When I am creating in the kitchen, I feel like I am leading you through the menu by the hand, and I stop and say, "Now look what she is tasting, look what she is doing, look what she is feeling."

Nadailia nodded. "It is exactly that. But no one else can know. And we haven't done anything inappropriate, we can't let the rumors start."

Dylan exploded passionately, "Oh, fuck them! Who cares? We are great at this. You have helped me begin to understand not only how to craft a perfect meal, how to put myself in the moment, in the dish and how to relate my feelings to the customer. Even more, how to elicit an emotional response through food."

Nadailia leaned her head on his shoulder. "Running a restaurant is a lonely act. That is why it has been so special having you with me on this romp. I sometimes feel like I am stealing from you."

Dylan kissed her head. "Boss, I have a lot of confidence in you and your ability."

"Thank you. I needed to hear that."

"You can't steal what is freely given."

The driver pulled up to his house, and Dylan turned to her and said, "I like the name. It fits the restaurant, even us: Consumed. Tonight was the first time I heard the premise. Erotic eating. Did we skip a part here?"

Nadailia reached over his lap and opened the door. "We are getting there."

Text

Dylan: Thanks for tonight. Food was amazing. Boss was more so. How is the menu and planning going? Will you send it to me?

Nadailia: I will, after I have polished it.

D: You don't want me to help?

N: What if you hate it?

D: No pressure AT ALL on your restaurant, you handle that in the way that is most comfortable for you.

N: It is our restaurant. This is much a team effort.

D: Boss, I'm not going to hate anything you do. I see how you create. I love your style, your passion and your openness. It's your restaurant. I am merely here to provide inspiration, to be your muse.

N: Thank you for that. Can we bundle you up and keep you under my desk?

D: Hahaha.

N: I promise to feed you. But you have to fuck me endlessly.

D: I like the terms you set forth.

N: When you are cooking next at home, I want you to make it sensual.

D: I am going to create a new dish tomorrow with only sex with you in mind.

N: I want you to feel the crispness of the ingredients, taste the filling as it marries the flavors together.

D: I have always thought of cooking as a mechanical process. Maybe like some view sex.

N: I want you to rub your crotch on the warm oven, and then move over to the freezer.

D: It's not mechanical. It's sensual, it's earthy. It is creative. You are helping me to understand this now.

N: I want you to feel the raw ingredients in your mouth and then see the difference after heat is applied.

D: Mmmmmmmmm.

N: It is as close to sex as you can get.

D: I never knew that. Until you.

N: I want you to open our best bottle of wine, and savor the flavor between bites. I want your description of the food to be sexual.

D: I've always enjoyed the sensual and erotic side of food. Now I see the comparisons.

N: Fire, heat, cold, wet, hard. Then, you are to write it for our menu.

D: And dutifully report to you?

N: That is right!

D: I have only one goal in my cooking now. To make a dish so delicious that I make the boss cum.

The Donkey of Early Spring

They went to a wine event together. The evening began with passed appetizers, White Gazpacho with Marcona almonds and chive oil, Caprese Brochettes with garden mint, and Sweet Corn Empanadas with a cilantro chimichurri. Empanadas were one of Nadailia's favorite foods, stemming from her Portuguese foster mom. Chimichurri was the one thing she brought back from Brazil. She wanted it on the menu, so she forced Dylan to try several. He agreed it is a sauce known to have been favored by the gods. Chimichurri is made from finely chopped parsley, garlic, olive oil, oregano, vinegar and a slew of the chef's favorite spices. These appetizers were paired with free-flowing exclusive Chamisal Chardonnay.

They were seated at long tables that provoked new friendships and lively conversation. Nadailia all but ignored Dylan; above the table. She talked to the handsome banker across from him and his plastic wife. Dylan was on her right and snuck continual touches to the inside of her knee with his strong hands. He felt the sharp intake of her breath as he stroked the inside of her thigh.

The first dish was Oak Seared Neiman Ranch Pork Loin with a Diablo sauce. They both were impressed with the savory flavors. Next was Rosemary Charred Free Range Chicken with a mesquite honey glaze, and Wild Mushroom Paella with chorizo, garden peppers and melted leeks. Dylan explained to her that paella, when done with a master hand like this chef's, is an awe-inspiring culinary event. He squeezed her thigh while proclaiming this fact. They served salad last, an organic heirloom tomato salad with shaved fennel and barrel-aged feta cheese, all sitting on organic arugula with shallot vinaigrette. This was served with Hush-Harbor rustic bread with a Bella Vista olive oil dipping sauce. All paired well with a Chamisal Estate Pinot Noir that stood up to the strong aromas.

Feeling full and a bit drunk, they went to her car, after air-kissing the chef and the winemaker goodbye.

In the car Dylan continued rubbing, sliding his hand higher up her thigh. She did not resist, his hand was burning a fire into her strong legs. She did not react. They sat like schoolchildren, erect and at attention, while their minds went to thoughts of long hours ravaging each other.

She turned to him. "I can't do this. It is exhausting wanting you and not having you. I get that you have a problem that I am married. I get that you are a good son. But damn it, I want you and I am used to getting what I want."

He looked at her, incredulously, thinking, 'How can someone so smart be so thick?'

"I get it; I will back off. Just boss and her boy from now on."

They dropped him at his house and he started to work on the menu on his laptop. Soon he saw an email from her.

To: Dylan

From: Nadailia

Regarding: Consumed

Dylan,

As you have seen, my brain is wired differently than most. It is creative, engaging and looking for new challenges all the time. It never takes the easy path.

You have already witnessed a sampling of my brain seepage. It can be surprisingly blunt and absolute. Then there are times that I'm filled with a longing; a lust so powerful, I'm sure it could fuel rockets.

With everyone else in my life, I have to watch my words, redirect my passion and carefully express myself. With you, I feel you can handle my truths, my exaggerations for the sake of telling a story, my verbal challenging. With you, I can tell the truth, stretch it for dramatic effect and share my emotional words. Please let me continue.

Take my words for the blunt truth that they are, a truth that is translucent.

Know that I want you and this partnership to go on forever. That is my dream. My one true wish is that we have this for a long time, learning, growing and creating.

When I tell you things, it is because they are swirling around in my head looking for a landing pad. You are the safest descent I've ever had, so I apologize if my thoughts are too heavy or incendiary. I do not ever mean to be cruel or in any way send negativity your way. You are the only place where my words are safe. You seem to draw out of my soul the raw material that has been looking for a safe place to endure.

When I said it was exhausting wanting you, I meant to say that all this unfulfilled passion is beginning to eat at me. That desiring someone is work. A chore I'm enjoying and yet feeling overwhelmed by the passion of it.

What we are doing is a dangerous game. We have done nothing wrong. There is an off-balance tip of the reward-to-risk scale.

If the main reason you do not want this to turn into a physical affair is because I am married, then tell me that. I do respect you for being an outstanding human being. I still struggle with that decision. So, like you, I'm on the fence. Except at night. Then, it is all I can do not to attack you.

Meanwhile, I work, you cook. With all this unrequited passion. I'm conflicted. Consumed.

I'm yours.

Nadailia

Heart Sharing Swallows

When her town car picked him up, she was wearing a short skirt and strappy camisole and her wild hair was loose and full of curls. She had told him they were going to try her favorite taco stand. It had no inside seating, but an authentic wooden-table patio. The owner, Jose, explained that this was Mexico City cuisine, so no rice, chips, guacamole or filler, just fresh food. Even the salsa is made in small batches, not stored in big buckets like at many other restaurants.

They started with the Alambre Plate that was a sizzling platter of shredded beef, bacon pieces, ham fragments, bell peppers, onions, cilantro and chipotle, all covered with a queso fresco and served with salsa, fresh pinto beans and blue corn tortillas. The flavors swimming in the melted cheese shocked Dylan. The complexities of the savors were as exciting as his boss returning the leg play under the table. He was awed by the brilliance of this chef.

They shared a Negra Modelo, Dylan loving their lips touching the same surface. He had started kneading her thighs, and she had accepted this as the only touch she would get from him. The power of his touch still incited her to waves of passion.

The Aztec Tacos were thick, house-made, blue corn tortillas wrapped around dried pasilla chiles with cheese inside and wet Azteca salsa, queso fresco, red onion and cilantro. They created a symphony of real mainland Mexican flavors, which Dylan had longed for but had never found here in the States.

Jose explained how they find the freshest of fruit, seafood and meat, and how they make their own marinated carrots and jalapeños. They talked for an hour about his techniques and his knowledge of this amazing style of food. Dylan instantly respected his passion and desire to create this cuisine that can reach deep down into a person's soul. He was beginning to learn this from Nadailia. From a carafe of the freshest strawberry juice, to the making of each tortilla and torta, there were no cans in this kitchen, only food constructed by connoisseurs.

They sipped like teens on a piña colada. Two straws in a whole pineapple shell filled with fresh coconut water, pineapple juice and a wine-based liquor was as refreshing as it was beautiful. Next they tried Hawaiian Tacos, featuring el pastor meat and grilled pineapple slices in those miraculous blue corn tortilla shells that also held bell peppers, red onions, cilantro and queso fresco. That aromatic, sweet surprise dripped down their arms, and he resisted the temptation to lick her wrist.

Nadailia was wiping the fire sauce from her lips, which were so swollen from the chiles that Dylan could barely take his eyes off them. He had not tasted them yet, but it was the one taste he longed to try.

Nadailia shook her head, smiled and touched his foot with hers.

Buoyed by the food and the colada, they climbed into the town car. This time she took his thigh in her hands and started to work one hand toward his crotch. Dylan kissed her neck and went to take her head in his hands to finally kiss her, when the car phone rang. The driver said in a polite but firm tone, "Madam, you need to go home. There is a problem with your husband."

As they drove toward his house, she marveled in her mind, the touching had been mind-blowing. She held his hand, it seemed they were having the same thoughts as he rubbed inside her wrist.

Energy and light beams were dancing through her soul. It was perfect, better than imagined. She couldn't believe she felt so much from so little contact. She believed that this had sealed the fact that they would be lovers for a long time.

But they did not kiss.

He let out a sigh. "I knew we would be good at this."

She rolled her head to his chest, listening to his heartbeat. She whispered, "Consume me."

He was shocked at this request, as they were in her car, with her driver, on the way to some emergency at home.

She needed him to release her so bad; she didn't care if they were on a stage.

"Take my nipple in your fingers and pinch it. Over and over. As hard as you can. And kiss my neck again."

He reached for her nipple. It sprang free from her shirt as if it had been waiting for him to come rescue it. He took it with his thumb and forefinger and started to rub. She moaned and threw her head back. He started with her neck – biting, kissing, owning her. She was covered with chills and electricity. He placed his other hand inside her bra and began to squeeze, twist and tease. Nadailia reacted immediately to this, panting. They returned to necking as she placed her hand inside his thigh, rubbing through his pants and feeling for the first time the size of his now throbbing cock. He whispered, "I want you more than I ever wanted anything. Please let me make love to you. At least give me a proper kiss."

Just then the car stopped. They were at his apartment. Dylan got out and adjusted himself as Nadailia stepped out of the car to hug him. "We have to wait; this is dangerous."

As the car pulled away from his house, she looked at herself in the mirror and was shocked by the reflection. She was flushed and looked more beautiful than she had seen herself in years. Then the rational brain took over. She had a thousand reasons why this would never happen again. "He is an employee; he is too young," she murmured unconvincingly to no one.

Later that night, she got a text from him.

Text

Dylan: I'm liking these car rides.

Nadailia: That was unexpected.

D: Do I need to apologize?

N: No, I am a big girl, I participated willingly.

D: Can I cook for you tomorrow at my home?

N: I'd love you to. You do cook from a magical place. I never had any idea food could be this sensual.

D: Same here.

N: It is the rawest form of intimacy I have ever felt.

D: I think, for me, I have never felt safe enough with anyone to express myself and put myself out there.

N: I haven't either.

D: I think cooking is one of the most sensual acts possible.

N: I agree, and a simple kiss.

D: That would be amazing.

N: We will get there. We have to be careful.

D: I want you.

N: I know.

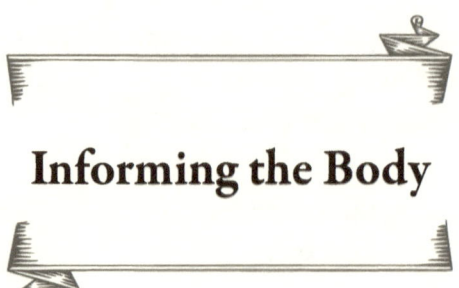

Informing the Body

After the fireworks and intense energy of their last encounter, her need for him intensified. She had never been able to bring herself to what she believed was completion, even using toys or water. It was only a small relief. It was never the sensation her friends described or what she read about in novels. The showerhead had always been her favorite faux lover, and she enjoyed a multi-speed, directional water flow. After years of fueling her imagination and turning the aqua goddess into a pulsating pleasure transmitter, she now left the shower unspent.

Her need for him was so grand, only his physical presence could bring her relief. And they hadn't even kissed yet. All that was needed was a touch, a phrase and a stolen blush, and she would come undone.

She was afraid of this power he had over her. Knowing that so little from him could give her so much. He would write sexy texts every day that were so sensual and cerebral that they filled all her pleasure centers. Then he would see her, feigning unfamiliarity that insulted her. Then sneak a touch so intimate and knowing that it would make her swoon. He would grab her leg under the table at a restaurant. Not a caress like an amateur lover, but forcefully pull her leg open and hold it there. These things drove her wild and made her know for certain that they would copulate like prizefighters.

She'd had too much wine that night, and the need for him intensified. She grabbed her phone and decided it was time to up the ante.

Text

Nadailia: Are you there?

Dylan: I am. What are you doing?

N: I am here and all yours.

D: Comfy?

N: I am. No bra or panties, silk kimono on.

D: Sounds yummy. I'm in bed.

N: I want to be in bed with you.

D: Yes. Tell me about your day.

N: I woke up shaking with desire for you. Literally quivering.

I couldn't get the food and your touch out of my mind.

D: What did you do?

N: First I went back to bed.

D: Hahaha.

N: I lay down on my stomach and recalled the back seat of the town car.

D: That is a good memory.

N: I got on all fours, put the big vibrator on my clit and pretended you where behind me, fucking me.

D: You'd like me dominating you?

N: Very much.

D: Sounds delicious. That made me hard.

N: When the moon is full, I become the lust monster and insatiable.

I want YOUR touch.

D: You need a huge hard cock stabbing your pussy.

N: I do, for hours.

D: Mmmmmmmm.

N: Then I had a bunch of appointments. I drove my Jaguar. I needed gas, so I drove into the drive-thru car wash. I thought to myself, "Dylan would fuck me here."

D: Yes I would.

N: As the windows filled with foam, I hiked up my skirt.

D: Ohhhhhh.

N: I pushed the Lelo vibrator that I always keep in my purse into me and rubbed my clit.

D: Mmmmmmmm.

N: Thinking of me on top of you. It took thru the second cycle, but as the dryer began to blow and the water stopped, I came, a bit.

D: Damn.

Ummmm, I got to go.

Talk with you tomorrow.

And he was gone. She was not sure if she took it too far and scared him away. Damn lust monster.

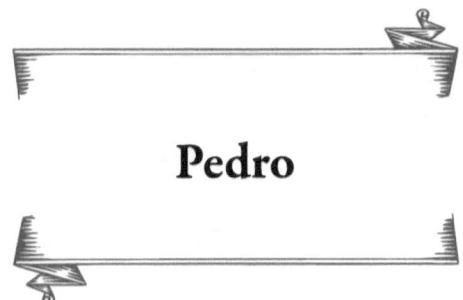

Pedro

P edro was a no-nonsense waiter whom Dylan had worked with many times. Playing the part of Dylan's best friend, Pedro loved to hear about his wild adventures. Mostly they were about cooking and new things he tried; occasionally he got to live vicariously through his friend's sexual escapades with a waitress.

He remembered the first introduction of Nadailia and Dylan, so he wanted to know how the "audition" went. Pedro was an older Spanish gentleman who was full of life – fun and flirty. He had a wife and three daughters, making family his priority. He did get away with murder at work, because he was comical and charming. Everyone loved him, and Dylan considered him his father figure. They had shared two bottles of Spanish Cava when Pedro finally asked.

"So tell me about the the interview meal? Did Nadailia like it?"

"I'm pretty sure."

"What?"

"She ran out."

"Why? I have never seen Nadailia run. What did you do? Put a spider in the dessert?"

Dylan was not sure whether to confide in his friend, he trusted Pedro not to gossip. He told him all the details and showed him that last text.

Pedro was shocked. "I never saw that coming."

"Neither did either of us."

"Wow! Things got complicated." Pedro was shaking his head and remembering the days when passion ruled his life with his wife. He smiled at the memory. "As a gentleman, you need to call her."

"I can't do that." The thought of talking to her made Dylan's knees weak.

"Don't be an ass; call the lady. Maybe she'll fire you so you can have a fantastic affair."

Text

D: I am drunk, what are you doing?

N: Thinking about your meal.

D: What is your fantasy?

N: A tub filled with truffles.

D: A real fantasy.

N: A man shopping, cooking, cleaning and rubbing my feet?

D: A sexual fantasy.

N: Really? We don't know each other that well and I am your boss. There will be no more touching.

D: But last night you told me your fantasy in words. Words don't hurt anything.

N: I was drunk. That won't happen again.

D: What is your fantasy?

N: Necking in the garden is my new favorite. You?

D: I am going to cover you in food and then lick you from top to bottom.

N: Hmmmmmmmmmmm.

D: You want details?

N: No, Yes, No, Yes. This seems highly inappropriate.

D: So was necking in my squash.

N: I love that memory.

D: Want me to cook you something sexy?

N: Yes!

D: Ok, tomorrow my place, 6 o'clock, leave your inhibitions behind. Wear something sexy.

N: The rules: No touching!

D: Not even a bit?

N: Promise, no touching or I am not coming.

D: You will cum.

Lauren

Nadailia invited her best friend, Lauren, over to drink a new wine find and to unload about Dylan. Lauren was a creative soul who owned a Burner boutique; a store dedicated to all things Burning Man 365 days a year. She was a hippy queen, and they had been best friends since kindergarten. She knew everything about Nadailia, she was frustrated by the fact that all Nadailia did was work and still had not known the power of *la petite mort*. She felt that all Nadailia's money was worthless if she didn't have a bit of passion. Nadailia had been adamant in the past that passion was a useless distraction.

She gave Lauren the blow-by-blow of the dinners, the back of the car, and then let her read a few texts. Then Nadailia did something she never did; she spewed emotion. Lauren sat there transfixed.

"I was drowning in desire for this man. All I could think about was his touch on my scorching skin, his breath coming in hot gasps in my ear. Then it was the taste of the food. A silent prayer of a flavor, better than chocolate and stimulating every taste bud. As if I were so hungry and yet too full to eat. My stomach felt sick, full, and longing to be rubbed.

"Wow! He really got to you. When are you going to see him? You are not going to keep him on as chef?"

"I see him tomorrow, and yes, he is the best, in every form, so of course I am going to keep him. I can manage this; I can stay hands off."

Lauren knew the sound of someone trying to fool herself.

Nadailia continued, "I can't focus. I got lost driving in a town where I have spent my whole life. I'm floored by my reaction. He is too young. My desire clouds my mind and takes my breath away. I know you said that desire is something we lose track of as we age. I remember this feeling as a teen, remember Don Famy? But, after years of being strong, calm and professional, this wave of desire not only took me by surprise but also floored me into decisions that only a lunatic would make.

You have to admit his texts are hot."

"Show me another one."

Text

N: I am flummoxed by this.

D: We will use this motivation to make the best restaurant anywhere.

N: I thought of you all day. This is unknown territory.

D: For me too.

N: I am obsessed with this right now, and it is motivating me like nothing else.

D: We have to overcome this.

N: I was sure if you touched me I would explode.

I like our little secret – it has to be ours.

God I loved touching you.

D: Yes. No chances of the staff finding out about us.

N: You make me tremble. I am not sure I can remember the food. I can give a blow-by-blow of every time you touched me.

D: I need to see you again. Alone.

N: We must be smarter and position ourselves so we can hide our touches.

Damn I wish you would get out of my loins.

I can't seem to stop squiggling, thinking about you.

D: Ok. Go to bed.

N: Dream of me sucking your cock.

D: I will.

Lauren smiled and handed the phone back. She knew her friend was on the fast track to desire, and that made her happy.

Dylan called his brother and told him about the texts. His brother advised him not to see her anymore or quit the job.

Dylan reacted powerfully. "Are you fucking kidding me? This new boss is beyond hot. I have never experienced such control. Wow! Each time I think of her, I get rock hard. I almost burned the head of my dick on the oven. I am keeping the job. I know she won't let me touch her again. She was playing with me, like a cat with a mouse. I need this job, so No. More. Fucking. With. The. Boss."

One Snake Head

N adailia was in her office working on the menu and schedule. She gazed at the couch where Dylan was sitting for a meeting with the staff that ended an hour ago. While the department heads gave their reports, she had spread her legs, giving him a glance at her lace panties. It was dangerous behavior; she was exhilarated and could not help herself.

She went to sit on the couch and texted him:

N: You there?

D: Thank you for the flash you gave me in your office.

N: I am sitting there now. It is fun trying to figure out new ways to entice without touching.

D: Yes! I'm still riding the high from that.

N: I wanted to be riding you.

D: I would have let you. Right on the couch, in front of the whole staff.

N: I know.

D: Just walk over to me and straddle my lap, lift your dress and cover us both, and ride my hard cock.

N: Fuck.

D: I'd have to pull your dress down enough to suck your nipples. Maybe pull you hair a little.

N: Yes. Please.

D: Maybe more than a little.

N: Clothes come off.

D: No.

N: Yes.

I am so sexed up.

D: We must maintain some decorum.

N: If you decided to fuck me tomorrow, I would posses you for 48 hours.

D: Absolutely.

But back to the couch.

N: Ok.

Sorry.

D: So, you are straddling me, no panties but a sundress on, and it covers our union.

I've pulled the straps down exposing your amazing breasts.

And I am biting on one nipple.

N: Perfect.

D: And pinching the other hard.

N: My breasts like the way you handle them.

D: My other hand is under your dress with my finger on your clit.

N: Nice.

D: We are both rocking and making my cock slide in and out of your wet pussy.

N: I like that you take care of all of my pleasure centers.

D: I release your nipple and pull back on a handful of hair.

And kiss your stretched neck.

N: Fuck.

D: From the top of your breasts to your jawline.

N: Yes.

D: Then I lick you lightly on your neck.

N: Bite me.

Leave a mark.

A reminder.

D: I nibble your ear.

N: I can feel you.

D: And pull your earlobe with my teeth.

N: Yes.

D: I put my hand on the back of your neck.

And pull your head to my shoulder.

N: Yes.

D: And nestle you into my neck.

You kiss me gently there.

N: Oh yes.

You're remembering.

D: Yes I am

The door to the office slams open, and in walks her stepson, Jeffrey. While a grown man, he still behaves like a child. Nadailia is forced to work with him, as her husband appointed him CFO.

She is slouched on her couch and not behind her desk, so he does not see her.

"Where is that stupid bitch?"

"I am right here." She surprised him from behind.

Jeffery had always been hard on her. Being a spoiled rich child, he possessed a sense of entitlement that baffled her. While she could care less about him liking her, she sensed that he wanted the entire restaurant empire to be his. He was the CFO, so all monetary decisions had to go through his office.

"Sorry, I didn't know you were in here."

"What can I do for you, Jeffery?"

"I want you to look for another chef."

"May I ask why?"

"He is insubordinate."

She chuckled at that, as she found he was perfectly compliant in all activities.

"You are not his superior. I am. If you need him to do something, run it through me first. He is the best there is, and I will not replace him because of your weak sense of self." He looked at her with sheer hatred and slammed out of her office.

Nadailia sent a list of rules to Dylan sure that it would set things on a straight line to happiness. In her world, once rules were established and followed, harmony prevailed. She was sure this list would ensure a carefree adventure for her and Dylan. She feared Jeffrey and needed to protect herself, first and Dylan second. She also realized she needed to protect her heart. She sent him an email:

To: Dylan

From: Nadailia

Regarding: Guidelines

Dylan:

As we embark on this adventure, a few rules need to be established. This is a path of artistry. A creativity outpouring expressed through intimacy. To make sure we both get the ultimate benefit of this creative magic, we must set guidelines.

Guideline #1. We only try one new thing when we are together. This is to be savored, not spent in the heat of passion.

Guideline #2. We will always respect the other's needs/desires without explanation.

Guideline #3. We will remember we were friends/compatriots first and that is the heart and soul of this relationship.

Guideline #4. Everything we try is in the art of experimenting. Since this is out of the "realm of norms," we are free to change likes, desires and expectations.

Guideline #5. We will never feel guilty for this selfish act. We deserve this pleasure.

Yours, Nadailia

He replied back, "All seems fair to me, I would like to kiss you."

Bamboos Converging on the Alter

He invited her over to his apartment to try out some new dishes and work on the menu. Dylan's surroundings were a surprise to her. Although he had no money, it was decorated with an aristocratic air. Antique books lined the walls, fine art reproductions showed his appreciation for beauty and aspiration. The walls were draped in fabric, giving off a harem-type of feel. It was cozy and beautiful. Nadailia was dressed in a comfortable wrap-around dress that was sure to give him access, if the evening went that way.

They started in the kitchen with a bottle of buttery Tolosa Chardonnay. She admired the ingredients for the feast he was preparing. This spread of epicurean delights was a testament of his resourcefulness and trained palate. Black and white truffles, foie gras, oysters and a charcuterie board were the main ingredients. Nadailia was perched on a high stool watching, taking mental notes, transfixed. He prepared everything with a delicate panache. She could not take her eyes off him. His movement was more like that of a dancer than of a grunting sous chef.

At each step, he loaded a bite of goodness and fed it to her. Each time his spoon came to her mouth, their eyes locked and the blue twinkling of mischief was not lost on her. She tried to remain neutral, not impressed and not breathing quite so hard, this moment of creating, tasting and laughing was catching her off guard.

"About your texts? Is this something I can expect on a regular basis?" She was trying to keep a conversation going when all she wanted to do was jump him.

"I think about you, and if I can't reach out and touch you, I write."

"Do you have a desire to write?"

"I have a desire to write for you."

This quiet declaration made her shudder. "I always wanted to write. My father was a writer, serious literary stuff, I am not talented enough for that, I'd like to try to write a sexy novel." He smiled, loving that she was opening up to him.

"Then we shall write to each other our passions. It will be a kind of literary affair. I send you the story inspiration, and you whip it into a legitimate and steamy prose." She glowed inside, thrilled by this idea.

"Here is the deal: It is my story. You can't share it with anyone else. I don't want anyone saying, 'Hey, I heard Dylan say that.'"

"No worries; everything I give to you is yours to keep."

Nadailia liked the idea of keeping him.

"We are going to be an unbelievably good team."

They toasted to that concept and went on to the meal.

His first dish was the white truffle. Dylan talked low as he fed Nadailia. "People say white truffles are sexy and they are mysterious, also delicious. Do you know it's against the law to carry white truffles on a bus or train in parts of France? It's the smell, pervasive and pungent." She moaned as she tried small bites.

"The white truffle is provocative on white toast with a simple, hard-poached egg."

She loved every bite, and what made it beyond a culinary distraction was the taste of his fingers as he fed her. The flutters began again.

She thought how wrong this was; he was an employee. She couldn't lust after someone she paid. She couldn't risk being the laughing stock of her partners and staff – or Jeffrey finding out. The next course would change her mind.

He brought out a dozen live oysters, three each of Blue Point, Morro Bay, Coromandel, and Hood Canal. Each variety extraordinary as its subtleties came out with a squeeze of lemon juice and a dab of hot sauce. To prepare them, he shucked the top shell and rinsed them in Tobin James Dream Weaver sparkling wine. To half of them he added a squeeze of fresh lime juice, horseradish and a dash of Sriracha. The remaining oysters were topped with a mignonette sauce of raspberry and balsamic vinegar with a touch of red onion.

The cool taste of the sea, the heat of the sauce and the bubbly they were rinsed in created a taste experience she had never felt. This was food porn at its best.

Halfway through the meal, they opened a bottle of 1997 Justin Isosceles, and the lushness of this wine took the food to another level. Dylan went into the history of the wine as he opened the bottle. "This is an estate blend of Cabernet Sauvignon, Merlot and Cabernet Franc from Justin Vineyards in the northwest corner of the Paso Robles region. It is a wine-lover's dream. The palate is quite lively, cherry and wet earth, some dark spices even a bit hot, but extremely delicious." Even the wine was conspiring against her not-so-level head.

The next dish was Truffle Arctic Char with black truffles. To indulge in the world's most expensive, and some would say exotic, erotic, mysterious and carnal – culinary offering was a dream for Nadailia. The European "Black Diamond" Périgord truffle, with the amazing fresh fish, kept this fervent feast going. The citrus-marinated Arctic char (imagine the freshest salmon sashimi) dotted with a balsamic reduction and anchovy pesto and topped with a generous mound of fresh black truffle shavings.

Next, there was a delicate chickpea pancake, cooked golden in a pan, cored with prosciutto. The pancakes were then filled with foraged forest mushrooms, butter, cream and truffle shavings, covered with foil and baked. Dylan explained that the dish "allows the scent from the truffles, the butter and the cream to hug and kiss each other and make love."

They embraced. He thought, 'I haven't known this woman yet.'

Then he kissed her. It was their first kiss. Not The first kiss. Their first kiss. They gently embraced. She felt his chest against her breasts and his strong arms wrapped around her. He felt the firmness of her breasts pressed against him.

He inhaled her scent and realized how he loved that smell. His hands caressed the hair at the nape of her neck. She put her hand gently on the back of his head. He pulled his head back slightly to look into her eyes. Those blue eyes that captivated him. He moved both his hands to cup her face, sliding his thumbs gently along the sides of her jawline. They both smiled. He leaned in, tilting his head slightly to one side.

She closed her eyes. He brushed his lips first against her cheek, then her eyelids. Feather-soft kisses, like butterfly wings. He slowly pressed his soft lips against hers and held still for a few seconds. Then he increased the pressure on the back of her head with his fingertips. Gradually they both started moving their lips to caress each other's.

She opened her mouth, inviting him to enter her. He slowly pushed his tongue into her mouth, feeling her tongue tangle with his. Wrestling for sensation. Beckoning further passion. He used his tongue to tease and caress the sensitive edges of her teeth, his lips still gentle and soft on hers. They felt like they were copulating with their mouths. They could not be more intimate at this moment. They felt the excitement in their loins, both beginning to moisten. They moaned together, with the promise of things to come, before they broke contact.

He stopped kissing her and placed a truffle on her tongue, letting her get lost in the sensation. She tasted it and then grabbed his mouth and filled it with lust. After each kiss, they sipped the wine, allowing the liquid to be part of their affair. She held her breath. "I am surprised, and so impressed."

"With the food or the kiss?" The mischievous twinkle of his sky blue eyes brought that feeling back to her stomach.

He returned to the kitchen and came back with the foie gras and a Châteauneuf-du-Pape Sauterne. They let it interrupt the Isosceles, as a Sauterne was the perfect pairing with the seared foie gras and Sonoma moulard duck. This was a shrewd combination resting on brioche toast, with red-onion jam and peanuts, all sitting in a bourbon maple syrup. The earthiness and richness of the gavage livers made everything in her body stand at attention.

The way he reached over her to grab a pat of butter, brushing her breast, setting the dish right below her nipple – she lost her breath, and her crotch became moist again. She knew the next move had to be hers. She had to be strong to keep the balance of the relationship and remain in control. The music was playing a sexy sax tune, so she took his hand, indicating she wanted to dance.

They came together and the electric shock almost knocked them both back. He held her tight and bent his head down to her shoulder. She began to rub his lower back, swaying her hips while pulling him close. Dylan was shocked at the wave of passion washing over him. She moved her hand down to his tight ass and began to knead his flesh. The front of her had a perfect rhythm that was hypnotic to him.

All at once, she panicked, knowing that to be with this chef was the most dangerous game ever played. As he bent to kiss her again, she turned, grabbed her purse and ran out the door. He began to text her immediately.

She responded when she was home and relaxed with a glass of wine.

Text

D: What happened?

N: I panicked.

D: About what? It was a kiss and a dance. I can't fucking believe you ran out on that meal and me.

N: Now that you've tasted me, let's talk.

D: I'm sorry. I was being a shit.

N: I don't see it that way. It was hot. I got scared. I gave us a forced timeout.

D: We could have fun in a lot of different ways.

N: You have no idea the plans I have for you.

D: Mmmmmmmm.

N: I am going to fuck you every which way possible.

D: It would be heaven.

N: I am pretty sure you will beg me to leave you alone.

D: You know I am very open to anything you can bring.

N: This one step at a time is working. On all levels. I do not want to lose this.

D: Me either. We must continue along this path.

N: This must be open and honest.

D: I get that. I have sexual feelings, and I don't think it's bad to have them.

N: I want to fuck you every 5 minutes.

D: Good, our cycles match.

N: You can be anything, even in a bad way. If it bothers me, I will call a timeout.

D: Fair enough.

N: I needed to break away.

Actually, you need to eat me until I scream.

I'm conflicted.

D: I'm fucking ready!

N: You promise to keep eating until I cum twice?

D: I won't stop till you fucking pass out!
That's my goal!

N: Promise?

D: YES!!

N: What else do you promise to do to me?

D: I have lots of ways to please you. Gently then rough.

N: I do NOT want you to be gentle with me.

D: I'd love spanking your ass.

N: I do not want you to treat me like a lady or like you love me.
I want you raw, hard and rough.

D: I can be rough.

N: I know that is part of the desire, knowing that you can and will.

D: I can make it hurt.

N: Please do. Take me seriously, I mean it.

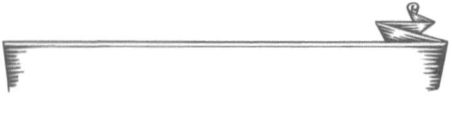

Dipping Pelicans

A s a team-building experience she invited the whole staff to dinner on the beach. They all stole away from drudgery of meetings and work to enjoy the spectacles of nature that the ocean provides.

The baker brought bread, the winemaker shared her favorite vintages, and the farmers picked fresh delicacies from their bounty. Dylan brought the seafood. He wanted to impress with the freshest seafood, so he went to Fresh Fish Market. Looking more like an aquarium than a market, because most of its inventory is still swimming,

Fresh Fish Market had been a staple on the pier for more than 30 years. BJ, the owner, is a salty dog that knew more about fish than anyone, and if you befriended him, he would save you the best finds. Dylan picked out a live halibut, a live yellowtail and four-dozen live oysters. He joined the group on the beach as the fire started raging.

To prepare the oysters, Dylan had Pedro shuck them, rinse them in Captain Morgan dark rum, add fresh lime juice, horseradish and a dash of Tabasco. The drunken oysters were a hit with the whole staff.

The busboy had caught three huge California king crabs. He boiled them over the fire in a seawater-filled pot. This sea arachnid is a rare treat, the shells might as well be made of titanium, so hacksaws are needed to get at the delectable meat, it was worth the effort, and no lemon or butter was needed.

Dylan filleted the seven-pound halibut, slathered it in butter and herbs, then made a cocoon out of palm fronds and set it on the fire. Next was thinly sliced yellowtail with a ponzu sauce, wasabi and ginger. The Poseidon celebration continued as pelicans dive-bombed, dolphins leaped offshore.

A pod of humpback whales had come to the port and were jumping, eating and frolicking in the water off Avila Beach. They were following a bait ball, where small fish swarm in a tightly packed spherical formation. It is a last-ditch defensive measure used by small fish when predators threaten them. The predators in the water at Avila included harbor seals, sea lions, dolphins, pelicans and those magnificent whales.

The diners around the bonfire watched as the whales breached at least 30 times, showing their majesty so close. Everyone in the group was awed. All knew this was a sight few witness.

Sitting around the bonfire and tasting vintage wines, the staff became closer friends. They told stories and laughed. Dylan and Nadailia were sitting dangerously close to each other. As darkness fell, they toasted S'mores and declared that they were officially in love with beach living as they watched the humpback whales breach into the sunset.

Dylan and Nadailia stayed after everyone had left and watched the bonfire burn down. When they were sure everyone was gone, they began to kiss. It was a kiss of exploration and finding each other's pleasure centers. They were tentative but hungry for each other. Dylan reached up and grabbed her breasts, loving the fullness of them and marveling at how her nipples were rock hard as he touched her. She reached between his legs, searching for his desire status. It was bigger than she anticipated, and she was thrilled. He was a bit surprised at this forward move in a public place and politely, yet firmly moved her hand away from his crotch.

"We need to go. Early morning tomorrow."

"But it was getting interesting," she pouted.

"Time to go, Boss. Need to get you home to your husband."

This simple yet declarative sentence told her he was not ready to be her lover yet. She would wait, and with their texts getting hotter each night, she was sure he would be in her bed soon.

Text

D: The first time you see my cock, where do you want it?

N: In my mouth.

D: Nice.

N: Are you shocked? I know you are a gentleman first and foremost, it is in your DNA, and that will not have to be the case in our bed.

D: I can be a gentleman when it is called for. I can be other things, and have been, when called for also.

N: Then I am calling for the "other."

D: Get my cock wet with your mouth and I'll ram it up you.

N: Sounds perfect.

I will buck you like a bronco.

D: I can ride you!

N: Better hold tight.

D: When's the last time you were fucked?

N: Too long ago.

D: Well, it will hurt at first, so get ready, I won't be timid.

N: I like the pain, and I already know how big you are.

D: Wait, What? From feeling me?

N: Yes!

D: So the order is you suck first, then I fuck you?

I think somewhere I need to finger you.

My finger buried in your wet pussy.

N: I think that is step two.

I think finger banging is so fucking hot.

But one thing at a time, remember?

D: So blow me then finger blast?
N: Yup.
D: Yes! I LOVE doing that!
That is one of my favs.
N: No wait; there is the nipple play!
D: It's an art form.
I've got to get to the pussy.
N: You will.

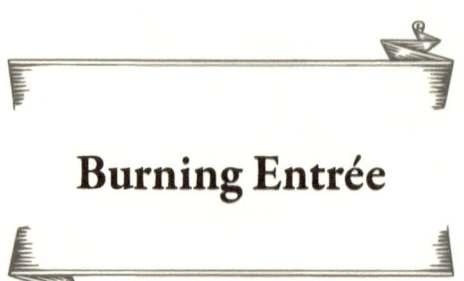

Burning Entrée

Dylan's brother Stu called. His Maman had been arrested in France for trying to steal two $400 bottles of wine from a rare-wine shop. It was not her first offense, so it was much more serious. Dylan booked a ticket to Marseille the next day with no regard for his job or obligations. The only thing that mattered to him was getting his Maman free and safe. He and Nadailia had a date that night to try her favorite Thai restaurant; he figured he would ask for the time off during the meal.

Her town car picked him up and he snuggled in next to her, ready to touch, explore and maybe get a kiss to wash away his Maman troubles. He got lost in the night and choose not to tell her about his not so "bon voyage".

They stopped at Thai Food Haven, Nadailia's favorite small, authentic bistro. Nadailia wanted Dylan to infuse some Southeast Asian flavors into the new menu. She explained that this family had owned a restaurant in Bangkok for more than 200 years, so there was a history and family pride that went into each dish. They talked about how to order a typical Thai meal. One should have a soup, a curry dish, a spiced salad, noodles with fish and vegetables, and a couple of stir-fries. All should be served communally and shared, as the harmony of tastes and textures is as important as the people with whom you share the meal.

Nadailia started with the creamy Coconut Tom Yum soup. As she spooned it into his mouth he moaned with pleasure. It was scrumptious, with mushrooms, red peppers and chunks of tofu. Dylan had the Fried Spinach Salad with flakes of spinach flash-fried with panko and topped with a vinegary hot dressing with ground chicken, cashew and ground chilies. It sat atop fresh organic baby greens. Their legs entwined underneath in a familiar dance of touching without touching.

The main course came; Thai Fried Rice with chicken, brown and green onions, eggs, Chinese broccoli, peas, carrots, cilantro and tomato. It was so full of flavor, and the rice was the perfect sticky consistency. The Kung Pao Chicken, with hormone-free chicken, stir-fried onions, bell peppers, dried chilies and peanuts, was as hot as their thoughts as they gazed into each other's eyes. Dylan started a tour of the curries, as they had three on the menu. The Red Curry had a long, sweet burn, with bamboo shoots, broccoli, zucchini, bell peppers, basil leaves and carrots swimming in a luscious curried coconut sauce. He also tried the Pad Thai, which was extra sweet (they have sugar on the table if you want to add more). A Thai lime wedge enlightened this traditional dish of fried tofu, tamarind and palm sugar sauce dusted with peanuts and fresh bean sprouts. They fed each other and discussed what flavors and which dishes to add to the menu.

"We will have to include a curry on the menu."

"I agree and some finger food. Don't you think eating is more erotic when you eat with your hands?"

"I think eating is more erotic with you."

Dylan was glad for the white tablecloths that hung down low so they could explore each other under the table. He liked to take her leg and pull it open, exposing her to his strong touch. This drove her crazy. No one had ever dared to touch her that way before. She went for his crotch, trying to coax it out any way or anywhere she could.

Next was the Mar Hor, which, for Dylan, was a new sensation of sweet and salty seasoning in ground chicken rolled into a ball, speckled with peanuts and served over fresh pineapple rings. It was marvelous. Then they tried the Corn Fritters, made with whole corn kernels, garlic and egg and seasoned perfectly. The fritters were served with a sweet sauce and a hot chili sauce. They were surprising and wonderful. Then, they had the Papaya Green Salad, a super-spicy dish made with shredded unripe papaya, carrots, tomato, green beans tossed with chili, garlic and peanuts in a spicy lime and fish sauce and topped with grilled shrimp. This was their favorite, as the textures, flavors and heat inspired them both, and they moved their hands from under the table for the first time to take notes. The main dish was Heaven on Earth, pan-seared tilapia with jumbo lumps of real crab meat in a savory, creamy panang curry coconut sauce with vegetables and kaffir lime and basil leaves. The dish was the product of a true master in the kitchen.

As they left the restaurant, the anticipation was as palpable as the lust. This moment seemed like it took a lifetime to manifest, even though they had met six weeks ago. Their first kiss was a couple of days ago; the physical realm of their affair was now burned into their psyches and their loins.

They went to his house. He sent his brother out to see a movie, so that meant two hours alone. Although they were together consistently at work, they were never alone. They certainly did not have the privilege of unbridled access to each other. Nadailia admitted she was frightened as he handed her a glass of Châteauneuf-du-Pape. That admission alone startled her. She was never afraid, and if she had a glimmer of fear, she certainty did not share it. With him, honesty was a gift, something she felt compelled to do, to not hold back any thoughts or feelings, for he had become her safe haven.

She had sent him her rules again before tonight's date, and he replied, "Let's see what happens." Sometimes his trite answers irritated her, and she disregarded this one.

Now, before the wine even touched her lips, his mouth was on hers. He cradled her head in his strong hands and kissed her gently, and then with a drive she did not recognize. This was real desire. He turned her around in her chair so her back was facing him and enveloped her in his arms. She could already feel his desire rising at the base of her spine. She trembled, a reaction she had never had with a man before. He bundled her hair into a tail and pulled her head back, giving him access to her long neck, which was now pleading for his lips. With her head tilted to the side, he caressed, and kissed, and bit. Then he lightly ran his hands down her back, like feathers, touching, exploring. She nearly fainted at the innocence and pleasure of this, and was surprised when he lowered the straps of her blouse off her shoulders and then did the same with her bra. He stayed behind her, kneading her breasts, softly at first, and then with more firmness and passion. This simple act was making her almost feeble with pleasure.

She mused that through their word play, he had paid attention to her erogenous hints. This man was going to own her, and right now she did not care. She swung around and threw her arms around his neck, devouring his mouth. He removed her bra, then he removed his shirt. Their blazing-hot skin was now touching, and she could now barely stand. He led her to the couch.

She was beyond ready for him, they kissed a bit longer. She moved on top of him, straddling his lap and began to kiss his neck, then his masculine chest, which had the right amount of hair and marvelous definition. She followed down his trunk and undid his pants, seeing for the first time the large glory of him. She slid to her knees and took the tip of him in her mouth. He was built of beauty and power. The size of him surprised her; never had she experienced a man with such a large cock. Her mind ticked off all the pleasing places he was going to put that gorgeous cock and how wonderful it was going to feel. She licked and sucked, when she tried to swallow him, it was too big. She was looking forward to stretching her throat to fit him.

With her head between his knees she sucked and idolized his fabulous cock, looking up to watch him watching her as he held her long red hair out of the way. She raked his balls with her fingers and began to consume him. Lost in the desire, she almost let him cum. She placed her fingers at the base of his cock and asked, "Do you want to cum on my face?" Greedily, he said yes, and stroked himself to completion as ribbons of cum soaked her face and her tits.

She was confident he would get hard again, so she sat back to take a break, as he gently wiped her face with his discarded shirt. He went to the kitchen and brought back a cheese-and-fruit plate to go with their wine .He sat next to her and began to massage her inner thigh. Then he pulled back her short skirt and began to caress and finger her pussy like a violin. Soft and amazing strokes of a maestro surprised and delighted her. With her head thrown back, he discovered every inch of her sex and then inserted his finger all the way up to her G spot. He rubbed with precision while his thumb found her clit, which was now engorged with passion. As she was about to crest, she whispered, "Kiss me."

When his lips found hers and their tongues began an erotic dance, she had her first small enlightenment with him. It ripped through her like a light beam. The force of the feeling took her by surprise, it did not sate her; it turned up the heat.

Now she jumped on to his lap, straddling him as he sucked her erect nipples. He had a small beard growth on his chin that he used as an erotic tool, grazing it on her nipples. These surprising erogenous pleasantries had her whipped into a horny frenzy. She felt a strong stirring with the nipple play, another first for her, and said, "You need to fuck me now."

He hesitated, and she saw a light in his eyes fade. Trying to regain the momentum, she straddled him again and tried sexy conversation. She placed her hands in his and pulled his hands over his head.

"Have you ever been tied up?"

"No."

"I am going to do that to you, and so much more."

He smiled politely; the fire was now barely an ember.

She tried several things to bring him back – joking, drinking, caressing and grabbing his cock.

"So what does your week look like?" he asked as if they were sitting across the desk from each other and not in a state of half dress.

"I do not want to talk about work," she half yelled at him, and dove between his legs to take his cock in her mouth again. He responded, it was only his body responding to the physical stimulation; she had lost him.

When she looked up from between his legs, she caught him looking at his watch.

This shattered her. She considered herself a sport fucker and most desirable, she seemed to have no affect on him; he had checked out. She moved off him, dressed and got up to leave. He crossed the floor and kissed her on the forehead. She nearly slapped him for that act of sibling love. She embraced him with one last attempt to bring him back, repair her battered ego, and whispered, "I love you."

No reply. Nothing.

She left his house as fast as her bruised ego could carry her.

At home, she wanted to talk to him, so she opened the chat window on her Mac and asked the familiar

Text

"Are you there? I got home safe. Want to chat?"

Their chatting had sustained and grown the relationship, so she thought he might give her some insight as to what had just taken place.

Dylan: "I have to catch a flight in the morning. Going to bed. Fun night!"

He was gone.

She wanted to cry, to run to him, talk to him, talk to anyone. She had promised him that she would not tell anyone, even her friends, for he was afraid of her stepson finding out and him losing his job. She was alone with her thoughts. So she wrote an email to him. Each word stung, it had to be said.

To: Dylan

From: Nadailia

Regarding: Confused

Dear Dylan,

I write this high on emotion. If I'm out of line, talk with me first before reacting to this. I trust you with my words. So here they are. Thank you for the most memorable night of my life.

Tonight was mind-blowing for me. I loved the sensual aspect of you touching me. I loved sucking your cock, tasting you and being able to freely touch you. There were many firsts.

I had so much fun touching, rubbing and kissing you. It was like Disneyland for my libido. I loved every inch of you. You are beautiful and strong.

You seemed to enjoy me, you were a bit distracted. Was it because it was our first time alone? Are you regretting this leap?

If you want to stop, I am ok and understand. We can go back to being friends. I have enough sexual energy from you to last a lifetime. Either way, be honest with me. I'm strong and will be fine. No hysterics.

I want the best for you. If you feel you've made a mistake touching me, it's our secret forever. I was devastated with how trite you were with me after; you seemed to want me to go away.

And for the first time since this started, there were no texts or words from you after (except pleasantries).

I guess I was surprised at your detachment. I never expect you to fawn over me. An acknowledgement of our activity would have soothed me.

No matter what our relationship, I took a huge leap of faith sharing my body with you. It was nerve-racking. It was frightening. And you acted as if it was nothing. Just another meeting. I am not sure what happens next, my ego is bruised and my anger barely kept at bay.

Nadailia

He did not reply or text for two days. When he finally contacted her, it was as her employee.

To: Nadailia

From: Dylan

Regarding: Family Emergency

Ms. Nadailia,

Family emergency has forced me to go to France for the next week. I am sorry for the inconvenience this has caused you. I will be back in the kitchen a week from Monday, and my staff will be on track and able to answer any questions you may have.

Warm regards,

Chef Dylan

The Soufflé Fell

L auren came over, and after a bottle wine Nadailia told her the whole story. Lauren tried to soothe her, she was inconsolable. She felt she had been used. She felt angry, hurt and devastated. Lauren listened and poured the wine as her friend agonized over this man. She suggested she write him a letter, never to send or share, to get her true feelings out. Nadailia loved the idea and took her poison pen to paper.

To: Dylan

From: Nadailia

Regarding: Fired

Dear Dylan,

I am beyond upset, pissed and mostly hurt. There are games being played that are not kind.

I get it. You think this is ok because you are young and have options.

But I'm destroyed. I should have known better. I should have kept to my rules. All I asked from you were a few touches; the words and the food seduced me. You wanted more. You pursued and broke barriers. I felt desired for the first time in years. I fell for your strong touch.

But whatever emotional minefield you're going through, I am not and will never be a priority. I feel betrayed. Left empty on the side of the road to bleed.

You knew that a few words via text would sate me, you willfully withheld attention to make me back away. I will.

You are lucky to have messed with a woman with no malice in her heart.

But I am human. I bleed on the page and rage in my heart.

Here's what I believe right now: You are only motivated by your dick, and my mind was never a subject of desire. It was a play to get off. And once you did, and saw and felt my body wasn't young and desirable, you moved on and I was no longer a priority. Stupid me.

I will fade away from you like a ghost you barely recall. I'll erase you from my heart, my thoughts, my contacts. My world. You were an aberration. A figment of my desire. It was a mistake. I will move on. It was a dangerous game. It has played out.

She was about to sign his termination letter when her text tone sounded.

Text

D: You there?

N: Yes.

D: Can you chat? I'm trapped at the Marseille police station for the next two hours.

N: Yes, writing you a letter. How are you?

D: Ok, considering. You?

N: A bit raw. Little too emotional.

D: What's up?

N: You.

D: How?

N: Not sure. Still processing.

D: Ok.

N: You have pulled me in. It feels too real. I'm not sure I'm making any sense.

D: Keep going.

N: I feel emotionally unstable. Needy.

D: My first chance I sent you a note. I wanted to tell you. That's not obvious?

N: Nothing is obvious to me.

D: Ok.

N: I'm not even sure what to say to you. I want to be honest, I can't tell if my emotions are real or make-believe.

We existed in a make-believe realm, and then reality crashed into it.

I'm in a quantum flux.

I could use a hug.

D: Yes. I don't want reality to crush what we had.

N: I find myself mad at you. I have no reason to be mad. Then I find myself wanting you and trying to talk you into moving forward. Then I find myself freaked the fuck out at the possibility of getting caught. I used to have one single mission.

D: We muddied the water didn't we?

N: We did. Like you said, it had to be done.

D: As far as getting caught, we may get busted for working too many hours together, but that is it.

N: I'm hoping time and being able to chat with you again will ease these feelings in me.

D: It will. And be prepared for me to grab your leg under the table.

N: I would like that.

D: Where's the conflict?

N: I feel hurt. Unwanted.

D: Because of the lack of communication?

N: I felt like I was being toyed with, not a priority. It was mostly your reaction after our rendezvous.

D: Ok, I think it's fair to say we were both a little surprised at that? We were both willing.

N: Yes.

D: I'm not toying with you.

N: I told you nothing I'm feeling is rational.

D: Last week was impossible for me. I had more on my plate than I could manage and felt bad for leaving you without a chef. I knew it might come across as not wanting to talk.

N: By the same token, nothing I've ever felt or done with you is rational.

D: I've done these trips to rescue her before they suck.

N: If I can't be honest with you.

There is no point.

I fully acknowledge my insanity.

That doesn't make it sting less.

D: You are not insane. You are like me, conflicted.

N: It will probably go away with one hug (that lasts 10 minutes).

D: Neither one of us has experience with these emotions.

N: I want to beat you about the head and fire you.

D: I'm pretty much getting punched around from another direction right now, so I'll defer any further beatings.

And there is no fucking way you are going to fire me.

N: I know!

And that's why I didn't want to be too weird.

D: I know one thing for positive, the day we stop being honest with each other is the day "this," whatever it is, is over.

I'll give you nothing less and demand nothing less.

N: I don't want this to be over. Ever.

D: Me either.

N: How is your mom? My life is a bit one-sided these days with "the patient."

D: Can I help?

N: No, he's just mean.

D: Two guys being dicks to you. I'll be less "dickish" when I'm in the same time zone.

Nadailia, give me a chance to get us back on track, ok?

N: Of course. That is all I want.

D: I feel we can ease back into our comfort zone. We touched the stove, found out it was hot, that doesn't mean we have to throw it out in the dump.

Jeffery came barreling into her office as the last of his text appeared. She knew he was a rage fiend, so best to nod and let him spew indignation.

"I can't believe you gave him time off. We are days from opening, and his kitchen staff is standing around with their thumbs up their asses with no direction. We don't even have a menu. Where the fuck is he, and what could be more important than Consumed?"

Nadailia took a deep breath, "He had a family emergency in France."

"Are you fucking kidding me? How do you know he is not on some beach in Marseille, fucking a hairy French girl?"

She was starting to get mad, but was wise enough and had dealt with Jeffery enough to stay calm and hide her feelings.

"Because I know."

The sneer of his lips scared her; he spat at her, "Really? And you know this because he is your current lover?"

The sting of him knowing this rocked her back in her chair. She thought they had been careful, that no one knew. Damn, this was a problem now. With too many emotions, she glared at Jeffery. "I am not having sex with him, and he will be back. Very soon."

Jeffery stomped out of her office, and she sank into her chair.

Now they had a problem.

Nadailia wrote him an email that night, as she deleted the first bitter one. She tried to explain her feelings.

To: Dylan

From: Nadailia

Regarding: Rewind

Dylan, I am at that crucial age when a woman begins to regret having stayed loyal to a husband she never loved, who was not faithful, and who is more a partner than an erotic adventure.

It was so wonderful sharing my body with you. I'm enjoying the afterglow. I'm resolute that if we can never be along together again, maybe a few stolen touches under the table will be enough.

You've become a staple in my life, my chef, my muse and my friend. I refuse to lose that for a few moments of physical pleasure.

Let's rewind. Go back. Back to the words. Let's remember the pleasure we got from creating the restaurant together.

I loved every second of our night, I do not believe at this point either of us is ready to take it any further or repeat.

I can say I got as much pleasure from you touching my back as I did with your fingers inside me.

I loved our kisses. I loved tasting you. I equally loved our hands touching.

Maybe we are looking for the wrong release? Maybe we are meant to neck for 40 years with stolen minutes and our words?

We can be passing-notes lovers.

Our time together is chiseled into my brain. I will never forget a moment of it, and I loved every second. I think we are meant for higher things, more cerebral events.

To quote you:

"I read your recent posts with eagerness and interest. The desire and passion you exude is palpable. We are both energized. Our creative neurons are firing, fueled by our passion. We are riding a high on new awareness. Awareness of the ability to create from this passion and desire. Confidence learned in the safety of love and concern. Development gained by no fear of failure. We must continue the passion, careful not to sate it. We will thrive by staying close enough to the flame to be warmed and strengthened by it, not so close that we are consumed by the thing that gives us new life."

Be safe. Someone in California desires to see you again (and be perfectly PG).

Nadailia

Dylan read this email over and over, not sure what she was saying or what was going on. He called his brother to give him an update.

"Hey Stu, how are you doing?"

Stu was studying, but always stopped working to talk to his brother. Dylan rarely asked for anything from his family. He was always giving.

"I am good. How is Maman? More importantly, how are you?"

"Frustrated, wanting to get back to my life."

"Is she out of the slammer yet?"

"No, I am talking to the police chief daily. He knows she will do it again. I think I need to bring her back to the States."

Stu feared this, as their Maman had a tendency to implode both of their lives.

"Fuck, that is raw. There is not enough good wine here to sustain her."

Dylan laughed for the first time in days.

"I know sacrifices have to be made."

Stu remembered Dylan's new job, and his new boss, "How is the new boss taking this?"

"Not well, but understanding. I need to get back there soon."

Dylan sent a text to Nadailia after he hung up with Stu.

D: Hey, how are you?

N: I'm good. You?

D: Tired. Long, long day.

N: I bet. Can I do anything to help?

Wanna chat, or are you too tired?

How's your head about us?

D: Ok. A little weird.

How about you?

N: Mine too. Big swings.

D: Yes. We need to take a breather and reassess.

N: Well, it's forced this week.

D: Oh, I get it - I'm in France.

N: Can't very well molest you there.

D: We need to stay in contact, pause the physical is what I meant.

N: Ok. It was beautiful. I could tell you were uncomfortable.

D: It was beautiful. I need to determine if I'm comfortable with that part of it, especially with you being married. No regrets at all.

Just not clear about what's next.

N: I have enough sexual energy from that night to fuel me for years.

Whatever we decide, it's good.

I would hate to lose you as a chef that would be harder to give up.

D: Nadailia that is not what I'm talking about. I don't want to take a chance on losing that.

N: Ok. You never will. I get it.

D: I'm afraid we can fuck our success right out of existence. I don't want to sacrifice that for the physical.

N: I 100% agree.

D: This "work" relationship and the restaurant's success are more important to me than anything physical.

N: Me too.

It was a big step for both of us. Quite frankly, I'm glad we got it over with.

No more speculation.

And technically a blowjob is not sex.

D: I agree! Bill Clinton made that clear!

N: I wrote some powerful stuff.

It felt so good to write again.

To harness the power and emotion and put it on the page.

D: That's great!

N: It's complicated, I'm glad I had an outlet for it.
Go to bed. I'm glad you texted.
I was like a cat on a hot tin roof.

D: Thank you for understanding.
It's amazing how much alike we think.

N: I know. I like it.

D: Me too! We need to be able to talk about anything 10 years from now!

N: We always will.

D: I will dream of you.

N: Goodnight Chef.

Maman

Dylan tried for days to get his Maman released from jail, but the Commissaire de Police would not let her go unless Dylan promised to buy a plane ticket back to the States for her. In between pleading with the authorities and sneaking his Maman wine in jail, he dined out, doing research on the local sea-to-table bistros. Most restaurants in the area only cook what they forage from the fields and the sea. It was a dream education. He sent menu notes and recipes to Nadailia, hoping to ease the sting of her executive chef being gone days before they opened.

Text

N: How are you?

D: Still negotiating to get Maman out.

N: I'm sorry.

D: Up at 6am, all day negotiating.

N: Tough. I can assist. I can be there in 24 hours.

D: No, I have to do this one my own.

N: Ok. I had a total loss of confidence today. Very weird.

D: In what way?

N: Every way. Like I can't do any of the stuff I signed up for. Extremely strange.

D: Distracted? I'm sure tomorrow will be better.

N: Yes. Before, the distraction gave me confidence.

D: Please don't take my lack of communication as anything other than what it is. I am trying to save my Maman, and I am halfway around the world.

N: I'm not. I can miss you.

D: I miss you too.

N: I feel better already. Stay strong, family is the priority! We will keep our relationship strong with our menu and texts!

D: Ok. No confusion. Nothing's changed. We had to go there. No choice.

N: Probably not the best timing for me emotionally to do that and then have no access to you.

D: I agree.

N: Some moments were beyond perfect.

D: Yes, it is keeping me going over here.

N: I'm trying to understand what these "Mommy Rescue" trips are like for you.

D: They crush me.

I'm fading.

N: Ok. Go to bed.

D: Already in bed :-)

N: Want a story?

D: Sure!

N: Once upon a time. Here is my plan for you with no time limit, nowhere to be and no chance at getting caught.

First I will undress you completely and marvel at the beauty of you. Then I will take my goat-hair whip and slap you gently from head to toe. You will feel a bit of the sting and a touch of indulgence.

Then I will start with me "driving the bus." I will try out my "drama-approved kiss moves" on your mouth and then work my way down your neck to your chest. I will lick and become familiar with every beautiful tan inch of you.

I know you will be over stimulated, so I will put a cock ring on you to ensure you don't cum. After that I will spend an exorbitant amount of time kissing, licking and sucking on your cock. I will graze your balls with the tips of my fingers and grasp your ass with my hands. You are not allowed to cum. Even when I swallow you completely.

After I have driven you to the point of destruction, I will let you go at my breasts. I am looking for a climax from your kiss and working my nipples. I am sure you are the man to do it.

After that petite mort, I will mount you on your lap, feeling the length of you inside my womb and reveling in it. I will rock back and forth so your pelvic bone is rubbing my clit while your fantastic shaft is stroking my G spot. We will be kissing and exploring each other's mouths, as we explode...............you will open your eyes and stare into mine. The whole time. No shutting, no fluttering, deeply watching our souls combine.

N: Now go to sleep.

D: Well, you haven't lost your magic touch. I'm hard as cobalt steel.

Thank you for that.

I feel better now. Quite a weird thing we have.

I'll convert that into hot dreams.

N: I miss you.

D: Miss you too.

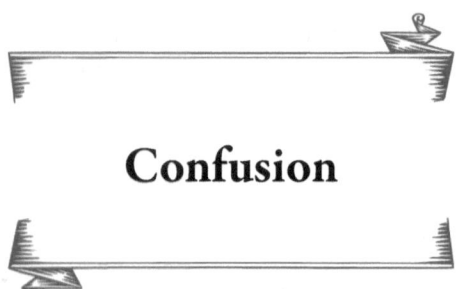

Confusion

They existed in a post-coital realm that was more dangerous and scary than the world had been when they were in discovery mode. Secrets had been shared. Body parts had been discovered. Fluids had been swapped. Fantasies shattered and uncovered.

It was real now.

And the biggest question was: What is next?

They both had the maturity of emotion to understand the change, their hearts and lust was still a factor. Not to mention ego. Both prided themselves on being exemplary lovers, that was only substantiated by their past lovers, who where predestined to be kind.

Did they please each other? Was it as each had promised? Did it hamper or incite the lust? It was a state of flux that neither was comfortable in.

But the memories were hot. Red hot. Each took away from their time together a few instances of fantasy fulfilled, lust reached.

They still decided to put on the brakes, suspend the physical. This was an easy decision when they were 5600 miles apart. Quite a different story as they sat across the table from each other with knees touching.

Nadailia was terminally horny, having spent 30 years with a man who was more interested in her as a 24-hour assistant than as a lover. She was sexually charged, looking for release, and did not tend to get attached to a lover, or so she had convinced herself.

She told Dylan she was fine with sliding backward, her mind and body craved him. She felt less confident without him. She felt lost.

She also knew not to push him. He was not a man she could manipulate. He was as strong of mind as he was of body. Plus, she respected him. She knew the key to their going forward was trust.

She would wait. Bide her time. He would come around, or she would get used to not having him. Either way, it would be okay.

Meanwhile she continued to write to and for him.

He would be hers if only in words and in her dreams.

The Rescue

S he woke up from a sensual dream about Dylan and was resolved to go and fetch him, solve his problems and make him her lover. She had her private jet ready to go in 45 minutes and was in Marseille for dinner the next night. Determined to help him, she went first to the jail and met with the Commissaire de Police. He was as taken with her as he was with the handsome check she offered to upgrade his jail. He agreed to let Dylan's Maman go the next morning. She could have one romantic night with her chef.

She went to his budget hotel and surprised him. Dylan was conflicted: glad to see her, sensing that she had over-stepped a boundary.

"How did you get here?"

"I have a jet."

"You own a jet? Are you kidding me?"

"You have to know that I am wealthy. Lets not talk about this now. Show me your special finds in dining here. I loved the notes; now I want to taste it."

On the way to Chez Ida, Dylan explained the distinctive style of cooking in Marseille. "Chefs focus on simple, fresh, healthy Mediterranean ingredients: low on the meat, animal fats and heavy sauces of traditional French cuisine; high on vegetables and fish.

And it's all spiced with influences from the city's successive waves of immigrants, in particular Italian, Spanish, Armenian, Turkish,

North African, Caribbean and Chinese. Today, it goes without saying that Marseille is not just about bouillabaisse."

She loved seeing him so impassioned, and she stroked his hand as he talked excitedly.

"The visitor to Marseille today is spoiled for choice; there is a selection of some of the best places to eat, each with its own unique selling points."

Chez Ida was a small but picturesque neighborhood bistro that immediately captured Nadailia's heart. A small board promised homemade specials to satisfy all tastes.

Ida came to the door and gave hugs and kisses to both her and Dylan. She promised to make them a meal to remember while they caught up on their amour.

They started with the traditional bouillabaisse, a provençal fish stew that originated in the port city of Marseille. What makes bouillabaisse different from other fish soups is the selection of provençal herbs and spices in the broth; the use of bony local Mediterranean fish, the way the fish are added one at a time and brought to a boil, and the method of serving. In Marseille, the broth is served first in a soup plate with slices of bread and roiled, and then the fish is served separately on a large platter.

They shared a *pieds ET parquets,* a genuine Marseille specialty, nearly impossible to find in any restaurant. It is commonly found in much of southeastern France. It consists of stuffed sheep's offal and sheep's feet stewed together. It was unusual, erotic in a strange way. They started on the second bottle of wine as the last few courses came.

The chorizo was the best Nadailia had ever had, and the orange chocolate torte was delicious. She was especially grateful for the white tablecloths, as Dylan spent the meal manipulating her inner thigh. They sang karaoke, a romantic duet from a 1970's band, and left full of fantastic food and two bottles of wine.

On the car ride home they kissed like starving people. He agreed to go with her to her opulent hotel, and she ordered two bottles of champagne.

Anticipation had built from the last time they were alone. They were ready to build on some of the previous explorations, both forgetting the emotional damage it had done. Their kisses were not tentative now, familiar and even more passionate. Dylan, without prompting, pulled the straps of Nadailia's dress off her shoulders and pushed the dress down to her waist, giving him unfettered access to her lovely breasts and nipples. He felt that efficiency was important now, time precious. Every second must be filled with sensory stimulation.

Dylan removed his shirt to feel her breasts against bare skin as they hugged. His nipples hardened touching Nadailia. He caressed her shoulders lightly with his fingertips, making her shiver. She reached down with her hand and felt his hardness through his pants. She unbuttoned his pants and pushed them to his thighs, freeing his cock and balls. She wrapped her hand around the shaft and stroked, stopping once to feel the wetness of his pre-cum on the tip. She stood up to reach his face, making sure she was not headed down that path of emotional destruction, and they kissed on the mouth, hard. She pulled her mouth away and immediately buried her head in his lap, swallowing his cock. She pulled back now and slowly began sucking him. He held her head and hair in his hands while she worked her magic. She licked and sucked aggressively, caressing his balls. As he built toward a climax, she decided to swallow his cum as she continued to drive him. He let out an "Oh fuck!" and she knew he was about to pop. She continued, finger and thumb encircling his throbbing cock up and down the shaft. He tightened the grip on her head and thrust his hips into her face as he moaned and began convulsing. She felt his cum erupt in her mouth and throat. Nadailia milked every drop, fingertips stroking his balls as he shuddered to an end. Once it was spent, she let his dick slide out of her mouth with a pop. She had swallowed every ounce of his juice. She lifted her mouth to his, and without hesitation they kissed greedily, tasting each other.

Nadailia was ready now, filled with more desire than she thought possible. She lay back on the bed, ready to have him ravage her. As he slid on to the bed, his phone rang.

"Please do not answer that." Her voice was scruffy with lust.

"I have to. It's Maman's number."

As he spoke with his Maman in French, she saw his face turn red. She could tell he was livid. He hung up and glared at her.

"What the fuck did you do?"

"I don't know what you are talking about. Calm down." She reached for him, and he slapped her hand away.

"You let her get out of jail? Unaccompanied? Are you fucking nuts? Who asked you to help? How is this any of your business?"

She pulled the covers up around her. "I thought I was helping."

"Well, you are not; you made things worse. I can't believe what a controlling bitch you are. I have to go fix this."

He grabbed his clothes and stomped out, slamming the door.

Wounded and still extremely horny, she called her pilot and left France within two hours. Not sure what to think, she was raw, vacillating between anger and hurt. Her rational side saw his point of view thought he was acting like a child with extreme over-reaction. When she got home, there was already an email from him. She was afraid to read it at first, thinking it would be his resignation.

To: Nadailia

From: Dylan

Regarding: I am a dick

Nadailia,

I realize I over-reacted and was a huge dick to you. If you never talk to me again, you are justified. Regardless of emotional

immaturity and being wound as tight as a clock about my family, I
adore you. I want to work for you and be your lover. I know it will
take time to gain your trust again. But you are a fire-starter. You see
that in me too. We can get this back on track. I believe there are two
kinds of people in the world. Those who start fires and those who
avoid them. Even those who put them out –temporarily are avoiding
them.

Those of us who do start fires recognize it in each other.

We also thrive on the kindling, the fuel source and how hot it
will burn.

Life doesn't allow you to rehearse.

Those who play each scene like it matters are fulfilled.

Passion, pleasure and pain drive the flame and fuel the creativity.

We have started a fire. It begs to be fed. It requires visual and
visceral. It asks for action.

This has become it's own life force.

This is attempting to become sentient.

This desires to be exponential with no point of reference.

It covets the burn.

At least we are not dying slowly.

We don't need to accept their rules.

It's our diversion.

Life is nothing but timing.

We own this.

This makes us incandescent.

Yours forever,

Dylan (the dickhead)

She was elated at his librettos. His words had always fed her soul,
almost as thoroughly as his food. She wrote back immediately.

To: Dylan

From: Nadailia

Regarding: I am yours forever

To My Dear Dylan,

I am not mad. I get that I overstepped. I tend to do that. Every five minutes I check for your text. It feels like a lifeline to you and the only way I've been able to express my affection for you. If our world never expands to more ways to share each other, it won't be so bad.

This longing is a new experience for me. Even in my wild youth, no one captured me as you have. I'm thrilled by the passion you've ignited. I create more freely and consistently. I like my conceptions. I want to keep having new experiences with you. This is a precious gift and one I will always treasure. You are miraculous. You will always have a job in my kitchen.

I'm Yours Forever,

Nadailia

To: Nadailia

From: Dylan

Regarding: Powerful gift

To Nadailia:

Very powerful.

Thank you for sharing; that was the greatest gift I have ever received. I'm excited the fire has been lit again.

To quote from Mark Twain: "The two most important days in your life are the day you were born and the day you find out why."

It has been hard to reconcile these new feelings, and our recourse was to express them physically. As fulfilling as it was, it derailed us, and we recognized it and changed course. Only you and I will ever know the cause of these changes. It is our lost treasure found. That secret will be the last smile on our lips as we pass to the next adventure.

Now, the physical and mental tenure of you is the same. I still want you. I desire you. I'm starving for you.

Dylan

That night she led him through their first sext-capade.

Text

N: What are you doing there in France all by yourself?

D: I'm naked under a sheet on my stomach in the dark.

N: In bed?

D: Yes, just now. Long day, Maman is safe with me. Sleeping on my couch.

N: So, here is what I want you to do.

D: Ok

N: Pull your dick under your belly so you are laying on it.

D: Done.

N: Now I want you to rock back and forth, side to side.

D: Ok.

N: Imagine me straddling your ass.

D: Mmmmmmmm.

N: My wet pussy leaving warm then cold marks on your back.

Now I'm kneading your ass.

Pulling it open. Pushing your growing cock down.

Keep rocking.

D: I'd love to turn over and plug one of your holes.

N: No touching.

D: Ok.

N: Yet.

Now spread your legs.

Feel the cold draft on your balls.

Imagine me licking you.

D: Yes. Good.

N: The saliva hot, then cold.

Keep rocking.

My tongue moves up to your ass.

I spread your cheeks and lick.

Kiss and suck you.

Are you hard yet?

D: I was hard at "Hello."

N: Good. Now I take my lips and lick your ass.

D: You have an amazing effect on me.

N: I know.

And you on me.

Focus.

D: Ok.

N: I'm licking your ass. My hands on your balls.

You beg me to take your cock.

But I won't.

D: Please.

N: You want it; rock it. My fingers graze and tickle your balls as my tongue works the outer rim of your ass.

D: Mmmm good.

N: My tongue goes in.

D: Fuck.

N: I suck and apply pressure you've never felt there.

My tongue is in you.

My hands are aggressive on your balls.

I place one finger in your ass.

I find your G spot. It's swollen and wants me.

D: Oh shit.

N: I reach around and grab the tip of your cock.

It's wet.

Just my palm over the top.

D: Ohhhhhh nice.

N: I'm biting your ass.

One finger in you. The other hand on the tip.

You are pinned and want to turn over.

But I won't let you.

I move my finger deeper.

I kiss your balls.

Lick them. Swallow them.

I turn you over and take you in my mouth.

Completely down my throat.

D: That's perfect.

N: My finger is still up your ass.

You are ready to cum?

I hope not. I've only begun.

D: Holy shit.

N: I take your dick in and out.

Blocking my airway.

Rubbing your G spot.

Over and over, I slam into you with my mouth.

Sucking. Licking. Devouring.

Fucking my face.

D: So hard and wet.

N: I take my face off your dick and work you with my hand.

Now!

D: Ok.

N: Take your fantastic dick in your left hand.

Feel me inside your ass.

Stroke it from top to bottom. Lightly.

Open your mouth. Feel my breast in there.

D: Yes.

N: Suck me while you stroke.

Remember the pressure in your ass.

Grab your cock at the base and squeeze hard.

Good.

Hold it there.

Now take the tip in your hand and rub under your head in circles.

D: Yes.

N: Feel the pre-cum.

Take your other hand and graze your balls.

Now stroke it.

Remembering me sucking it.

Remember every sound. Every sensation.

The look of my head bobbing on you.

D: Mmmmm.

N: Now think of slamming that cock into me.

Up against a wall.

Skirt hiked up.

No panties.

Fuck me hard.

Now cum.

D: Cummmming.

Oh shit!

N: You like?

D: Mmmmm. Be right back :-)

D: Wow, nice! Thank you!

N: Your welcome. Would be happy to do it in person when you come back.

D: That would be delicious.

N: Go to sleep.

Dream of me

D: I will sleep like a baby having adult dreams.

N: Know that you have my heart.

D: And you mine.

The Back of The Tiger

Dylan took his Maman to dinner at a quaint little seaside bistro overlooking the ocean. The rumor was that this chef was dazzling with his small plates and creative uses of flavors.

Their waiter started them with a palate cleanser of a puff pastry holding duck and kumquat zest sitting in a vinaigrette reduction sauce with micro greens. They were both surprised at the complex, yet simple, flavors of this little first dish.

"Maman, I need to get back, and I need you to come with me. I have a fantastic job there now with a great boss. I don't want to lose this opportunity."

"I think you are hot for this boss. No?"

"I think you should mind your own business and know that I can't support you if I don't have a job."

"So I come live with you, and you baby-sit my every move?"

"No, Maman, you can have your own studio and do whatever you want, as long as it is legal."

They were joined by five of Maman's friends. The restaurant offered meals in four-course options. It was the most creative, brave menu Dylan had seen and clearly was created by a chef that possessed colossal talent. He artfully brought together flavors that dazzled and delighted the senses. Even the names of the dishes were inventive and promised culinary relishes. They ordered literally everything on the menu and passed it around. They had pommes frites with garden herbs and truffle oil, astounded to find that these simple potatoes could taste this good. The Blue Crab Frites were flash fried soft-shell crab dipped in a saffron aioli, another testament to this chef's extreme talent.

The Soft-Shell Crab was a tower of flavor. The crab is flash-fried with a light breading, stacked over fried green tomato, mustard greens, avocado, Nueske bacon and cherry tomatoes. The freshness of the sea, the taste of the earth, all mixed with precision.

On the parade of amazing dishes: squash blossom fritters, crispy veal sweetbreads, and liver and onions. Dylan was beyond impressed, and the main courses had not arrived yet.

Artic char is a fish that is seldom found on any menu and is highly prized. This was prepared with succotash, paté à choux gnocchi, garden herb butter and the char's roe. Maman was over the moon in love with this. Dylan proclaimed from his end of the table that his entrée was the best: day-boat scallops with forbidden rice, baby bok choy, lemongrass buerre blanc, and pickled vegetables. They also feasted on wild Alaskan halibut, rabbit with wild mushrooms, and prime Angus strip loin steak. Every dish was creative, amazing and palate pleasing beyond their expectations. Dylan was taking copious notes on every dish and presentation.

The dessert was called Coffee Hour, a French doughnut with hazelnut croquant and espresso semifreddo with chocolate sauce, a delicious delight that sang through their taste buds. The Mixed Berry Shortcake was amazing, with a cake soaked in berry caramel sauce with peaked whipped cream. The French chef impressed Dylan with an aptly named American dessert, One Bourbon, One Scotch, One Beer: a testament to the American George Thorogood. It was three startling desserts served in tandem: peach bourbon bundt cake, butterscotch ice cream and a chocolate stout pot de crème. All were happy and full when the chef came out to chat with them. They sang his praises, and Maman offered a marriage proposal.

As they drove home, Dylan put his foot down and, reveling in this sumptuous meal, told Maman he was leaving by the end of the week, with or without her.

Text

N: I'm missing you terribly.

D: I miss you too.

N: The quiet seeps into my subconscious, and I make up shit.

D: Like what?

N: My mind is a scary place. It thinks of the worst of the worst. I have to remind myself to stop making up worse case scenarios.

I like my mind better when it's sex soaked. LOL.

D: Ok. I think I get it. Listen, it's weird over here. It's like I'm in some other dimension. No time of my own, constant pressure to rescue Maman from her latest scheme.

N: I TOTALLY understand. I couldn't do it for more than three days.

I'm not putting any demands on you.

Letting you know I miss that thing we have.

Especially since I'm immersed in it.

D: I know.

I miss it too, and that's part of my angst and impatience with this chaos.

N: A few more days.

D: It's like I'm treading water.

N: Without you, I feel like I'm in an eternal dentist's waiting room with static Muzak and 20-year-old magazines.

And someone did all the puzzles in Highlights!

Returning to America

D ylan and his Maman flew home, where he set her up in the spare room, hid all the wine and was eager to get back to his kitchen and his life with Nadailia. He turned on Turner Movie Classics for Maman and went to Consumed. He entered his office and found Jeffrey in his chair, counting a stack of money while shredding dinner tickets from what looked like Nadailia's other restaurants.

"What is going on here?" Dylan crossed to his desk to grab the last of the tickets. Jeffrey grabbed the cash and screamed, "None of your damn business. I thought that bitch fired you?"

"No luck, Jeffrey, I was doing R & D. Do you want to explain this?"

"None of your fucking business." Jeffrey grabbed the cash, slammed out the door and was gone.

Dylan knew exactly what he was doing: taking the cash sales for himself and destroying the order tickets. This is a classic restaurant scam. Nadailia is going to be furious. Problem was that there was no way of knowing how much he had stolen or how long this had been going on.

Seaside Resort

For the celebration of returning to the states, Stu, Maman, Dylan, Nadailia and Lauren went to a seaside five-star resort, as they had been told it was a trifecta of culinary perfection, unmatched anywhere in the county. With spectacular views, an unequaled wait staff and a touch of panache rarely seen in this area, it was something to aspire to.

The amuse bouche was an awe-inspiring and palate-cleansing tomato gazpacho with a panko garlic covering. They moved to a favorite, Cayucos Abalone and Crispy Pork Belly. The abalone, sitting on a bed of crispy pork belly with brown butter and ginger, broke out the compliments. Every bite was perfection, and Meyer lemon sauce made the dish as delicious as it was beautiful. Dylan touched Nadailia tentatively, and she responded wantonly pushing his hand up her thigh. Next came the Seared Ahi with roasted beets, tempura asparagus and a signature salsa verde. They were excited to move on and share more. The group saluted with 3 bottles of 2013 Santa Ynez Valley Cabernet Franc from Lo-Fi Wines. Dylan and Nadailia gazed into each other's eyes for the first time in seven long days.

Next, the salads; an Heirloom Tomato Caprese Style with tasty goat burrata cheese, tangy wild arugula, white balsamic pickled onions, pesto and house-made country croutons, a virtual party in their mouths. Their legs wrapped around each other below the table, sneaking touches across the table and risking everything for the slightest of touches.

The flatbreads were astounding. So much texture, essence and flair. They ordered two more after tasting one bite. These housed a myriad of flavors, including whole roasted garlic, olive tapenade and gorgonzola dolce cheese. The savory flavors blossomed as everyone's favorite, which had huge slices of fresh green figs, a smattering of blue cheese, delectable prosciutto and a light salsa verde for heat. They toasted Dylan's return, beaming secretive smiles. Maman watched them like a hawk, and Lauren tried her best to distract the devoted mother with talk of wine tasting.

The Cedar-Planked King Salmon, lying on citrus-scented basmati rice with wilted summer greens and a cilantro pesto, was cooked to perfection, and the marinated tomatoes brought out the acidity that made this fish whirl. The Burrata Ravioli, a house-made pillow of pasta and savory cheese, rested in a bed of slightly roasted heirloom baby tomatoes with local herbs and extra virgin olive oil. This was a sensuous dining experience, and the room fell away. They fell in love with the Black Summer Truffle-scented Chicken, which had tantalizing flavors that danced on your tongue. The Parisian gnocchi and the prosciutto wrapped Treviso, a red radicchio, which is also called "the winter flower" – was delightful in its sherry laced natural pan jus.

Then came the desserts: a milk chocolate pot de crème with house-made graham crackers and toasted marshmallows; a stone-fruit crostata with sour cream; and a brown sugar ice cream with a raspberry sauce that was so robust they fought over licking the bowl. Next came a trio of ice cream sandwiches. Each was a combination of sweet and frozen: a ginger snap cookie with plum ice cream; a snicker doodle cookie with strawberry ice cream; then a chocolate chip, pecan and date cookie with vanilla ice cream. All miraculous in mixture and preparation that lust was ignited in everyone, most of all in Dylan and Nadailia.

Text

D: You alone?

N: Yes, thinking of what I would do to you if you were here now.

D: Do tell.

N: Where are you?

D: In bed on my stomach.

N: I'd straddle you naked.

You can feel my wetness on the back of your thighs.

I rub your gluts and your magnificent ass.

D: Mmmmmmm.

N: My hands dipping between your legs.

Quickly and lightly.

While I massage your lower back and down.

At the base of your spine, there is a pleasure point.

When rubbed correctly, it will make a man cum.

D: That's new.

N: It even works on many paralyzed people.

I'm full of tricks.

I find yours and give it the proper amount of stimulus.

You feel my hair graze your back.

One hand on your spine, the other between your legs.

N: You're so hard now it's uncomfortable.

I adjust you so your cock is up and under your belly.

I'm rocking you back and forth while rubbing.

Deeply massaging your ass.

D: Sounds good.

N: While I work the magic spot on your spine.

The orgasm surprises you.

But you don't come.

D: Interesting.

N: All the feelings, no ejaculation.

I roll you over and take your cock in both my hands.

I roll you like dough. Up and down.

You start to cum again.

D: I'd explode by now.

N: This time, I place light pressure on your perineum.

You have another orgasm.

Still no ejaculate.

All the same sensations, just no juice.

And you are still hard.

Steel hard.

When your breathing returns to normal

I massage your chest and work down to your groin.

This time I take your cock in my mouth.

D: Mmmmmm.

N: I suck and lick you like a starving woman.

Devouring you.

Tasting you.

Massaging your balls.

This time when you cum, I let the juice flow

You are like a fire hose.

All over my tits and face.

D: Nice.

N: You actually scream as you climax.

My goal.

Fish Eye to Eye

Dylan and Nadailia were not sure what was coming next, the time apart and the feeling of passion for each other frenzied them. They booked a suite at an oceanfront hotel the next day. They heard the door lock behind them and stared at each other, eyes burning with desire.

She moved him over toward the wall, and her softness suddenly turned to stiffness as she shoved him against it. He was surprised out of his stupor and raised his hands to shove her back. As he did, she dropped to her knees and started to rub her face on his pants, searching for the top of his dick with her mouth. After finding and nipping the top and placing him back in his passion coma, she quickly unzipped his pants and took him into her mouth. As Nadailia sucked and licked his cock, he moaned and rocked. Her mouth was perfectly tuned to play his instrument. He started to cum.

She took her thumb and placed it firmly on his perineum with deep, strong, steady pleasure. This stopped the ejaculate, he still had an orgasm. When he finished convulsing, Nadailia released him and he dropped to the floor, stunned. She sat next to him, brushed his thigh and said, "What do you think, Chef?" with a sly smile.

"What the fuck was that? Can you do it again? What happened to me?"

"You had an orgasm without ejaculating. It is a Tao practice."

"I am still hard!"

Nadailia explained that the Taoists of ancient China looked upon sex as a vehicle for enlightenment, provided the sexual urge was properly harnessed. To them, sex and spirituality were interdependent. "That is the benefit of the practice," she said as she folded over and took him into her mouth again.

This time she licked the underside of his dick and sucked lightly. He was about to cum again; there was a knock at the door. He rolled onto his side to get up so as not to poke her with his rock-hard penis.

Room service delivered a Passion Pizza. More like a flatbread, this amazing amalgamation of flavors included La Quercia pancetta, butternut squash, apples, gorgonzola and caramelized onions, all diced and dispersed evenly around the pie, making each bite remarkable. On the top was a poached egg, which enhanced each flavor as it dispersed around the pie. As they ate the heavenly dish, each planned the next move. He was blown away that his desire had grown instead of diminishing, as it usually did when he came. He wanted to learn more, the Tao practice scared the hell out of him.

They followed the pizza with a chocolate-hazelnut terrine and salted caramel ice cream. This fantastic dessert had texture, flavor and panache. They had a late-harvest Foxen Zinfandel to wash the rich creaminess of the chocolate from their mouths. The room had fallen quite as the music had stopped, and their desire of the food had momentary distracted them from their unbridled passion for each other.

As the candlelight flickered between them, their eyes met. The gaze was so intense, so burning, that they both looked away, almost embarrassed.

Dylan mumbled, "What the fuck is happening?"

He jumped up from the table, grabbed his coat and ran for the door. "Where the fuck are you going?" she said, astounded that he was running. He did not answer. All she heard was the slam of the door.

Later that night she got a text:

D: I'm conflicted, hotter than Hades and confused.

N: I guess. You left me stranded in a hotel room.

D: What was that fucking trick? I'm still fucking hard.

N: It's something I want to teach you more about. It's called The Practice.

D: I am not sure I want that, damn – your touch, your mouth was like wildfire. I got pretty excited, as you may have noticed.

N: You ran out the door.

D: I guess part of the passion is in the "We shouldn't be doing this."

N: What are you afraid of?

D: I am not sure. I want you, and I want to learn, not get entangled. Is that even possible?

N: No. Both are not possible.

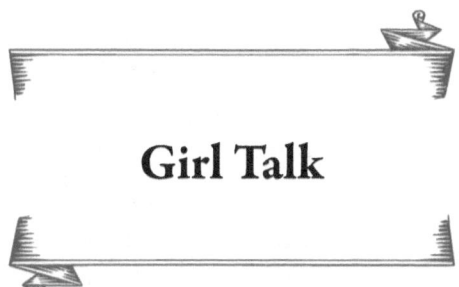

Girl Talk

Lauren sipped her Clesi Malvasia Bianca and listened to Nadailia obsess about this man/chef. The fact that Nadailia was so connected and still had not had him fuck her, this was making Lauren crazy. She loved her so and wished that this man would uncrack her damaged heart. He seemed to take his pleasure and run, and that worried Lauren.

They started with the Green Bean Casserole, which was a combination of haricots-verts, diced smoky bacon, crispy won ton chips, basil and mandarin oranges, all sitting in a hoisin-miso glaze. The sauce was so good that Lauren embarrassed the waitress by licking the plate (She made sure their bread bowl was full after that.) Their appetizer was from the dessert menu and featured three kinds of fresh figs, black mission, Texas and green, all sliced in half and resting over an orange-cardamom Bavrois with honey-cardamom syrup and a triangular sugar cookie. It was so original, with freshness and sweetness shining through, that they ordered another.

"What am I going to do?" Nadailia lamented while spooning figs into her mouth.

"Finally get fucked, I hope."

"This is so amusing to you, isn't it? I am confused, lusted up and not sure what to do with this man."

Lauren looked at her tortured friend and smirked. "Good. I think you not controlling everything is why this is lasting."

Jack, the maitre d', opened a bottle of 2005 Foxen Range 30 West Pinot Noir and shared his current anecdote. Nadailia got the feeling that many diners came to chat with Jack. He was "zippy" personified. She made a mental note to hire him for one of her restaurants. He made instant friends of everyone and would be a pronounced addition. They shared a Caesar salad, which was flawlessly arranged with the hearts of the romaine still intact and Spanish white anchovy, crostini and parmesan cheese. Lauren went for the Chilled Zucchini and Basil Soup; it was magnificent with Arbequina olive oil drizzled on top. "Have you told him?"

"That I am frigid!?! No!"

"You are not frigid; you just haven't found the right stimuli."

For their entrée, they had the Caramelized Pork Belly, which was perfection. It is the love handles of the pig (basically uncured bacon), reduced down to a delectable treat. It was served over udon noodles, sautéed shitake mushrooms and market cabbage with an Elephant Heart plum sauce and sweet, spiced pork jus. This was the best pork dish Lauren had ever had. They did save room for one more desert, a house-spun watermelon sorbet.

Nadailia was slightly drunk when she got home, so she decided it was time for another sext-capade.

Text

N: Where are you right now?

D: Kitchen.

N: Standing?

D: Yes.

N: Go over to the sink.

D: Ok.

N: Put your hands on the cool tile.

D: Ok.

N: Close you eyes and remember me there.

On my knees.

D: I am.

N: Sucking you.

D: Yes!

N: You are pulling my hair.

D: Mmmmmmm good.

N: Holding it out of your way.

D: Yes.

N: Rub against the tile.

D: Ok.

N: Think of my head bobbing.

Conquering.

Sucking.

Swallowing.

N: Grabbing your ass.

D: And your wet panties.

N: Tickling your balls.

As I try over and over to swallow you.

You noticed each time I get better?

You know I'm practicing.

D: How?

N: Big fucking carrots.

You've seen them.

In your garden.

D: I'm still there and still hard.

N: Go to the freezer.

Get one ice cube.

Go back to the sink.

D: Got it.

N: Set the ice cube on the counter.

D: Done.

N: Unbuckle and drop your pants.

D: Done.

N: Take your shirt off.

Turn on the hot water.

Let it run.

Pick up the ice cube and rub it on your lips.

D: Ok.

N: See me. I'm on my knees in front of you.

D: Mmmmmm.

N: Move it to your nipples.

D: Ohhhh.

N: Left then right.

D: They are hard.

N: Train it down your belly.

D: Cold.

N: Stroke your cock with the ice cube.

Feel the sensation of cold.

Take your left hand.

Put it in the hot water.

D: Ok.

N: Keep moving the ice cube around.

Try it on your balls.

Move it to the back.

D: Mmmmmm.

N: Now take your warm left hand.

And envelop your cock.

I'm left-handed.

It's me. Warm, and full of desire.

Devouring you.

Wanting you.

Sucking the cum right out of you.

D: Holy shit.

N: Now cum in the sink.

Think of fucking me. Hard.

D: Wow, I needed that.
N: I'm going to sleep and dream of you.
And plan my attack.
D: Thanks for the warning!

Joined Mandarin Ducks

The next day at work, Nadailia was short and curt with everyone. Funny thing so was Dylan. Both had a feeling of restlessness in their bellies and a cloudy perception of what is right or wrong. After about six hours of burning from the inside out and not being able to concentrate on the easiest task, she barged into his office.

"What?" He looked up at her and instantly was filled with happiness.

Nadailia smiled and was suddenly more relaxed as he sat. "I love the texts. I always wanted to be a writer, so this hot role-play is pushing my buttons. You are coming over to my house tonight, and we are going to figure this out once and for all."

"Aren't you a bossy cow?"

"Are you coming or not?"

"Apparently I have now choice."

"I will take that as a yes."

Dylan squirmed in his chair. "In my defense, I was sitting in my kitchen and started thinking about you not wearing panties."

She smiled shrewdly. "I'm not. I'm an eternal optimist."

"This is an almost impossible work situation."

She agreed, "Yes it is a bit tricky."

Dylan walked around the desk and looked into her eyes. "I want to slip my hand under your dress and put my hand on your pussy and my middle finger in you."

Nadailia shuttered, looked back at him and said, "Oh, I about came with that sentence."

"Tomorrow while I'm working, I'm going commando, for your mental entertainment."

She smiled. "I love that you are ready for an impromptu blow job."

"Always."

Nadailia shook her head to clear her thoughts. "We have to reconcile this. Here I was, trying to say that you were bad for breaking the touch rules, and the first chance I get, I grab your cock. Seriously, I am obsessed. I am flushed, wet and ready to disrobe you at any point. I have been a good businesswoman for too long. I couldn't get sexed up enough to teach someone The Practice. You came along, and problem solved."

"I don't mind being your plaything."

"It may come to more than that, because I am only thinking about fucking you."

Nadailia was pacing now. Like a tiger ready to strike. She knew what was right, she wanted this man anyway. He had told her about Jeffery's theft, and it had been made clear that Jeffrey's only desire was to get Nadailia thrown out of Consumed and for him to take over. If she stayed out of trouble, Jeffrey would implode himself. The trouble was impossible to avoid when this hot chef was standing in front of her.

"This is new territory for me," she said. "I don't trust easily. That being said, I trust you completely. This puts me in a precarious situation. That is my issue, not yours. In a short time, I have become devoted to you."

Dylan smiled and moved toward her. She held up her hand, motioning him to stay put. "I am fueled by your passionate words," she said, and by your work and your longing for me, and it keeps intensifying. Devotion is not something I have ever given to anyone.

Not a cause, religion or person has ever caused me to feel this strong pull. Until you. From the first, your desire was intoxicating. It drew me in like a moth to a flame. I have been wanted, never desired. It was word play until you touched me and the infernos ignited. And they have stayed kindled for weeks now.

Then I got to taste you, to feel your real appetite for me through your lips and hands. Even your breath spoke of your longing. It has created the strongest memory for me, one that fills my unconscious and keeps my loins stirred every day."

Dylan was leaning against the wall, feeling like prey, he began to speak:

"I passionately await that moment of your release, as I have been greedy and stupid. I have fantasized about it in many different variations. I welcome your touch, your lips and your arms around me. I love your planning; I desire the fulfillment. I want the heat of my breath on your breasts, my teeth on your nipples, pulling them, hardening them to attention. I want you to tease me, to coax my cock to hardness and make it throb with excitement, leaking pre-cum in anticipation of your mouth and your pussy. I want to build and delay until we can stand it no longer. I want to explore your wet pussy with my fingers, mapping your most sensitive spots. Then slide my rock-hard cock into you and exploit those newly discovered territories. I want to bring you almost to completion, then finish you with my hands in your pussy and on your clit, feeling you shudder and moan with release."

She almost fainted from the wall of passion his words brought to her. It was more powerful hearing him speak them than reading them. She crossed to him, and took his face in her hands. He pulled them down and looked sadly into her eyes.

"I am still not comfortable with having an affair with a married woman, especially someone who is my boss. I am crazy about you, lust after you, it seems wrong. I love us creating in the restaurant and with our words, I cannot reconcile having a physical affair with you – until I see you, and then all my convictions get thrown out the window. I am so conflicted. I don't want to stop, ever. This is a lovely mess, as my Maman likes to say, who, by the way, is driving me crazy."

The words stung, and she spun on her heals and left him standing in his office.

Text

D: Sorry about today.

N: I get it. You were honest.

D: I think I always do and say the wrong things.

N: No, it's fine. I was thinking about touching.

D: And?

N: Lightly touching your hands. Up the inside of your arms.
Around your neck and ears.
Down your jaw. Then landing soft kisses.

D: Nice.

N: Light feather kisses on your lips.
Slow and easy. My tongue finding my way around your mouth.
Deep and full, but still soft.
Biting your lips gently. Taking your face in my hands.

D: Mmmmm.

N: And kissing for 10 minutes.
Lost in the sensation of your lips and tongue.
Running my tongue over your teeth.
And then your lips.
Still gentle, like I have all the time in the world to devour you.
Moving my hands down your hard chest.
Feeling the power of you.
Stopping to feel your heartbeat.
The rhythm of you.
I haven't spent nearly enough time on your neck.
Nibbling, caressing.

Finding your neck spot.

D: We never have enough time.

N: Then to your ears.

My hot breath echoing.

Biting your earlobe.

Finding your pleasure centers with sound and feel.

D: I'd love to be stretched out naked, face down on a massage table for this.

N: I think I would stop there and make you beg for more.

I like you face up ;-)

Then on your back. I have a whole other plan.

D: I would be dripping by now.

N: Want to hear it?

I'd lick it off.

D: Mmmmmm.

N: I'm too quick to take you in my mouth.

I need to explore more of you.

D: Time is our nemesis.

N: Not really.

We need to learn to manage it better.

D: I am trying not to burn out the fire.

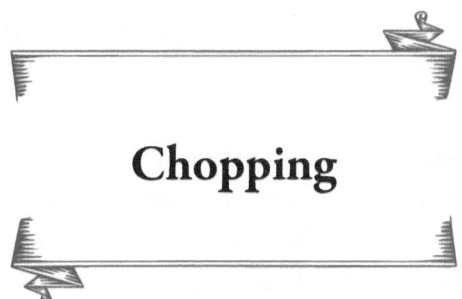

Chopping

The next night after the staff had gone home, she watched him closely as she perched on the chopping block while he cleaned up and prepared for the next day. She was eerily silent, which made him uncomfortable. It was like being stalked by a tiger.

"Tell me a story while you watch me slave."

Intrigued by the concept, she poured another glass of wine. "What kind of story?"

"Of your past, your sexual past. Tell me about your lovers."

"Really? You can handle that?"

Dylan looked at her and winked. "I can handle anything from you."

Nadailia took a big swig of wine and started talking in a low, sexy voice.

"The knock on the window startled me.

Then I remembered it was the first Monday of the month. And I smiled and got instantly wet.

I was glad I had remembered to wear my pink pinafore. But no panties.

I threw back the covers and walked to the window.

I saw he was like a toddler with his face pressed against the glass.

I opened the window, and he climbed in.

As I went to shut it, a voice yelped.

I turned to Doug. 'What the fuck?'

He smiled, his two different colored eyes twinkling. 'I brought a friend.'

In climbed Doctor Number Two.

These once-a-month booty calls were a great source of pleasure for me, a source of need for him. He got an eight-hour window once a month to fuck. And he liked to fuck me. He ate my pussy like a starving man. So I indulged him.

We went into the living room, and I poured tequila shots for the three of us.

The rules were no talking about med school or real life. We discussed Tom Robbins novels, sailing, food and theater.

He loved that I was running an experimental theater and wanted stories from the land of misfits. He also liked that I only took lovers. No boyfriends. I was strong and uncomplicated. I loved to fuck and experiment. I was the perfect partner for a medical student.

I sat on his lap as we discussed a recent sailing race. Running my fingers around his ears, knowing this kick started him. He stopped mid-sentence and kissed me on the mouth, hard. Tongues intertwining and breathing each other in.

Sam watched from the couch. Doug asked if I would share. I took a shot of tequila and said, 'Why not?'

Sam walked over, his enthusiasm showing through his scrubs. He kneeled in front of us, and Doug turned me 180 degrees and opened my legs that were resting on his. Sam dove between my legs head first. Anatomy class served him and Doug well. Sam licked and plunged his tongue as Doug played with my tits beneath the pink chiffon. He kissed and bit my neck.

Sam ate me until my juices were dripping off his chin. Doug rose, lifted me up and turned my face to the back of the couch, knees pulled up, my dripping pussy exposed.

Doug entered my pussy, and as always, the size of him shocked and delighted me. Sam came around to the back of the couch and pulled down his scrubs. His small stature did not prepare me for the size of his dick, which he placed in my open mouth. As I sucked and attempted to swallow Sam, Doug fucked me hard from behind. It was always his first move, fucking his stress of med school. He pulled out and came all over my ass. I stood up, and Sam rested on the floor. Doug took my hand and led me down, lying on top of Sam. Sam kissed me – not as powerfully as Doug, but pleasantly.

Doug rubbed my back and ran his hands down my ass and spread my legs apart.

He literally slid Sam's dick into me. Sam began rocking. And I moved with his rhythm. Doug climbed on my back and slid his dick into my ass. The feeling was so overwhelming. I made them both hold still while my body adjusted. Then I said, 'I'm ready.'

They both started moving slowly. I asked if they could feel each other's dick inside me. This started a back-and-forth rhythm as they alternated in and out, feeling each other through my pussy wall. Doug came again inside me. Poor Sam had not cum yet and was pinned under two sex-crazed idiots.

Doug cumming makes me even hornier, so I said, 'Sam, sit up!' He did, and I straddled him. I rode his pony, taking his huge cock all the way in. As I rode him, Doug fed him shots of tequila. Sam started to cum, so I quickly jumped off and stroked him until he came on my tits.

We went to the kitchen and cooked naked, then started Round Two. They left at 5 a.m.

10 years later I took my nieces to a new pediatrician. When the doctor came into the room, it was Sam. He smiled and kissed me. He said to the kids, 'You have a great aunt.'"

"No fucking way!" Dylan was staring at her with his dick in his hand, not even realizing it.

"Way," was all Nadailia said as she crossed to him and kissed him hard on the mouth. She dropped to her knees and took him in her mouth. He was rock hard and ready for her. He gathered up her long red hair and wound it like a rope while he gently pulled, and she drank him in completely, taking him all the way down her throat, and then swirling around the tip, trouncing on the underside, and then sucking him again. Her fingers tickled his balls as the other hand grabbed his ass. She encouraged him to fuck her face, and he obliged. When he came, she continued sucking long after he was done, and he was comfortable with her continued contact. The result was another sneaker orgasm, which made his knees buckle.

She kissed him on the lips and said good night as he stood there panting over his butcher block.

"Damn woman is going to fuck me to death," he said to the dark and empty kitchen. The clicking of a video camera turning off caught his attention as he pulled up his pants and looked for the voyeur.

When Dylan got home, he found an email from Nadailia.

To: Dylan

From: Nadailia

Regarding: Sexual Feelings

Dylan,

This might clarify my position. I've always been a sexual being. I remember my first sexual feeling was when I was 8. I was pressing my feet against a sliding glass door in winter. The sensation was hot at first, and then as I pressed and held, it became cold. It made me feel things. In my stomach. Up my spine. My mind wandered to fantastical places. I did not know what it was then, I recognized the feeling when I was older and had the vocabulary to explain it. The difference with me, compared to the rest of the world, is that I never did (and still don't) equate romantic love with sexual desire. I was a sexual experimenter young and learned how to control, expand and sustain my sexual power and pleasure. I never had boyfriends. They seemed cumbersome and demanded emotion that I never felt they were worthy of receiving. I took lovers. And treated sex like a hobby – a sport that I could excel at and gain perfection. I practiced, experimented, learned about my sensuality and my partners'. My pleasure was my main goal.

When I married, I chose a partner based on life skills, not on sexual desire. Marriage was a contract fulfilled with a partner witnessing my life. I always planned on having a lover and a husband. And never felt weird or guilty about possessing both.

Maybe that is why we are so apart on the lover equation. I don't want anything from you but loyalty, your words, honesty and sex. I never want you to replace my husband, live with you or be anything but a pleasure-giving entity. I don't want to be your mistress – just your lover.

But I see that because you started your sexual adventures in the confines of romantic love, this is an impossible concept for you. I can imagine why it's nearly impossible for you to reconcile what I'm wanting from you. I want for us to be lovers. You are hesitant, and rightly so. I do want to share my body with you, along with my raw desire for you. You bring out the real Nadailia. I know that is why "This" exists. Either way, you remain my friend. The only one I trust with my words and secrets. My crazed desires. We will always exchange words, fuel each other's creativity and have each other's raw souls held in a safe place.

As always, this important realization came from you forcing something out of me. This time, real memories of who I am. When I chose who I was, I chose my path, not society's, not being married or a boss. The things you instinctively pull out of me make me better at being myself and more true to who I am. This is a gift I can never repay and will fight to keep until my death. You made me *Me* again.

I love you in a way neither you nor I have experienced before. I desire you in a way that is raw and untainted by rules. I will always be there with and for you. You fucked my mind and made me better.

Made me go back to when I was just Nadailia. This powerful gift will serve me forever. Thank you.

Nadailia

IYF

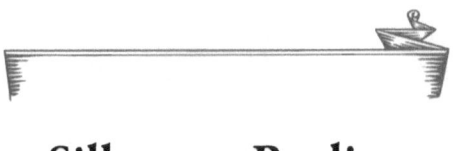

Silkworm Reeling

A renowned female chef opened a new bistro in town, and Dylan wanted to take Nadailia there to try everything. He explained, "With this new place, she can experiment and give us the freshest and tastiest renditions of French countryside-inspired dishes."

This hip space felt and looked like something you would find in a big city. It had an industrial feel with cool decorating touches, two bars, a lounge and a wine shop that stopped them in their tracks with its creativeness and hand-selected varietals.

Nadailia began with a Chateau Guibot from Bordeaux and a Pinot Noir from Stasis to go with the first round, which was from the Burrata Bar. Dylan explained that burrata is a fresh Italian cheese made from mozzarella and cream. The outer shell is solid mozzarella, while the inside contains both mozzarella and cream, giving it an unusual, soft texture. The first one they tried was the Lemon and Garlic, with lemon crème fraîche, garlic chips, an Italian dipping sauce called bagna càuda and small, anchovy-like fish called boquerones. The second was the Chanterelle, with an egg yolk vinaigrette and an earthy chanterelle conserva. The menu read, "Cheese – Milk's leap to Eternity," and they agreed with this after tasting these amazing amalgamations of flavors and textures. When they ate and drank like this, they always found a way to touch. Even if it was toe-to-toe, they found a way and encouraged feeding each other.

They moved on to the starters, which were all unique and prepared flawlessly. The Smoked Duck Crostini came with large slices of levain bread cooked until crisp. On them lay thin slices of smoked duck breast with an orange marmalade and Pozo Tomme, a raw sheep's milk cheese from Rinconada Dairy. Next was the Smoked Trout Lyonnaise salad with winter greens from Windrose Farms, king trumpet mushrooms, fresh croutons and a perfectly poached egg. Then came Nadailia's favorite dish, Rabbit Molé Tacos. An unbelievable combination of flavors that caused her to exclaim, "This is the best thing I have ever put in my mouth." Dylan smiled because he knew better.

Dylan raised an eyebrow as he tried the chocolaty Oaxacan molé, Mexican crema, orange slices, avocado and spectacular rabbit breast meat. It blew his taste buds away.

This executive chef, Julie is a rare and wondrous delight in the kitchen. She is brave and understands the complexity of flavors better than most, and insists on using the best ingredients.

They moved on to their favorite new find in wine, a Barton Wines Cabernet Franc. This wine was astounding by itself, it harmonized flawlessly with the next round of dishes. Dylan suggested the Pan Roasted Skate. Very few chefs even attempt to prepare it, he knew Chef Julie would wow his boss with this surprising combination of skate wing, coconut, fried peanuts and lychee. It was a delectable gift from the sea. Dylan began to pull on Nadailia's thigh, marching his fingers up to her always hot sex. Then came the next dish, and his hand went to cut and eat. The Quail and Cocoa Maltagliati Pasta mesmerized them with a hand-cut chocolate-infused pasta served with celery root, orange brown butter and pecorino, an Italian hard cheese similar to parmesan. They shared the Pavè Au Poivre, which was an impeccable 6-ounce Wagyu filet with wild mushrooms and a brandy cream.

In between they massaged each other's legs, not wanting anyone to see them in rapture. They moved on to desserts and ports. Each dessert was served in a small Mason jar, and each captivated their already-full bellies. There was a lemon-with-olive-oil cake layered with Meyer lemon curd and crème fraîche. Nadailia's favorite was the Tcho Chocolate Torte with macerated strawberries, rose petal jam and a black pepper anglaise. They all tasted extraordinary.

The service was impeccable, and the staff seemed to have the goal to make sure each diner had a magnificent experience. The check came with a packet of seasonal seeds to plant and grow your own organic Toscano kale. Nadailia and Dylan loved this little gift and vowed to plant it in their own garden by the light of the moon.

They went to his house and fell into a rapturous coma of food and wine, forgetting to have sex.

The next morning he was gone before she awoke. Although it had only been a few months since their affair started, and he still had not fucked her, it felt as if they had always been together. Her brain remained steeped in memories and fantasies about him. Upon waking, when a free moment appeared in the day, and especially at night, he swirled inside her head, the thoughts leaking down to her heart and loins. If someone had told her she could sustain a constant state of arousal for three months, she would have laughed them out of the room. Now she couldn't imagine life any other way.

Their private time was limited because of the secrecy of their relationship, they always managed to touch, brush each other's hands and, when a moment of solitude was presented, embrace and kiss as if they were drowning.

Text

D: Hey, thinking of you.

N: Specifically?

D: I need to fuck you.

N: Yes you do. When you are ready.

Just got out of the shower.

I'm dripping.

D: Love the visual.

N: I've been writhing all night.

Want to know what I did in the shower?

D: Yes.

N: Only if you promise to touch yourself.

D: Well that might be a problem since I'm sitting at a cafe. I will if you insist, I may not be welcome back here anymore.

So you know, you already have me hard before you even start the description.

N: First I rubbed my tits until my nipples were as hard as glass.

D: Mmmmmm.

N: I pinched them, pulled on them.

D: Nice.

N: I turned on the vibrator to the lowest setting and rubbed it on my tits, down my stomach to my clit.

My pussy was still dripping wet (pretty sure I have been for days now), so it slid nicely into my cunt.

I turned the power up one more notch and held it there with my clenched muscles.

I took the showerhead and turned it to pulsating.

D: Oh fuck. I love this.

N: I grazed the pumping water on my still hard nipples.

Then slid it down to my clit. The sensation was immediate.

D: Ahhhhhhh.

N: I was running a tape of you in my head.

I could feel the hotness, taste your cum and hear your heavy breathing.

D: Ohhhh maaan.

N: The shower was pumping, inside was vibrating and my brain was recalling every detail of our last encounter.

D: Sweet mental picture.

N: When I hear the words, "Tell me a story," I get wet.

D: Hot shit!

N: And I am hornier after.

When I get out of the shower shaking and dripping, and the text sound goes off on my phone.

I climax again.

All it takes now, a sound, a memory, or a well-put phrase.

D: Well. I'm so hard right now I could cut diamonds.

N: Words are our most inexhaustible source of magic.

Shifting Turning Dragons

The restaurant was full and lively, everyone enjoying the evening, from the staff to the patrons. It was a point of pride for them both that Consumed's atmosphere was one of joy and discovery. It mirrored their affair.

She was in her office printing new menus at the end of the evening. Dylan walked in. She was standing in front of her desk, leaning over and sorting the menus, her strong legs encased in intricate thigh-high hose and her skirt lifted, revealing a touch of silk panty. The sight overwhelmed him, and he quickly locked the door. Before she could turn, he was on her. One arm reaching around and grabbing her breast. The other hand taking her hair, pulling her head back as he attacked her neck with his lips. She turned her head to find his lips and responded with the same raw passion. Her hand reached over her shoulder and caressed his head as he kissed the back of her neck. Her other hand reached back and found his crotch. He was hard, and she rubbed his dick through his pants. Finding his zipper, she freed him.

He pushed her over the desk, face down, pulled her panties aside and slammed his cock inside her. He held her hair like a bridle and rode her hard. About to come undone, he picked her up and turned her around, forcing her to kneel in front of him. She opened her mouth like a baby robin begging to be fed. He held her head in his hands and fucked her face. She moaned with pleasure, the sound waves vibrating on his engorged cock. She was so damned good at

122

giving head and loved it so much it was intoxicating. He was about to cum when she jumped up and laid back on the desk, legs spread like a wanton whore and whispered, "Eat me."

He complied, immediately burying his head in her crotch. He worked the inner folds with his tongue, stroking up and landing on her clit, which was hard as rock. Her hips rocked and plunged toward his face as she grabbed his head with her hands, forcing him to go deeper, bite harder. As he nibbled and flicked her clit, she experienced a shock wave. He placed his finger in her pussy to feel and assist the waves. She released his head and brought him up to her face, and she licked her love juices off his lips and chin. He slid into her dripping pussy and came on the fifth stroke.

He collapsed on top of her, nuzzling her neck and panting, put still not sated. She did not want him to know. "Well, that was not how I saw our first time. Sorry, I couldn't help myself; you intoxicate me."

Just as they dressed, Jeffrey stormed into the office, using a key Nadailia did not know he had. They were covered and clearly flushed by the encounter. Jeffrey started screaming, "Are you two fucking in this office?"

"No!" Nadailia stomped, it wasn't convincing. Jeffrey had seen nothing except their flushed cheeks.

"I'm going to have you thrown out of here, you whore. You are cheating on my father and fucking the help."

Dylan strode up to him, red in the face, "You do that and I will have you brought up on grand larceny charges. I know you are stealing from the restaurants, and when I prove it I will have you removed and jailed."

Jeffrey spun on his heals and moving away from Dylan.

"You little fucker, you will not survive this." Pointing at Nadailia, he said, "This cunt will eat you alive."

Dylan leapt at him, grabbing him around the neck. Nadailia crossed the room quickly and separated them, showing a strength that surprised both men.

"Knock it the fuck off, both of you, and get out of my office."

They both filed out like scolded schoolboys.

Text

D: What are you doing?

N: Thinking about you. What do you want? Please resume the hot text.

D: If you were here right now, what would you do?

N: I would sit on your face.

D: Mmmmmmm I love that taste.

N: Tell me how you will eat me.

D: One of my favorite gourmet meals.

I can spend hours at that feast.

I would lick your labia on both sides first.

N: Wow.

D: Then slowly from the back to the front run the tip of my tongue up your wet pussy, flicking your clit with the tip of my tongue.

N: More.

D: I would then slowly roll my tongue around your clit to the right.

Lightly and slowly.

N: Fuck.

D: I would use my lips to suck on your clit, drawing it toward my teeth.

N: Bite me.

Holy shit my head is going to explode.

D: Barely holding it with my teeth, gently adding pressure.

No pain, biting down with steady pressure.

N: More.

D: Once your clit is between my teeth, I would flick it with my tongue while holding it captured.

N: Yes.

D: When I release it, all the blood would flow back and cause some pain.

D: I would stick my right pointy finger in your tight ass.

N: OMG!

D: Pushing all the way in to my knuckle.

Then harder.

N: Yes! My panties are off, finger inserted.

D: My thumb would be in your wet pussy and moving in and out at the same time.

N: Dylan.

D: You would feel like you were being double penetrated.

I would take my other hand.

N: Holy fuck.

D: And, palm up, insert two fingers into your pussy.

N: Dylan. Stop. No don't.

D: Using those two fingers to slide across the ridges on the roof of your pussy.

Then I would stop sliding those fingers and put pressure on that G spot.

N: I.

Am.

Ready.

D: I would lean up and take your hard nipple in my teeth and bite down slowly.

N: I am dying here.

D: Harder and harder until you squealed stop.

First pain then pleasure.

Good?

N: I am going to fuck you senseless next time I see you.

Count on that!

I must fuck you for at least 12 hours.

D: If only it were that simple.

N: It is. No one has to know.

D: I'm not sure when I'd be ready to say stop.

N: That's easy, when I make you crazy.

D: Already there.

N: It would be pleasure that would last us both a lifetime.

D: We could disappear for about a week.

N: Please

A retreat. You are on a food trip.

On some tropical island.

D: Yes!

N: We can fuck in the waves.

Fuck in the hut.

D: I love tropical!

N: Fuck in the jungle.

D: Nonstop.

N: I would tear you up.

I bet you would give in first and beg me to stop sucking your cock.

D: I'd let you try. I can give as good as I get.

N: I am insatiable.

D: You've never been load-tested properly.

N: That is true.

Please test me.

D: I wish.

N: I am booking a trip to St. Thomas right now. It is a spa retreat for me, food exploration for you.

D: Be reasonable.

N: Why not? With the shit we have been through, a week of pleasure is the least that is due. No one will ever have to know.

D: Just how would we ever wipe the smirks off our faces?

N: We wouldn't. Everyone would love how happy we would be.

Your kitchen staff is already bitching about what an asshole you are.

D: I'll dream of you.

N: Goodnight, handsome.

She sent him an email:

To: Dylan

From: Nadailia

Subject: The Caribbean Dream

Us on St. Thomas: The warm water engulfed us. They dove into the sea and held each other close, so happy to be able to touch each other openly.

After scooping up the soft sand under the water, the sensation erotic in her hands. She swam up to him and wrapped her legs around his waist. She kissed him long and deep. As the waves batted them around, she clung to him. She found his dick hardening, and she moved her bathing suit aside, pulled his cock out and placed him at the entrance to her cunt. He entered her with the rhythm of the waves, and he began to move in a circle.

She released his neck and fell back into the water. Floating, with her arms stretched out like a resurrection, and still connected to him. He moved in and out as she floated on the water, pure bliss on her face. As they swayed with the cadence of the ocean, they both had a slight release that they knew was the start of a week-long sexual exploration.

A dread-headed man yelling from the shore startled them, "You stop doing that in my ocean." They moved to their hotel room and fucked for days.

-N

IYF

The next day she circled his kitchen like a hawk looking for a tasty rabbit. "How is your Maman doing?"

"She is bored out of her brains. She needs a job, a hobby or a lover."

"How about all three?" Nadailia teased.

"Nadailia, if you could help her find a purpose, I would love you forever."

"You are going to love me anyway." Dylan took her into his arms, dipped her like a 1940's movie star and kissed her deeply. He raised her up and slapped her on the butt. She was so shocked by this move that she did not see Jeffrey standing in the pantry.

Dylan left the restaurant, as he had to pick up his Maman early for a job interview that she had been granted. Her English was sparse, so he wanted to be there as an interpreter.

He drove, absent-mindedly chatting with Maman about new Paso Robles Zinfandels she had discovered and how California might not be in the wine dark ages, as she had suspected.

What Dylan did not realize was that he was taking his Maman to his restaurant. She hopped out before he could protest too much and was greeted at the door by Nadailia, who smiled innocently at him and waved as his Maman stepped inside.

While his Maman was interviewing for a job that he was sure would ruin his life, he decided turnabout was fair play and went to Nadailia's house. She had given him the key when he was looking for a rare wine in her cellar.

He entered her house and quietly walked from room to room. Nadailia had told him the nurse and husband was away for a long medical procedure, so he was alone there. He stood in the doorway of each room, looking at each item as if he were determining its reason for existence and why it was placed where it was. Dylan liked the way she had designed the interior of her home, sure that she had designed it herself. As a chef, he had always felt a kinship with interior designers. He felt they both had to have a sense of what is pleasing to the eye and how to arrange objects in their proper positions.

Nadailia's house was expensively, not ostentatiously, appointed. All her furniture was well constructed. An excellent balance of form and function. Several rooms, the ones she apparently never used, looked almost staged, as if they were ready for a photo shoot for Architectural Digest. The area she lived in was more pleasing to him. In her bedroom he could smell her essence. He saw where yesterday's clothes were dropped on the bed, and he withheld the desire to smell them. Her nylon gym shorts, sports bra and a T-shirt on the floor. Her bedcovers were askew as if she had jumped out of bed. He wondered if she slept in the nude, and he felt a little stirring in his groin at that visual. He felt himself being pulled to her bed and reached down and felt the high-thread-count sheets. The material was smooth and cool to his touch. He sat on the edge of the firm mattress. He ran his fingertips along the edge of her nightstand and turned on the bedside lamp. He noticed the bottom drawer was slightly ajar. The top of a metal box reflected the lamplight. Curious, he pulled open the drawer. He felt a little invasive, his curiosity got the best of him and he lifted the lid of the box.

His eyes widened at the sight. Inside the box were a myriad of sex toys. For a moment he stared. Then he began imagining the purpose of each one and pictured Nadailia using each toy. The excitement and anticipation she must feel as she chose her joy for the night. As Dylan visualized her probing, thrusting, massaging and vibrating with these sex aids, he felt himself begin to stiffen. He removed the box from the drawer and sat it on the floor, removing each toy and examining it. He removed a clear glass dildo with a cast cock head on one end and a red glass rib cast into the side, spiraling down the shaft to a turned-up taper on the other end, seeing her feminine hand sliding the cool glass in and out of her wet pussy. Next he removed a stainless steel butt plug with a handle on the end. Dylan felt himself leak juice from his now steel-hard erection at the thought of seeing her double penetrate herself. There was a pair of nipple clamps. They had black rubber on the end and a stainless steel screw for tightening, with a chain for tugging. He had never touched them and was impressed with their heft and seriousness.

One particular item caught his attention. It was in a case that resembled what an expensive watches come in. He lifted the case out of the toy box and placed it in his lap as he opened it up. Inside, a velvet lining surrounded what looked like a large lipstick tube, dark rose in color. He plucked the "lipstick" from its nest and noticed the heft. It felt and looked like quality. Twisting the top off and saw a tapered end that had "LELO" printed on it. When rotating the base, and the toy began to vibrate quietly. He loved the sensation in his hand and could imagine Nadailia touching her clit with it. The exquisite pleasure she must feel.

A noise startled him from his reverie. He heard Nadailia opening the front door. He quickly placed the toys back in the box and jammed the box back into the bottom drawer. He rose to meet her with a sheepish grin. She arched one eyebrow then glanced down at the huge bulge in his pants and gave him a sexy laugh.

"What are you doing here?"

"Invading your space. I felt it was apropos after you interviewing my Maman to work at my restaurant." He sulked, she wasn't affected by his pouty pose. "You hired her?"

"Why yes, I did, and it is my restaurant, and I believe she will make a wonderful addition as a sommelier."

"Are you crazy? Putting a wino in charge of our wine cellar?"

"She will be fine. You told me to find her a job or a lover. This seemed like killing two birds with one stone. Now she has access to good wine and something to keep her busy. I find her palate quite sophisticated. She and Jeffrey met, and they hit it off, I'm maybe killing three birds with one wine cellar."

"It's your profit that she will be drinking. Don't say I didn't warn you."

Nadailia smiled and said, "As long as you are here, let me cook for you."

While she cooked, he toured the rest of the house. It was a work of art, located on a high cliff beside the beach with a 180-degree view of the Pacific Ocean. He was not comfortable with this opulence, he calmed down once he saw her Chagalls, Monet and Dali. He marveled at the beauty of these original works of art and loved that her bookcases held many of the same books as his. It occurred to him again that this woman was über wealthy. Instead of this thought bringing him pleasure, it frightened him. She was too powerful, too rich and too married.

She brought over a bottle of Cristal with a tray of seared scallops with artichoke duxelles, bacon brown butter and radish sprouts. The scallops were perfectly prepared, and the subtle flavors came shining through. He was impressed that she could cook too. "Is there anything you are not good at?" She looked at him through lidded eyes. "Following the rules."

They shared a hoisin-marinated-chicken lettuce wrap – several leaves of fresh butter lettuce stuffed with chicken, toasted peanuts and soy wasabi. Amazing finger food and a bit messy, which made them both fidget. As they licked the sauce off each other's fingers, their eyes became dense in a lustful glance. They shared a Cohiba pork wrap with black beans, soaked with Cuban flavors.

For dessert, a chocolate cake with raspberry coulis and crème anglaise was sweet precision. Afterward, she took him by the hand and led him to her bedroom. It had a sheik theme to it with the walls draped in silk, water fountains and fireplaces. The art was erotic and expensive, he was momentarily distracted. She appreciated that he saw the beauty of the room and led him to her huge bed. She quietly undressed in front of him while he took in every amazing site as it appeared. His mouth began to sag open, and she nipped him on his bottom lip. He staggered back and took off his clothes as she lay back on the bed.

"Dylan, I love you, and I want you to promise to remember that."

"I promise."

"Good, because I am about to fuck you like I don't."

He laid on top of her, their naked bodies in full frontal contact. He kissed her and reveled in the moment of their bodies meeting. His hard cock, pulsing with each heartbeat, was poised just outside her soaked pussy, pausing, anticipating the next second when he entered her. It felt like the first time. He slowly slid into her. Their natural lubrication combined to give him that warm, amazing feeling of being enveloped and pulled into eternity. First the head, then the shaft, slowly pushing into her. Finally stopping as he felt his pubic bone resting against hers. She arched her back to fully feel the pressure of him on her clit.

They began to rock slowly, at first an inch at a time, not even thrusting yet. He could feel her hard nipples against his chest. Then they slowly began to build a rhythm, a little faster, a little longer stroke. Slippery warmth, pressure, a feeling of her gripping his full length as she tightened the muscles of her vagina around him as if she were milking him.

They continued this way for what must have been an hour. No awareness of time or sense of urgency. He cradled the back of her neck with his hand and pulled her to him, their bodies taut with anticipation. He increased his speed and intensity, his cock seeming even harder than before. She rose to meet every thrust in perfect unison, perfect timing. Now he was a steam engine, pounding into her with determination. Love gone, just raw lust. Each time he slammed into her, she sensed a small flash of heat and light. The head of his dick intentionally riding across the folds of her G spot as he almost withdrew and re-entered her with each stroke. He felt her tense, arch her back and moan. She shuddered against him, no longer in control, gripping his ass and pulling him deeper into her. He continued his long strokes, taking her over the edge again. They made love uncountable times that night, each with a different rhythm and touch. Hard, fast, slow, loving and always full of wonder.

He rose from the bed at sunrise and marveled at the hues of color on her beautiful sleeping form. He kissed her and placed a rose from her garden on her bedside table.

Next afternoon text:

D: I loved being with you. Now we are going to play a game.

N: Sounds fun. Monopoly?

D: Hahaha!

Are you moist?

N: Yes. Eager.

D: What are you wearing?

N: Beach clothes.

D: Ok, good. Now try and relax.

N: Fuck you.

You know that's impossible.

D: Hehehe.

N: Brat.

D: Yes. But fun loving.

N: Yes you are. You like the build-up. Making me want you more. If that is even possible.

D: Ok. Ready for Pleasure Play?

N: Yes!

D: Go gather the following:

Medium mixing bowl half full of ice.

A water bottle with a small hole in the cap.

A wooden spoon.

Your new chrome butt plug.

N: Wait! How did you know?

D: I saw it in your box.

Also get: Two thick towels.

A room with a locking door.

A chair.

A table.

One chip-bag clip.

Some massage oil heated to an almost painful temperature.

N: OMG!

D: Then:

Make tiny hole in bottle cap.

Fill bottle with hot oil.

Go to room, lock door.

Strip.

Put towel on chair.

Sit on towel.

N: Stop.

Let me get the list.

I don't eat chips.

This is elaborate.

D: When you have everything arranged, send pic of the stuff on the table.

N: Give me a bit.

D: Just do it. No more lightweight plays for you.

N: Fuck you.

D: You've got 15 min.

N: My husband his nurse are literally one wall away. If I am going to get caught, I want it with your dick inside me.

D: What is the proper response?

N: Yes sir.

D: Good girl.

N: The door to my office does NOT lock.

D: Well that's your problem.

N: No chip clip.

D: Ok, get nipple clamp.

N: This is too much.

D: Ready for your adventure?

Too bad. Want to stop?

N: I am, but....

D: Stop?

Or go?

N: No, proceed with caution.

Go.

D: Ok. Strip.

N: Yes sir.

D: And put your butt plug in the bowl of ice.

Is the oil hot?

N: It is a slow process; it's warm.

D: Put folded towel in chair and sit on it.

N: Ok.

D: Is the heated oil in the water bottle with the hole in the cap?

N: No.

D: Pour it in the bottle.

It needs to be almost painfully hot.

N: Ok.

D: Are you in the chair?

N: Yes.

D: Spread your legs.

Is the toy in the ice?

N: Yes.

D: Put your left hand in the ice.

N: Ok.

D: With your right hand take the spoon and spank your clit and pussy lightly.

Use the flat end.

Tell me when your fingers are numb from the ice.

N: HOLY FUCK!

Numb and wet.

D: Yes.

Let them get REALLY cold.

N: They are.

D: Use you wet cold fingers and pinch your left nipple.

N: You have to promise to do this to me.

D: I will.

N: I mean it. No bullshit.

D: I will, no BS.

N: Good.

Continue.

D: Now do what I say.

N: I am.

D: Pinch your nipple.

Now same process for other nipple.

N: Ok.

D: Use spoon handle on clit now.

N: I like that. It's new.

D: Yes.

Take ice cube from bowl and rub it on your nipple.

N: Yes.

D: Put spoon handle in your pussy.

N: Ok.

D: Remove it.

N: Why?

D: Just obey.

N: Hehehe.

Ok

D: Good girl.

N: Ice has melted on my nipples.

D: Put new ice cube in right hand.

And put cold toy in left.

Put ice on nipple and toy in pussy.

N: can't type wet hands.

D: Ok.

N: It's in. HOLY fuck that is cold.

D: Put clothespin on cold nipple.

N: And uncomfortable.

D: Yes. Warm it up with your hot pussy.

N: Ouch! Sensory overload.

D: Take the hot oil and pour it on your clit right now.

Warming things up.

N: Shit.

D: Yes.

N: Thank you.

D: Thank you, sir.

N: Fuck you, sir.

D: Please :-)

N: Feels amazing.

D: Now take your left hand and put your middle finger in your pussy as far as it will go.

N: And the toy goes where?

D: You know where.

N: I do not. You have to tell me.

D: Put massage oil on it and slide it in your ass.

It should be cool, not cold, by now.

N: I warmed it up in my mouth.

It's in.

D: Now if you were bent over a chair, that's how I would have fucked you. My dick in your ass and my fingers in your cunt.

N: Please do.

D: I was so hot it would have gone quickly.

N: Me too.

D: Pounding you hard.

N: I adore you. That was amazing.

D: Wish I was there.

N: We need to grab that moment of pleasure.

D: Yes.

Pleasure Play.

N: Most people never find this, most only pretend.

D: No. Too scared.

N: I want to live happily ever after every now and then.

The Butterfly Opens

The artsy lighting in the tree, opulent heaters and a warm welcome from the staff instantly dazzled them. This place looked like it stepped out of a Woody Allen film with its drama and elegance. Dylan snagged the waiter, Matthew, and ordered for them both. He had brought epic magnums from Grey Wolf Cellars (a Petite Syrah and a Tempranillo). They started with Matthew's suggestion of a sparkling Cava from Spain, which was wonderful.

The first course was the charcuterie platter, a bacchanal of house-cured meats, including peppered salami, chorizo and prosciutto, with a hard Gouda and two kinds of brie. This beautiful dish was sprinkled with gastronomic delights such as blue cheese and honeycomb, nut clusters, candied apples, cauliflower, red peppers and a Hush-Harbor baguette. They snacked slowly, enjoying the sensations of delectable cheese and house-cured meats.

Knowing Nadailia's love for bacon and blue cheese, the next dish was Bacon-Wrapped Medjool Dates. This amazing amalgamation of flavors floored them. The apple-smoked bacon was wrapped around the dreamily sweet dates and stuffed with Valdeón blue cheese. This was her version of epicurean paradise.

Matthew paced each passage flawlessly, and the next course was a Caesar salad with stems of romaine lettuce peppered with shaved parmesan, boquerones preserved in olive oil and a dreamily prepared dressing. They also had The Wedge, an iceberg lettuce quarter with bacon lardons, smoky blue cheese, cherry tomatoes and blue cheese dressing. The house-made croutons were of note, this was rabbit food worthy of men.

Then they moved on to Dylan's favorite, Paella. He told her he would swim to Spain for this done right. This swirling dish of risotto rice with house chorizo, prawns, organic chicken, mussels, clams and local halibut with a sprinkling of peppers and onions was a symphony of flawlessness and flavor. Each fish was stewed to excellence, and the melding of the savors, an enchantment. Just when she was thinking it couldn't get any better, they brought what Nadailia considered culinary fulfillment when done decorously, pasta carbonara. The Black Truffle Carbonara Linguine rocked her world. This dish, when organized precisely, will make you see spirits. And not only was this done right, it was completed with black truffles. Dylan explained to her the cooking procedure.

"This is how I make a carbonara. Start with house-made linguine cooked al dente. Add shavings of black truffles, snap peas, prosciutto and parmesan. When the pasta is done, place a raw duck egg atop the noodles. The steam from the pasta poaches the egg to perfection, and then you mix it all together. The dish was first made as a hearty meal for Italian coal miners. The etymology gave rise to the term 'coal miner's spaghetti.' It is now comfort food from our Roman roots, and this is the best I have had in the States." She loved it when he got passionate.

Next they had the Hand-Cut Local Beef Tartar with brioche toast, Meyer lemon, herbs and sea salt. This dish was a rare treat. Raw beef pounded and rolled, with the crunchiness of the toast and the acidity of the lemon making it something to remember.

Dessert was from Dylan's favorite ranch, Windrose Farm. The Apple Galette was a small apple tart with a dolce de leche crème fraîche, a flaky buttery crust, and apples infused with a hint of rosemary, which had been planted around the orchard and seeped into the fruit. It was served with house-made vanilla bean ice cream, simply erotic. The Chocolate Pot de Crème with a lavender pinion cookie and a chantilly crème made Nadailia sigh with exultant satisfaction.

Nadailia got up and went to the parlor to gather her thoughts. This meal seemed too sensual; she was feeling a heightened awareness of him.

She had had plenty of sex. She had been sexually active since her first real crush at 16. She experimented with a woman or two along the way. She had always found sex pleasurable, whatever she was doing with Dylan was growing into something else, and it was confusing and distracting. Their last session was still burning in her mind. Dylan was an attentive sexual partner. He was fully "in the moment," and for a young man with limited sexual experience he was aware of where she was, emotionally, during their sex time. This last time seemed to move past the sweating, touching, stimulating, thrusting cliché of fucking. Transcending into what? Lovemaking? And that was part of the confusion. It felt to her that, God help her, an element of love was replacing her lust. Like the convergence of two rivers. One body of water continuously blends with the other until the two become one. Damn it! She was not ready for emotional involvement. And that was the reason for the distraction. Her learned skills and instinctual talents failed her as she tried to make sense of this new feeling she was experiencing.

She couldn't make order of this particular emotionally chaotic event. And that was what she was best at. That was how she had amassed and managed her fortune. Of all her traits, Nadailia was noted for knowing when to take charge of a situation. And this situation necessitated her taking charge. She fixed her hair, noted her flushed cheeks and joined him at the table. There he sat, grinning like the Cheshire cat.

"We have to go now," she said.

"Is there a problem?"

"Yes."

They left abruptly, and she had her driver drop Dylan at his house. She said not a word on the trip, was glued to her iPad. When they arrived at his place, she leaned over and pecked him on the cheek, a sure sign that she was not going to come in.

"I am sorry, I have to get to work. See you tomorrow."

She slammed the door, and as the car sped off, he stood there bewildered.

Text

D: What was that?

N: I feel I am losing control.

D: Ok.

N: Don't be paranoid. I will get over it.

D: You need a distraction.

N: Yes I do.

D: Where are you now?

N: On the couch.

D: Perfect.

I have fantasies about you and that couch

You in a blouse, no bra, skirt, no panties. Bending you over the arm of the couch.

Spreading your legs from behind.

N: I like that.

D: Pulling your skirt up to reveal your naked ass.

Kneeling behind and licking your pussy with my tongue.

Using my first two fingers to probe your wet pussy.

Fucking you with my fingers first.

Then standing behind you, spreading your legs further with my hands.

N: Fuck.

D: Allowing the tip of my hard cock to barely caress the outside of your pussy lips.

Moving it with my hand in a circle around the wet outside.

N: Perfect.

D: Then barely in, and up and down the slit.

Not penetrating.

Then slapping the insides of your thighs.

N: So perfect.

D: And pulling it up to rest on the crack of your ass, dripping pre cum down the crack toward your waiting pussy.

My balls pushed against your wet lips.

Making circles with my hips.

N: I want you so much.

D: You have me.

N: It is complicated. Tell me more.

D: Pulling your hips back hard against me to grind like that.

N: You already know what I want.

What fuels me. The way I want to be touched.

D: After a few minutes, me slowly pulling back, positioning my cock in your slit and slowly sliding into you.

Then stopping. Not thrusting.

N: I'm so wet.

D: Feeling you tighten your pussy around my cock like a fist.

Then you milking my cock with your pussy.

I slowly start thrusting.

Very short ones at first.

Then longer.

Almost all the way out then fully back in.

N: I'm going to come unglued.

D: Then faster like that, slamming hard against your pussy and ass.

Faster and faster.

N: You're perfect.

D: My hand is flat on your shapely butt.

My thumb, wet from your juices, slides into your ass while I fuck you.

N: Yes.

D: I keep it there.

And move it in and out.

N: This is hot.

D: You feel like you have two cocks in you.

N: Yours will fill me.

D: Now I'm driving hard, hard, slamming into you, raw power and hard fucking.

N: Oh my.

D: I can't last long like that and I groan and spasm into you.

You actually feel my cum gushing inside you.

N: Perfect.

D: I continue fucking until I'm soft.

As I pull out, my cum leaks down the inside of your thigh.

N: This is amazing.

D: You push off the couch and kneel and take my soft, butt-cum-soaked dick in your mouth.

N: I was going to ask if I could do that.

D: And slowly and lovingly suck me while soft.

N: Holy fuck! Wow, that was amazing. I am dripping for you.

The Beast With Two Backs

The next day at the restaurant, she left her office, determined that she would pay Dylan a visit and talk this out. It was not in her nature to allow distraction and confusion to rule her. She would manage these emotions as she had managed countless business problems in the past. Head on, with rational discussion and sound business practice. He was not in his office. She was told he was at the Farmers' Market, buying ingredients that were not in his own garden.

She decided she would drive over to his house. Like any hormone-driven 16-year-old would. What the fuck was happening here? If she were a guy, she would say she was thinking with her dick.

No car in his driveway. She knew Maman was out wine tasting.

She sat there for a minute, not sure what to do next.

She called him.

"Hey, I'm in your neighborhood and thought I might stop by."

"I will be there in 40 minutes. Let yourself in."

"Well, OK. I'll see you then."

She found the spare key where he told her it would be and let herself in. She had another brilliant idea: She would cook dinner for him. She found the Chez Pannise cookbook and all the items she needed quickly. Now she felt her strength and power returning. She was back on familiar turf. She scalloped potatoes and seared ahi, salted and peppered, then topped with baked strawberries in a balsamic vinegar reduction and crumbled gorgonzola.

She started opening the kitchen drawers one by one and was amazed at his organizational skills. All his utensils looked to be oversized (like him, she giggled to herself) and restaurant quality. She searched for an apron but failed to find one. Then she had the genius idea of the day. Removing her clothes so she wouldn't soil them while she was mixing and blending completely naked.

It felt freeing. Her breasts were exposed and moving freely with every step, which was arousing. Her nipples hardened. Fear of discovery is a powerful aphrodisiac. She felt herself moisten. She immersed herself in the preparation of the meal, turned the stereo on high blasting Boz Skaggs and completely losing track of time. As she was plating the courses, she felt Dylan behind her.

"That is amazing." She turned to him, holding the spatula she was using to place her finished product on the plate. Completely focused on her project, she had forgotten her nakedness until she saw his eyes. She started to cover up with her hands.

"No, don't move. You are a vision." He wrapped his arms around her and pressed his lips against hers. He reached low and cupped her ass with his hands and pulled her into his hardness. She molded herself to him. After a long embrace, he lifted her off the floor. She wrapped her arms around his neck and her legs around his waist. She could feel the material of his pants rubbing her clit.

He carried her to the kitchen table. The wooden chopping-block pattern was smooth but cool to her bare ass and back. He pulled away and with a half-turn opened one of the kitchen drawers and pulled out a large metal whisk. He used the solid stainless handle to tease and rub the outside of her pussy and slowly stoke her clit up and down. He then carefully inserted the now warm and wet handle into her pussy, gradually increasing the depth. He angled the whisk down, forcing the handle upward against her rigid G spot, and moved it in and out an inch at a time, blinding her with chromatic flashes of pleasure. He switched the tool to his left hand and retrieved a small-diameter pastry roller with his right. He brought it into play against her now hard and throbbing clit, rocking the rolling pin from side to side over the most sensitive part of her body.

She was losing control quickly. He stopped undulating her clit and grabbed the olive oil. He poured a generous portion in his hand and rubbed it over the pastry roller. He then took his finger and lubricated it by sliding it into her slippery, wet pussy. Then he inserted that finger into her anus. Slowly at first, then deeper, and sensing her sphincter relax, he shoved the oiled rolling pin into her ass. Her eyes widened, her mouth gaped, but no sound emitted. Just a sharp intake of air.

Now he was working the whisk against her G spot and using the rolling pin to fuck her ass. She had never been so hot. Her world was reduced to the intense sensation she was experiencing at his hands. Nothing mattered. Only that this feeling continue. Her brain was completely saturated with sex. Only the final climax mattered. She determinedly drove toward the goal. It was almost tangible.

Text

N: After what you did to me tonight, I am more satisfied and at peace than I have ever been.

D: Oh fuck, Nadailia. I love to hear you say that.

You like?

N: Yes, it was perfect.

D: You're sweet.

N: No! I am not. I am honest.

D: It's all yours, my dear.

N: I want more.

D: I would love the opportunity to help you experience that type of toe-curling orgasm.

N: Your words, like your touch, are magic.

Lets play, "What if?"

D: Ok. Love this :-)

N: What if we both found ourselves unencumbered by work or obligation and we could be anything we want?

Where would we go first?

D: Someplace tropical.

With ocean.

Warm water.

Some boutique hotel.

20 or 30 rooms.

N: I like.

D: Gourmet meals.

We could suntan naked.

And hold hands while we fell asleep on the beach.

Put a towel around us and walk to the tiki bar for drinks.

N: Would you rub me with lotion?

D: All over.

Maybe pausing at some special places.

N: So we don't touch until we are in our room?

D: I would love to rub your nipples till hard.

N: I like your pausing.

D: Yes.

N: Growing anticipation.

Knowing there will finally be a release.

D: Once in the room, we drop the towels.

I turn you toward me and press against you.

N: Yes.

D: You feel my hard dick against you leg.

I can't kiss you fast enough.

My tongue forces into your mouth.

N: I want you to possess my mouth.

D: You push back with your tongue.

I put my hand behind your head and pull you tight.

I feel for your nipple and squeeze it.

N: The waves of pleasure are building.

D: Then reach down and put my hand on your pussy.

I insert my middle finger in you while we are still standing.

You are wet.

N: Yes, I am.

D: I guide my finger slowly in and out.

And walk you to the bed.

I push you back on the bed.

And stretch our full length.

Covering you.

We giggle.

Your legs are off the bed. Your feet dangle.

N: Yes.

D: I kneel before you.

N: Holy fuck.

D: I spread your legs gently with my hands.

And lean in to your sweet glistening pussy.

N: OMG.

D: At first I breathe in your essence.

Then I slowly run my tongue.

Up to the place where your labia and leg meet.

First one side, then the other.

N: Dylan!

D: Then I put my mouth over your whole pussy and I taste you.

I slowly put my tongue into your slit.

N: I'm dying here.

D: Licking from back to front.

Then pushing it deep inside you, fucking you with my tongue.

I draw your tiny clit into my lips.

N: My God!

D: And suck it till it is gorged with blood and lust.

N: Please.

D: Flicking my tongue on it.

Then you stand up.

Then I stand up.

N: Couldn't if I tried.

Wait, what?

D: Smiling I lay on you and....

N: Ok, better.

You big fucking tease.

D: Let you lick your sweet juices from my lips and mouth.

N: Yummm.

D: As I ease my cock into your juicy wet pussy.

You love the way it feels that I am completely shaved and smooth.

My hard cock pushes to the depth of your pussy.

My pubic bone resting on yours.

N: You are killing me.

D: My balls resting against your ass.

I slowly begin to pump in and out.

You are holding my ass.

N: Yes.

D: We move as one. Like we've been fucking for years.

It's like we invented fucking.

N: I like that.

New but familiar.

D: So warm and wet. You using your muscles to milk my dick on each stroke.

I have to pause a couple of times to keep from cumming too soon.

You are too much for me.

N: I like that.

D: It feels like I am fucking you and getting sucked and a hand job all at the same time.

I love your experience level.

I love learning about sex from you.

N: I will be your teacher.

D: We go like this for an hour, maybe two, ebbing and flowing.

Edging.

But never cumming.

N: Good.

I like the edge.

D: Finally I explode into you, filling you with my hot white cum.

You thrust against me.

N: Yes.

D: We lie still for a moment, afraid to break the spell.

N: Seriously hot.

D: My cum leaking from your cunt and tracking toward your ass.

I stay inside you.

As I get softer.

We lie like this for a long while.

Slowly you start moving your hips.

My dick responds and hardens.

N: No way!

D: We begin again.

N: Yipeeeeee!

D Hahahha.

N: Did you used to be a woman? How can you know this?

D: I don't fucking know!

N: You are special.

Beyond empathetic.

D: I'm a little drunk :-)

N: I like that about you.

You have a real talent with words, young man.

D: The first "inappropriate" text I sent you (while semi-drunk) was "I would fuck you stone cold sober." I meant that.

Did that shock you?

N: No. It should have, somehow it felt comfortable, safe, right.

D: Mmmmmmm.

N: Men talk shit to me all the time because I am strong and rich. But this felt honest.

Rear Flying Wild Duck

The restaurant was in turmoil. True to his prediction, Maman had emptied the cellar of their best wine and shared it with the staff after the restaurant closed. The staff spent all night drinking, cooking and fornicating. When Dylan got there at 8 a.m., there were passed-out bodies strewn throughout the dining room and his kitchen was a disaster. He yelled in English, Spanish and French, so mad it looked as if the veins on his neck would explode.

He called Nadailia. Her job was to keep Jeffrey away, for his reaction to this debauchery would be to fire everyone. She took Jeffrey to a restaurant supply store and spent hours arguing with him over items she did not need or want but knew he would object to. When they finally showed up, the restaurant was clean and ready to go for the night, like nothing ever happened, except all their top-tier wine was gone. This would be harder to cover up. Jeffrey had taken a liking to Maman, so Dylan told her if she did not flirt her way out of this, she would lose the job.

The anger fueled his creative juices, and Nadailia was thrilled at the resulting menu. She had Lauren join her so she could taste and gossip. They shared the Rangeland Wines 2010 Syrah-Mourvedre mix that was as elegant a California wine as either had ever tried. They started with the Dungeness crab salad, with in-house-shelled crab (penance for the staff party) and an apple-kohlrabi slaw with a pasilla aioli and Bloom microgreens. The salad was a perfect mixture of salty and sweet.

Lauren was impressed with both Nadailia's calm and her hunger. She knew something was up. "Why are you so.......... Hmmmmmm.... What's the word? Serene?"

Nadailia smiled as she inhaled the last bite of salad. "Oh, nothing much. We are fucking regularly now. Looks like it is a consistent thing now."

Shocked, Lauren dropped her fork, and half the diners turned around to see what the commotion was about. "No. Way! Have you orgasmed?"

"I think so."

Lauren was happy for her friend but knew that there is no gray area in knowing weather you have cum.

Nadailia smiled as Pedro dropped off the next dish, oak-roasted brussels sprouts with a La Quercia pancetta, stone ground mustard, red onions and a demiglace. He smiled at Lauren as he explained the dish, and then whispered, "They make a lot of love."

Nadailia was startled that he knew and wondered how much everyone else knew. She didn't think of Dylan as chatty, maybe she was wrong.

Lauren loved seeing her unusually stoic friend undone, and placed her hand on hers. "I am sure Dylan didn't spill any vital information about your epic encounter, so don't worry. Now I want every tiny detail."

Over Sicilian-style swordfish with Italian white beans and a pine nut currant relish, Nadailia told Lauren the juicy details of both the physical act and the texts afterward that brought her even more waves of passion. The grilled lamb and duck sausage became a phallic symbol for their story. It was also an amazing amalgamation of flavors with sunchoke-potato purée and a mushroom ragu. Their dessert was a dark chocolate napoléon with brownie bites, candied hazelnuts and a mild chocolate crème chantilly.

Lauren looked at her friend, "You say you had and orgasm and I believe you. Then you all say it did not sate the passion. Are you sure?'

Nadailia smiled at her friend, "I think I am sure. How can you explain the taste of chocolate if you have never tasted it? I do know this, Dylan makes me feel something and no one else has ever done that to me."

With the wine emptied and the chocolate consumed, Nadailia finished her story and had the driver take Lauren home.

Meanwhile she went to find Dylan in the kitchen to compliment him on the amazing dinner and see how his anger was holding up. He was in the dry storage, alone, doing an invisible inventory. She knew he was tired and overwhelmed, even a bit embarrassed for his Maman's behavior. With the door closed, she knew they had five minutes tops of privacy, so she took his face in her hands and kissed him deeply.

"It's okay; the boss is not mad," she said.

"Thank you for that, it is still bad. How am I going to replace the wine?" She kissed him again.

"You are not the one responsible for the missing wine, your Maman is, and she and I have already worked out a deal on how to replace it."

"How?"

"She is going to work her magic on local winemakers and replace it with vintage stock from Paso Robles."

Nadailia began to kiss him again, and he kissed back, hard, the stress and the emotion of the day feeding into him consuming her mouth.

She went for his chef's jacket and undid the buttons, marveling at his magnificent chest. Then she grabbed his crotch, not surprised at all that he was rock hard. She freed his cock from his chef pants and dropped to her knees. She took the whole thing in her mouth, swallowing him completely. He nearly came undone and pulled her wild, long, red hair into a ponytail, using it as a rein to guide her mouth. In and out she sucked, conquered and engulfed.

He bent her over the potato boxes and started to finger-blast her. Inserting one, then two, then three. Finding her ridges, curving up to her G spot. Now that her floodgates had opened, he believed he could make her cum with the power of his intention and some rubbing on her clit. She reacted strongly and it forced his fingers out of her pussy. He always mistook the strength of her vaginal muscles for an orgasm. She turned and sat on the case of potatoes, breathing hard, flushed and beautiful. He approached her, ready to stroke himself and cum in her waiting mouth, when she yelled, "Stop!"

"What's the matter?"

"Why is my pussy on fire? Why am I burning?"

"Oh, my God! I was chopping jalapeños! I didn't wash my hands before I came in here. You took me by surprise. Holy shit, my dick is on fire."

They both started laughing, as they discussed ways on put out the fire in her vagina.

"This is why it is dangerous to have clandestine touching sessions in the kitchen," he said.

As they were laughing and crying at the same time, the door to the pantry opened and Pedro strolled in with a bag of potatoes.

Pedro saw the scene and moved quickly back to the kitchen, while Nadailia and Dylan washed and dressed. Nadailia left to go home, not catching the eye of any other member of the kitchen staff as she raced to her waiting car.

Text

D: Are you there?

N: I am here. What do you need?

D: Not sure. I feel deprived. It was a total shit day.

N: You pulled it off well. The new menu items were amazing.

D: I am never fucking needy.

N: Sorry about the interruptions.

D: I want to be coarse and vulgar.

N: With me you can be. I am not alone, and neither are you.

D: I want you.

N: You've become accustomed to having me at night.

D: Yes, I have.

N: I love that.

D: I want to fucking rip your clothes off. And push you against the wall.

N: I like that.

D: I want to bend you over the arm of the couch.

And slam my dick into you.

Hard! Then turn you over.

N: Keep going.

D: And bite your nipples till you scream and begin to fight.

Then I want to kick your knees open with mine and jam my dick in your cunt and pound you till you whimper.

N: I am loving this.

D: I want to spit on your tits and then slap them.

N: You got me wet.

D: And pull my hard dick out and slap your face with it.

I want to bite you.

I want to lick you.

N: Holy fuck, this is good.

D: I want you on your back with your legs over the arm of the couch.

There I can fucking eat your pussy hard.

I want to be rough, not gentle. I want to use my teeth and pull your pussy lips.

N: Shit.

I love this.

I want you so much.

D: And lick your clit, then bite it.

N: I want your hardness and your strong sense of desire.

D: While using my hands to squeeze your ass HARD!!

I want to fucking own you and fuck you.

N: I want that so much. That is a dream.

D: Wow!

I'm tired.

I don't know where that came from.

N: Nice.

D: Really?

N: We are playing.

D: I think I sounded like a real dick.

I guess I'm frustrated.

N: Not at all. I love this.

I would let you do it all to me.

D: I know. And I am yours. Thank you for letting me rant.

N: That is why this works.

We get to do the fun stuff.

That wasn't a rant. That was fucking hot.

I wish I were there so you could take it out on me.

D: What a lot we have to explore.

I've never met anyone like you.

And I never will.

N: And me you.

Yes we can do tender, violent, soft, hard, fast, slow.

So much to explore.

D: I like the lack of boundaries.

Ok. I got those subtle comments off my chest.

Have a good night.

See you tomorrow.

N: Goodnight, Hot Hands.

Kingfishers Intertwined

They met first at her biggest competitor's restaurant. Nadailia said it was for research, Dylan got the distinct impression that he had become arm candy for the boss.

They started with the Bodegas M 2011 Albarino-Querida, and the sommelier explained how God and soil made this an outstanding selection. Chef Brad came out of the kitchen and introduced himself to Dylan and thanked Nadailia for coming. Abalone bisque with an arugula purée offered pure essences of the ocean served in an espresso cup. It was high on richness. The salad that accompanied it featured charred abalone with persimmons and Asian pears, a dusting of almonds and a spicy roasted daikon, thinly sliced. This was a complex salad with multi-layers of flavor, all surprising and prepared impeccably.

Between courses they toured the kitchen and walked through the garden. With its fantastic view of the ocean, this had always been a favorite spot of Nadailia's. They positioned themselves so they could always be secretly touching. She would breeze by him, and her hand would magically graze his crotch. He would adjust his feet under the table and lightly touch her calf.

The next course they enjoyed was russels-style abalone stew with corn soufflé-stuffed baked cannelloni. The broth was light with a spice on the end, and it was teeming with impeccably cooked squid, shrimp and octopus. One exquisite abalone steak rested on top. Swimming in the stew was sausage and red kale. This was Nadailia's favorite dish. The wine pairing of Wild Horse Pinot Noir brought the strong, subtle flavors to the palate.

Nadailia got up to visit the water closet, and he followed. The outside area held a sink where everyone could wash. The lights were muted and candles swayed over the copper sink. She left the private area seeing him standing there waiting for her. Not a word was said as she kissed him and grabbed his cock. The shock of what they were about to do frightened them both, and she ran out.

Back at the table, they began to savor the braised beef short ribs with roasted butternut squash purée, roasted Brussels sprouts, heirloom carrots and quince jam. The meat was bursting with flavor and fell off the bone. The combination of sweet and savory went dreamily with the wine pairing, a Hearst Ranch Winery 2011 Three Sisters Cuvée. The last plate came with the instructions to indulge, and they did, on a four-layer devil's-food cake with hot fudge drizzles and vanilla crème anglaise. The dessert was flawless, not too sweet, and brilliant with the Roxo Port Cellars 2008 Magia Preta.

As they walked along the beach, she turned to him and they touched foreheads. He let out a sigh. She said, "All I do is want you." Her head rolled to his chest, listening to his heartbeat. She whispered, "Fuck me."

He was shocked at this request, as they were in public, on the beach. It was dark, but still, they were on a public walkway. Dylan wanted to please her, he knew it was the wrong time and place.

"You said no more public CTS."

She looked at him incredulously. She was not used to anyone not jumping to do her bidding. "What is CTS?"

"Clandestine Touching Session. Remember, we were going to call it that? Like, 'Meet me in dry storage for a CTS.'"

"Our secret is going to get out."

"Going to?"

Everyone who worked at the restaurant knew they were lovers. It was a gossip center. Since many careers are started when one chef gets fired and his sous chef must step in to replace him, they were playing a dangerous game. Also, Jeffrey hated them both and would do just about anything to get rid of them.

Text

N: How are you at fried chicken?

D: Gourmet fried chicken?

N: But of course.

D: It takes three days. Must soak in buttermilk. I'll make the buttermilk

N: With your superior stroking skills?

D: Yes! I have well-developed forearms, from stirring, of course.

N: Yes, I've noticed them.

N: Stamina is your forte.

D: I like the delay because it makes the ending better.

N: Me too.

D: And a hint of jalapeño.

N: Unless there is jalapeño involved.

N: Haha, we are getting in sync.

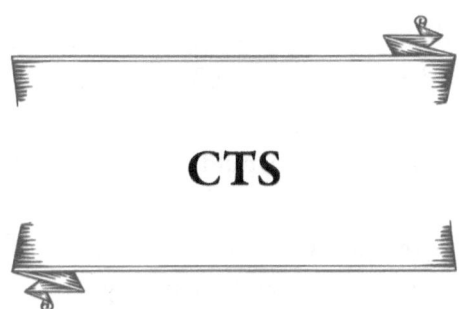

CTS

After the restaurant had closed, they were sharing an employee meal and intimately talking and touching. The ricotta gnocchi with wilted spinach, artichoke chips, browned garlic butter and parmesan cheese was breathtakingly tasty. It paired so well with their new find, Caparone Winery Nebbiolo. Thinking no one was there but the cleaning crew, they were openly touching and occasionally kissing. Jeffrey came through the back door, claiming to be looking for a bottle of wine for a party, and he caught them kissing. Jeffrey was definitely breaking the rules, so he did an abrupt turnaround and headed out. Nadailia followed him out to discuss what he was doing, he was gone.

Text

D: No more CTS or PDA. I scared myself tonight. I know without a doubt that if you had locked the door, I would have bent you over that table, hiked your dress up and rammed my cock in your pussy without a second thought. It scares me how much I want to fuck you in public.

N: I know. Me too. We can secretly touch, right? Don't dampen my spirit. We are both highly intelligent people who should know how to pull this off without hurting anyone.

D: I have no experience in this. You are right; I feel safe with you. You know more about my sexual side than anyone else. I have never shared this fetish with anyone.

N: I am glad you feel safe with me, I have not done this either. As wrong as it is, damn, it feels right. You are safe with me. I won't let anything happen to your job.

D: If I had any doubt, we would never have gotten this far into this.

N: Can I tell you now how much I loved the meal tonight?

D: I enjoyed the touching and the kissing.

N: Me too. And my body has always been honest with me.

This longing for you, if it were just fleeting, would have been gone in 2 days. But it is not going away. And public fucking is the best!

D: Mmmmmm. As delicious as that sounds, I'm not sure how to resolve that. I'm pretty sure it would change things, especially at the restaurant.

N: We are not going to resolve anything. We are redirecting this energy into the menu. Then our passion has a path; it's in the food. When the day comes that we can be together, it will be wonderful.

You need to cook my love.

The Seagull Soars

N adailia was frustrated. She had gotten used to the constant state of arousal that accompanied working with and being around Dylan. Their late-night texts became her favorite part of the evening, and she anticipated them with a 16-year-old girl's yearning. She wanted him now.

The party celebrating Consumed success was entertaining, filled with employees and board members, so she could not touch him. He was dressed to the nines in a silky shirt and pant combo that was hard to resist touching. Nadailia was dressed as a chorus girl, rumba panties and all. Every time he breezed past her, she reached out to touch him. They danced in a group on the disco floor, she wanted to slow dance with him, grind him into a state of excitement and then take him upstairs and fuck for hours.

With the rare exception of everyone leaving at the same time, this scenario was not to be, so she took the short cut and, after dancing, walked out onto the back patio, beckoning him to follow. She had had the staff clean out the woodshed, making sure there were not any errant protruding nails. She entered and lit a candle. There was one potting shelf and a couple of old ropes used for trellising. As she waited, her breath became quicker, anticipating this hot and fast CTS rendezvous. The anticipation was liquefying her as she heard the door creak open. He crossed the room and took her mouth with his, hard and full of need. She responded with the same raw need. He lifted her and set her on the potting shelf, and she wrapped her legs around him with a python-like grip. He moved down her neck and pulled the straps of her dress down, exposing her swollen breasts and hard nipples. From his back pocket he pulled nipple clamps stolen off a pimp's costume and fastened them to her erect nipples. She gulped at the pain as he pulled the chain and lifted her dress up to her waist. He quickly grabbed the trellising ropes and tied her hands together, then fastened the rope to the hook above her head.

Their mouths met again, this time is was soft, passionate, breathing each other's life essence and softly touching tongues. While it was soft up top, the bottom halves were becoming hard and wet. He ripped off her thong, tearing the silk to shreds. He found her first with his hands, stroking her lips, squeezing her clit, and then he thrust three fingers into her. She was dripping wet.

He removed his fingers and thrust into her. She was milking his hard cock with her strong pelvic muscles. He then started long strokes, all the way in, his pelvic bone touching hers, and then all the way out. Slowly at a maddening pace. She thrust to make him move faster, he knew this was a move she loved and hated equally, so he kept the steady pace as he pulled the chain on the nipple clamps. She squeezed with a force that knocked his dick out of her. He loved her strength.

When he was ready to cum, he withdrew, and she said the magic words: "Cum on my tits." He leaned back and his white pearls of essence covered her tits. He kissed her. Gently at first, and then with the greedy desire they had both come to expect.

Then he whispered, "This was a bad idea. We could have been caught and lost both our jobs. You are to be punished now." He smashed his lips into hers, blew out the candle and left her in the dark.

Text

N: You asshole.

D: Did I get my point across?

N: Yes! I'm super worked up. Beyond horny.

D: How are you planning to resolve that?

N: Not sure. Any ideas?

D: MANY!

N: Tell me.

D: First I'd have you lean on a chair facing the back of it.

Then I'd pull your dress up over your back.

I'd grab your panties with both hands and yank them down to your thighs.

Sorry, got to go!

N: Holy fuck! Are you still punishing me?

D: Yup.

The Paired Dance

They started acting stoic to each other at work to keep Jeffrey at bay, and Dylan would come to her house after the kitchen had closed. She had moved her husband's hospital bed to the far end of the house, as far away as possible. The beeping of the machines that helped him breathe at night kept out any escaping sounds of passion.

Dylan was interested in the Tao, and she enjoyed teaching him techniques and positions. She explained to him that the practice was open to both sexes and had a unisex purpose, namely to 'transform the boudoir into an altar for body-mind enlightenment through meditative enrichment and spiritual transmutation of the sex urge'.

Her housekeeper, Loo, and gardener, Alan, were Taoist, and while she had read many books, she had not had a partner with whom to explore the sexual Tantric practices. The house staff was more like family than any she had ever had, and she respected their friendship and opinions. They were sipping tea when Dylan knocked on the door.

He was there to cook, so he made them all a meal of seared, bacon-wrapped scallops sitting atop fried spinach with a delectable lemon aioli and goat cheese spread around the plate for visual stimulation as well as palate pleasure. The scallops were bigger than silver dollars and perfectly cooked with the essence of the sea shining through the crispiness of the bacon. Dylan paired the dish with a bottle of crisp Barton label Blanc y Blanc, a white blend, which was a new and delicious offering from Joe Barton of Grey Wolf Cellars.

Next was the beef carpaccio, its thin slices spectacularly prepared and resting on mustard vinaigrette with capers dotting the top and adding a perfect blend of flavors. Resting beside this heavenly dish were baby arugula leaves with shaved parmesan and a sprinkling of black sea salt to enhance the essence. This deconstructed dish was pleasing from every perspective as they launched it into their mouths.

The next dish was a subtly delectable lobster vol-au-vent (French for 'everything is better in puff pastry'). This amazing shell-shaped and multi-layered tartlet was swollen with sautéed lobster, grilled asparagus and cubes of fingerling potatoes. It sat upon a cloud of lobster cream sauce and green onions. Every bite was perfect and rich, creating a harmonious experience. Dylan deemed it "50 Shades of Lobster," likening the cream sauce to bisque and the meat inside – tasty morsels of the tail – to kings. It was absolute flawlessness.

The main course was a large pork osso buco confit. A succulent meat shank from the thigh bone, cooked for hours in its own fat, was a favorite of any food-obsessed creature. Add to it sheared fried beets and carrots; rest it all on a purée of cauliflower with oven-roasted tomatoes, caramelized onions, spinach and a thyme jus; and it can make for a quiet table. The amalgamation of flavors, textures and sauces made this a most memorable indulgence. They paired it with a Turley Zinfandel. Both the wine and the meat were so impressive that they were not sure if they could or should go on eating, but were enjoying the under the table exploration.

Dessert was a light apple crostata with See Canyon apples baked to a sweetness known only to the apple connoisseur, with a buttermilk vanilla bean ice cream and a drizzle of caramel sauce.

Afterward, in a private room they sat facing each other, naked on the soft leather couch. They had been instructed by Loo and Alan that this was the first step in the Tao practice, designed to build intimacy. They were not to touch, only talk, and speak of intimate things. Loo had set a timer for 30 minutes and left them alone.

Dylan looked at Nadailia lustfully. "That bra was beautiful."

Nadailia blushed, another thing she only did with him. "I buy things like that for you. It's a first."

"Smoking hot!"

"There is a matching thong."

"Whatever you were wearing Saturday night made your breasts look amazing. I was staring."

"Thanks. It was a new dress. I was so comfortable in it. Lauren saw it with the bra and said Dylan's going to stare at your boobs."

"I fucking did. I had to send the 'you're beautiful' text as soon as I saw you."

"That made my night. No one says that to me but you."

"I knew it was something different. Well, my Truth Meter voted full staff."

Nadailia sneaked a look at his crotch, and his Truth Meter was at attention.

"I think you've met the Truth Meter."

"I did. It's heavenly."

"Truth Meter doesn't lie."

Nadailia wanted to change the subject.

"Tell me about your last girlfriend?"

"Now? Why?"

"I don't know. Want to hear about my last affair?"

"No, if you feel I should?"

Nadailia thought this would be a good time to tell him about her curse.

"Bottom line: I scared the hell out of him. I'm kind of insatiable. He was overwhelmed. So after one long weekend, where I was even more so, he didn't talk to me for a couple of weeks. After six months of him basically ignoring me, I missed my friend. He married a 'nice girl' and is happy. Sound familiar?"

Dylan looked at her, amazed at her candor.

"I am not afraid of you or your insatiable appetite. I hope to feed it."

This warmed her heart. She went on.

"Here is the difference. You already know that about me. It will not be a surprise. I'm not going to move into your life any more than I am in it now. We are held together at the restaurant every day."

"True. Like any good thing, moderation is the key to an impeccable dish. And our main ingredient is desire. We have to take it slow."

"Are you fucking kidding me?"

"No. Texting you makes my cock hard. It makes my imagination fly, and it weirdly has made me a better chef. We still have to be careful of work friends and enemies."

"I know that."

"Nadailia, I want you so much it scares me, scares me that this will end if we give in to it."

Dylan touched her arm, breaking the rules.

"This, my love, is never going to end," he said. "Our minds are wrapped around each other. It will grow, change and morph, but it will never end."

"Perfect. I want to nurture this."

"We don't have a choice, do we? It's like breathing to me."

"Honestly. There have been days when I wake up and say I am not going to do this anymore. This is dangerous, for this I could lose everything I have worked for. I'm resolute. Then you text, 'You there?' and I am yours again. Absolutely."

"We both feel love for each other and obligation to others and the restaurant."

"I love that our words are so freely given to each other. This is real. Concrete. Beautiful."

"We still need to have a mindful burn. Take things slowly. It's not something we should be casual about."

"That's bullshit. And fear talking. We are both bright people."

"Bright enough not to have to touch a stove to know it's hot."

"That logic of the stove is lost on me."

Nadailia was getting frustrated, having to stick to a conversation and not being able to touch this beautiful man sitting right in front of her. She changed the subject.

"Let's talk new menus."

Dylan loved to watch her try to regain control over things she could not and decided to mess with her.

"I think the No-Panty Pie is a good choice for dessert."

"Fucker."

"Followed up by Free-Wood Shorts.

We'll need to stir the two together.

And make some cream.

Maybe a décolleté dessert."

"Nice."

"With two perfectly proportioned breasts.

That requires kneading.

Then a dash of kisses hidden in the preparation.

Pantyless Pot Roast.

Hot Kitty Short Ribs.

How's that sound?"

"I'm going to rape you."

"It's not rape if it's consensual."

"I'm going to attack you and make you do bad things to me."

"I'll pretend to object while I fuck you."

"I'm going to whip up a batch of buerre blanc and spread it on strategic places so I can lick it off."

The timer went off, and they both jumped. They dutifully put on their clothes, both quieted by the intimacy this strange exercise had brought them. Dylan's kiss at the door was long and full of power, and he sighed as he left.

Text

D: I am semi-drunk. I got home and drank a whole bottle of wine. That exercise unnerved me. I am not responsible for what I say tonight.

N: I love you drunk.

I think last time you tried to take me in a bathroom.

D: It's because I'm, "easy" when I'm drunk.

N: I need to touch your flesh.

D: I visualized eating you all through my drive home tonight.

N: I would have liked that.

D: Next time, the hot oil massage. It will feel amazing to you.

N: Next time, you warm it up and administer.

D: I'd love to.

N: Me too.

Hot and cold rocks.

They will blow your mind.

D: I had that once. Spa in Paris.

N: With sex?

D: No, sadly.

Just rocks.

N: With sex, they will turn your body inside out with pleasure.

D: Tell me.

N: Your body can only feel one sensation at a time.

Which I experienced tonight from talking to you.

D: Your pleasure is my pleasure.

N: You place the hot and cold rocks alternating down your chakras, and your energy is confused. Looking for a nerve ending.

Then you move them to your love place, all cold and then all hot.

D: Sounds yummy.

N: Your nerve endings are exploding with energy.

Then I move my mouth to your cock, which is confused by the hot and cold but encouraged and wanting to be stimulated by one source.

D: You are good at that!

N: I suck you until the body temperature overwhelms the nerve endings.

D: Nice.

N: Here is what I think you need.

For me to suck you. Assault you. Overwhelm you. But never let you cum.

Then the emotion is longing.

That overwhelms the other garbage.

D: Maybe. I like to cum. Just like you do. Right?

N: Honestly, I am not sure.

D: About cumming? You are kidding right?

N: You need to get your emotions ready for me.

I can be a bit much. I am a pleasure you will never forget.

D: I wish I had that kind of control over my emotions.

N: You have no idea the effect you have on me. I am a lust monster.

D: And you know I am a creative sex monster. Perfect combo.

The Wild Horse Leaps

They take Maman out to eat at a local wine bar and bistro. Nadailia was trying to win her over, since getting her out of jail in France, giving her a job and turning a blind eye to her nightly thievery had not been enough to impress this woman. She still considered Nadailia unsuitable to date her son.

They started with warm, fresh goat cheese with honey and truffle salt, a perfect combination. They also tried the white-bean-and-garlic hummus, served on crostini with fresh cucumber and tomato. It was an enjoyable taste arousal. Maman had a bottle of NV J. Lassalle Champagne from Champagne, France, while Nadailia had a Cava Cocktail that was Spanish Cava with a splash of Pink Port. Dylan enjoyed the Reutberger Export Hell, which the bartender told them was made by nuns. It tasted like a clean German lager.

Maman grilled the owner, a sommelier named Ali, on the wines she carried and told her that if she needed help tasting she would offer her superior palate. They moved on to tapas, sharing a plate of Boquerones and Red Peppers, then a plate of Chorizo and Manchego, a Spanish cheese with a nutty flavor that they all adored. Marcona almonds and Castelvetrano olives filled out the small plates that were filled with unexpected flavors and went well with the beverages.

Dylan got up to purchase another bottle of Champagne, when Maman set upon Nadailia like a rabid dog. "You think you own him?

He is my petit garçon. He will not settle for being your paramour. He needs a proper wife who will give me petits-enfants." Nadailia was taken aback, not deferred.

"Dylan is a grown man, and if he wants me as his lover, then you cannot stop him. How about you acting more grateful and less bossy?"

Maria hissed at her, "If you do not stop putain de my Dylan, I will tell Jeffrey and make sure you get fired."

Dylan approached the table, and the conversation hung in the air between the two women. Nadailia was beyond furious, so she resolved to keep her mouth shut until they got this horrible French thief home.

They shared the carnitas salad with slow-roasted pork, black beans, roasted corn, onions and heirloom tomatoes, served with avocado-cilantro dressing. Maman made a toast, and the waiter asked what she was celebrating. "That I live in California and can have such wonderful food," she said. He told them that all the restaurant's produce comes from local organic farms and that each dish was chosen for its ability to pair with their wines.

Maman was excited about the Panini Croque-Monsieur, a classic French sandwich with Gruyère cheese and cured ham, and it was perfection. Dylan went South and had a Cubano with house-made Niman Ranch pulled pork, grain mustard, pickles, prosciutto and Gruyère. It was perfección. Nadailia had the traditional bocadillo, a sandwich served on a Spanish roll cut lengthwise. Traditionally seen as a humble food, its low cost has allowed it to evolve into an iconic piece of cuisine.

Maman promised to come back for the Bubbles Bar and oysters on Friday night, Dylan reminder her that she worked at their restaurant on Fridays. The car ride home was silent, which Dylan thoroughly enjoyed. He braised his hand up and down Nadailia's thigh and every now and then stuck his thumb into her panties to get a feel for her dampness.

They dropped Maman off at Dylan's house and went back to Nadailia's. His stroking up and down her thighs had softened her fury, she knew she had to get this affair under control or lose everything.

Having spent multiple hours contemplating where this could go and what it could be, and heeding Maman's issues, Nadailia came up with a plan as to how they should proceed in order to make their affair a creative, secret and long process. She knew it would never follow a conventional affair, she would not give him up.

Nadailia explained, "I need you to make me a promise that you will always look to your own pleasure first. This is not a relationship based on anything but pleasure and creativity. Absolute honesty is imperative. You are not looking out for my pleasure or happiness. You are looking out for yours. This is selfish in its makeup and direction. The more honest we are about that, the easier it will be.

"I need you to be bossy and confident. Tell me what to do, even if it's finding us a safe place to do it.

"I'm here for our pleasure. I know that this kind of desire requires rules so it doesn't burn out."

Dylan was shocked at her honesty and replied, " I adore you. Every bit of you. I need something different from this. Something I am sure that you are uniquely able to provide. We will be safe. We will be secret forever. I love you no matter what."

The phone rang breaking the spell. It was Maman calling feigning being afraid to be alone, so Dylan kissed Nadailia on the head and drove home to rescue his Maman.

Text

D: You still up? Sorry I had to leave. Hope you didn't have any plans for us.

N: I always have plans for you, it is safer that you go home at this point.

D: Are you still hot for me?

N: Next time we are sitting across from each other at a table, I am going to somehow prove to you how wet I am every time you are near.

D: If we pick the right table and restaurant, I'll put my toes on your wet pussy.

N: I just gasped at that.

D: Then I would dip in with my fingers.

N: Mmmmmmmm.

D: Then show you my wet fingers.

N: Butter for your béchamel.

D: I would need to figure out an excuse to suck the wetness off them in front of everyone.

N: Flavor! We can blame it on flavor.

D: I have stopped wearing underwear under my chef pants in your honor so you can clearly feel the head and shaft of my hardening dick.

N: That is kind of you, Sir.

D: It's fleeting but long enough for you to get a good estimate of my hardness.

N: I got that last week. Still makes me crazy thinking about it.

D: I love the feel of your long fingers when I push my crotch slightly against your hand. I look for an opportunity to reciprocate.

N: Write to me. Tell me a dirty story.

D: I'm sitting beside you in a darkened restaurant. We are with Stu and Lauren,

and we have been drinking and laughing.

The other two are engaged in some banal conversation, and you reach down and grab my cock through my pants under the table.

N: I like.

D: You slowly hike your dress up above your knees.

We both go to the restroom at the same time.

My hand flies to your lap.

Pushing down to your wet, wet pussy.

My middle finger finds the slit, and I ram it into your pussy.

Quickly curling my finger upward, I search for your rigid G spot and rake it with my fingertip as I withdraw my soaked finger.

As we are walking back to the table, I look at them and suck your sweet juices from my finger as I inhale your essence and smile.

Reaction?

N: Oh my!

D: Hahahaha!!!

N: Please promise to do this.

D: Gotcha!

N: I am fucking dying here.

D: First fucking chance I get.

N: I have got to get relief.

The pressure and lust wake me from a dead sleep.

This is insane.

D: Sleep well.

The next night they had Nadailia's house to themselves, as the husband was staying overnight in the hospital for tests. She wanted to cook for Dylan and impress him.

Nadailia had made a proscuitto-wrapped artichoke that was lying on a bed of wild arugula with burrata cheese and Calabrian chile salsa verde. The prosciutto clung to the artichoke heart like a glove and enhanced both of these savory favorites. Dylan took three bites and then said, "To say this is the best thing she has ever put in my mouth is an understatement, well so far." It was perfection on every flavor front and unique in its pairing with a 2011 Daou Cabernet Sauvignon.

Ahi was the next dish, piled high on a bed of avocado and soy chile marinade with Kendall Farms crème fraîche. Using high-quality tuna, cut perfectly and paired with impeccable taste, she was off to a good start in the culinary corner. Now, she was going to blow his mind in the sensual corner.

They moved to her room. She wanted to teach him to trust her. She needed to run the next chapter of their sexcapade. She lit the candles, opened a bottle of Cristal Champagne and melted some pure-cocoa chocolate for painting and tasting. She made sure there was silk rope at each corner of the bed to secure him.

He entered the room as if he were ready for battle. His slight smile dazzled her as he noticed the box of toys at the foot of the bed. "I am not comfortable with losing control," he said. His eyes pleaded, the passion and curiosity showed in his flushed face. Nadailia smiled and took his hand.

"This is about pain and pleasure, and you will be receiving bucket loads of both, not any control. Tonight, I call the shots," she whispered in his ear as she removed his jacket. He twirled to kiss her. It was long, hot and wet with their tongues weaving, dancing, and searching for more. Removing his shirt, she sucked his nipples and gave them a quick bite. She shoved him down on the silky soft blanket laid on top of the bed and brought out the scarf that would serve as a blindfold. Quickly the mask was in place, and she brought his hands above his head and tied them together. As she lightly nipped his ear, neck and lips, he began to squirm with anticipation.

Removing his pants and releasing his beautiful cock made her gasp as she licked the insides of his legs. She secured each leg with a silk rope; happy that she had spent time learning to make a knot that he couldn't escape. Now she backed away from the bed. He was writhing and begging, the blindfold making his other senses more alert. She blew on his neck, tweaked his nipples, and slapped his hard cock. All this was to get him unbalanced, out of his head and into pleasure.

She covered him with the hot chocolate, and he winced as she painted it into his more sensitive spots. Then she started from top to bottom, licking off every bit. He was blown away by the eroticism of this and couldn't help but struggle. She was slow and deliberate, a testament to her patience and passion. When she was done, the places were her tongue had been where cold and alert with pleasure. Then she upped the anti.

She started with a leather riding crop, gently rubbing him and then giving it a fast slap all over his body. Making sure there was no rhythm or trail to help him anticipate her next strike. He began to moan after each slap and panted when the crop connected with his cock. She was silent and concentrated on his erogenous zones; soles of his feet, inside his thigh, along his neck and under his arms. She would work an area and eventually always end up torturing his cock.

He began to beg for release. "That is not going to happen. You will cum, over and over, no release will happen. I am going to teach you to climax without coming, so you will last forever and always be ready for me."

"Impossible!" He yelled. She smacked his balls as punishment.

The next step was a frozen treat. She put an ice cube in her mouth and rubbed all over his neck and chest. The cold/warm sensation was almost too much for him when she suddenly took his whole cock in her cold mouth. She swallowed every inch as the head slid down her throat, she stroked him in and out of her until he was ready to explode. Nadailia released his cock, then filled his mouth with the taste his essence as she kissed him deep and hard.

He started to beg again, praying for release. But she flipped him over and brought him to his hands and knees. "We are going to be playing with your G spot," she whispered in his ear as she poured warm oil all over his ass. She played with his taint, massaged his balls and did 20 hard strokes from the base of his penis to its tip. When he started thrusting his hips, she spanked him with an open hand, a hard slap on his rear end. The sensation was both excruciating and pleasing. She rubbed the spot, stroking him and then hit him again. Now he begged to be hit again. With an open palm, she smacked and clapped his red ass cheeks, making sure to always get a bit of ball in the attack. When he was welted and moaning, she slid her head underneath him and took his cock in her mouth. This time she sucked and moved the head with her tongue. Then she would swallow him whole, sucking every inch into her throat and then release. Grabbing the base of his rod, she encircled and held his cock in place while she moved him in and out of her mouth. When he was about to cum, she stopped abruptly.

He moaned and begged. Then she started with small kisses all over his red and fiery skin.

"Next level?" she whispered in his ear, and all he could do was choke out a "Please."

She poured more oil on his ass and began to work on his asshole, loosening it and getting him to relax. First she inserted her pinky. He gulped, grew less panicked as she stroked his shaft. When he was good and pliable, she inserted the butt plug swiftly and deeply. He whined, but a few whacks and he begin to enjoy the full sensation.

Flipping him on his back, she went to work sucking, swallowing and devouring his cock. She released her mouth and straddled him. His cock sunk deep into her, and he nearly came until she tightened her pelvic muscles around his cock to stop him. She set the pace with a slow swaying movement, and the plug did its job, stimulating his prostate. These were all new sensations for him. She moved faster and harder, kissing his neck as her tits pleaded for his mouth to take them in. She whispered into his ear as she rocked and orchestrated his cum.

"Now baby, feel the plug, feel my G spot, fuck me, let go. I am going to let you cum in 5, 4, 3, 2, 1." And then she lifted her pelvis so the top of his penis was inside. She swayed in and out. He began to whimper. Pulling the whole of him into her, she began to kiss him deeply, passionately.

He came and the electricity coursing in a circle back and forth between them, so much energy was produced that his orgasm lasted three minutes. He wept when she climbed off, and as she untied him he pulled her close.

Afterward, he got dressed, mumbled about meeting his brother, and once again ran out the door. She was beginning to think this was how he would always be post coitus.

Text

D: Sorry for the abrupt exit . . .again.

N: I am getting used to it, like it is a natural way to end great passion.

D: I am a bit over my head with you.

N: Part of the reason this is so intriguing is you're not afraid of me.

Everyone else seems to be. You take me at face value. You see my strengths and weaknesses, and neither intimidates you.

You would as soon laugh with me, fuck me, have an argument with me or confide in me.

I adore the intimacy we have and love even more that at work, we are just colleagues.

D: That was amazing tonight.

The Pampered

Nadailia and Lauren were lunching and then having a spa day. Nadailia called for it, as she needed to talk, to vent. Lauren was happy to oblige and get a day of pampering.

"What has got you so flustered?" Lauren asked. "I have never seen you act like this."

"He is taking over my brain. I can't lose this feeling, this uncontrolled desire. It has moved down into my heart. I feel like I'm hungry all the time. It's been more than two months. I truly expected it to leave after a day or two. It grows stronger. This is ridiculous. My loins are still literally tingling.

I watch the clock like an algebra student, waiting for the minute that I can talk-text-touch him."

Lauren smiled and enjoyed listening to her best friend finally being happy.

"Maybe you are in love?"

"Well we say that, but no, that is silly. Lust definitely. When I have a moment to think, my brain is fuzzy with lust. This is the behavior of a teenage girl, not a grown woman. I don't understand it, I'm loving every minute of it. It's like someone has filled me with a balloon of pleasure and it's not popping."

Lauren nodded and moved into the hot tub.

"Well, just enjoy it. It won't last long with Jeffrey hovering over your shoulder waiting for you to make a mistake so he can take the restaurant."

Nadailia joined her in the swirling hot water and again was amazed at how sensual everything felt.

"I love this, I worry about control. How much he already has over me, and he doesn't even know it. What happens when he realizes the kind of control I am willing give him? What happened when he realizes I will do pretty much anything to be near him? His Maman threatened me the other night. I need to take that wine-soaked woman seriously.

There's a part of me that wants it all to go away. Forget and ignore the feeling. That is impossible. I am trying to conquer the feeling. Push it down. Stay away from him. Lord, is there ever any end to this?"

Lauren smiled. "Well, you could fuck him to death."

Mean to Me

They met at a local restaurant where no one would expect to see them. She was there to talk about all the new feelings, her desires, his Maman's threats, and to see if they could come to an understanding.

Dylan was there to eat, then fuck.

He barely listened to her, focusing on the food.

"Hey there." He stood and hugged her, and she went weak in the knees from the proximity of him.

He pulled out her chair, took her hand. This simple declaration of affection rattled her, and her hand began to tremble. She looked into his eyes. They cut like lasers into her soul, and she lost her breath.

"We need to talk," she said.

"Yes, we do. Why are you being so mean to me at work?"

"I am sorry for that. I don't want anyone knowing we are having an affair." Dylan looked as if he had been struck by her. "Is that what you are labeling this? And you don't think they all don't already know?"

Nadailia grabbed his hand again and felt the energy flow between them. "I am not sure what this is. It's new territory. I have had lovers and a husband before, I have never felt the feelings that I do feel for you."

Dylan brushed her cheek with the back of his hand and said, "C'est l'amour."

Nadailia nearly collapsed at the words and the gesture, she continued. "This is a first in my life. I have never had real before you. I had passion, not the mind-blowing desire. After our last time together, I finally understand what the poets are talking about. I am more like a male in the ways of love. I am not big on snuggling. I don't need to hear sweet nothings. With you, everything is different. I can now fell passion anytime, as long as I have a memory of you, or even reading a text from you. It all started with that first text."

"So, what do you want to do about this 'problem'?"

"I have no idea. We can't get caught. I am finding that with each equally impressive coupling, I desire you more. You have moved from my loins to my head."

"Honestly, I like being in your loins."

"This desire for you builds and builds. I am glad you were bold in the garden that first night and in your texts."

He had now removed his shoes and was stroking her leg with his foot. She could feel the tension building. She was shocked that after years of chasing this sensation, now it would not subside. She swooned at his touch and was about to reach a peak when the waiter came over. She changed the subject.

"Honestly, I was shocked. I never thought in a million years you would be interested in me."

Dylan smiled at the intimate feelings she was sharing. He could love this woman.

"I love being your inspiration and chef."

Nadailia said quietly, "I fell for you the first time I met you. I felt it was impossible. I never thought you would go for me. Then those first hot texts."

He was always shocked when she seemed less sure of herself. It was like she didn't believe anyone could love her.

"Really? You are smart, sexy, uninhibited and outspoken. What's not to like?"

"Honestly, most men hate that."

"I am not most men."

"No, you are special."

He grabbed for her hand again, twirling little circles in her palm. "I don't want to mess this up. Whatever it is."

She gazed into his eyes. "I don't believe you could, we have to be careful. I have learned that passion makes life better. Even if you are passionately mad, as long as it is genuine, it is gold. Complacency causes death." She paused, needing to say something true and meaningful to him.

"One thing that men do not understand is the bequest of desire for women. When men feel aroused, they either take care of it themselves or take it out on their companion.

A woman's desire lives in her brain.

It travels to our loins and fills our hearts, this desire is sparked or squelched in our brains. So even if a lover's hands are magic, if his thoughts and words are not, I would not be sated. Women, like animals, can feel a man's intention. If I am desired, I am fulfilled. If it is an obligation or a need, I know it. I can go through the motions, I'm not satisfied. What I feel from you is 100 percent longing. A wanton desire that has never surfaced before. You awoke in me a primitive need."

Dylan caressed the inside of her forearm. "It is a invasion of my mind too, as my every thought is focused on having you, possessing you, pleasing you."

Nadailia continued, "While we are at work, I respect your need to protect me. In fact, that makes me want you more. Your resolution is hot. A weaker man would have taken me and seized the opportunity for smoking-hot sex. You are resolved to keep us both safe and professional, functioning as responsible adults, and colleagues."

Dylan looked at her with deep admiration.

"I like the way you think. The desire has to be received and welcomed by the other party. Many times, expressed desire is used as a weapon against a man or dismissed as not important."

Nadailia was outraged at the thought of anyone wounding this wise man. "Oh, Sweetie, desire used as a weapon is terrible."

He moved over to touch her hand.

The affection she felt for him surfaced again. "Let me be your safe place for a while."

She resolved herself into being a responsible, card-carrying adult and not implode either of their lives, the passion and love she felt for this man had to be manifested.

So far, through their work, exchange of words and an occasional coupling, they both found it kept them blissful. Each time circumstance found them alone, they fell upon each other like starving people.

Text

N: So, I am going to run the game for tonight.

D: Ok, I'm ready.

N: First, are you comfortable and have access to your non-texting hand?

D: Yes, and I'm so hard I'm ready to explode.

N: I will be fast. Just stroke and read.

They went to a movie and sat in the last row.

D: Ok.

N: It was a movie about food, their favorite subject besides sex.

She always brought a bottle of wine, which was now swirled in her mouth as she bent to take his rod. She knew he was enthralled by the food, she wanted him to have a bigger memory, and so she prepared to suck him off like no one had done before. He took a sip of the wine and began to concentrate on the big screen.

D: Fuck.

N: She unzipped is pants, let his passion spring forth and took all of him into her mouth.

D: Nice.

N: After having thought about him all day with her loins tingling.

Unsatisfied, she had to have him, pleasure him.

Make him scream for more.

After fondling and slurping, she swallowed him completely.

Engulfing him was the best sensation in the world.

D: Holy shit.

N: She rocked and sucked, swallowed and stroked until he was ready to explode.

D: Now?

N: Pleasing him was as satisfying as cumming herself.

He shot a load of cum into her mouth that went on forever.

D: Perfect. Yes.

N: She swallowed every drop, loving his flavor invading her taste buds.

D: Oh wow. Love it.

The Rhythm of The Sea

They were lunching at the seafood restaurant at the end of the pier. Teetering over the ocean, with tabletops of glass so you could look down and see the seals swim by, this place was intoxicating. They were there to try some of the amazing offerings that the fishing boats brought in every day. Dylan and the chef were old friends, so he pulled out the best of the best.

They started with Morro Bay oysters on the half shell served with a mignonette sauce of raspberry and shallots. It was served with a crispy 2013 Sauvignon Blanc from Tolosa Winery. The oysters were fresh and small, with a wonderfully subtle taste. They each slurped a dozen, hoping the siren of the sea would take over their passions that night.

The crab bisque was a rich, creamy soup with minefields of lump crab meat, sherry and a hint of cayenne pepper. It was served with 2012 Tolosa No Oak Chardonnay that was a light touch to the spicy soup.

Next they moved to an uncommon delicacy from the North, Alaskan king crab tails. This regional favorite is usually only found on menus in Alaska. The crab tail is a meaty, rich part of the body of the crab, and these were breaded, fried and served with a sweet and spicy Thai dipping sauce. It was astonishing in flavor and texture.

Next came the photo opportunity. It was a Kodak moment as several whole Alaskan king crab were presented to them, with each leg weighing almost a pound. Beyond its amazing size, the flavor was so virtuous they did not need butter or lemon. Large pieces of crab came out of the shell easily, and it was so rich that they could barely finish it. Served with a 2011 Tolosa "1772" Chardonnay, this tasting proved that the rarest crab in America is the finest fare. The chef explained, "The crab's freshness is enhanced by a program called Total Tracability. Each huge crustacean comes with a record of the date and time it was pulled from the depths of the Bering Sea. It is then sent overnight to our restaurant and served by the pound when in season."

They ended with a house-made Key lime pie that was as authentic as any you would get driving down the Keys in Florida. Tangy lime juice in a cream cheese-based pie with a graham cracker crust.

After lunch, Nadailia took Dylan shopping for clothes, which he loved and resented in equal amounts. He admitted that he needed to dress to impress, he hated her paying for it. He resolved himself into acceptance by calling it a working wardrobe and having Nadailia promise to buy equal amounts of sexy lingerie. After they had purchased enough chic clothes for two centuries, they wandered into Panty Pantry. They worked with a panty consultant who showed them all the latest outfits. She placed 15 items in a dressing room, and Dylan settled in on the big overstuffed chair while Nadailia tried on everything.

Five minutes in, Nadailia called Dylan into the dressing room. He paused outside, not comfortable with going in, she said she was stuck and needed his help. He acquiesced and went inside to help her. She was wearing the hottest pair of red crotchless panties with garters and a demi bra that had her magnificent nipples hiked up and exposed.

She smiled at his reaction to her outfit. "I need some help out of this outfit; I seem to be stuck." He stared at the clothing that was clearly designed for seduction that now skimmed her curves with a sexy, scalloped-lace trim. He had seen this style in the Paris fashion market, and he had always wished to see a real woman in this kind of outfit. He was rendered speechless and moved to her, taking her in with his eyes. She grabbed him and started to rub his now blossoming hard-on and nibbled on his neck. He started to leave, she held him tight. "Let me go; this is not right."

She held him tighter and began to rub her protruding nipple with her thumb and forefinger. He gulped at the sight of this and promised to lock it into his brain forever.

Then she took her other hand and stuck it between the red lace and her pussy. He stood there dumbfounded. She began to moan, and not at a whisper level. He placed his hand on her mouth and whispered, "Shhhhhhhh!!!"

She smiled and kept working herself and moaning.

He put his mouth on hers, intending to quiet her, she took it as a sign he was all in. She rubbed his cock with her groin as she continued to pleasure herself. He was beginning not to care if anyone heard and was lost in her seductive masturbatory dance.

When she was sure he was fully captivated, she turned her back to the wall and wiggled her unrestrained crotch at him. Free from reason or inhibition, he took his cock out and inserted it into her welcoming pussy.

Lost in passion they finished with expansive energy as the panty consultant was knocking on the door.

"I know we are known for our playfully seductive heritage," she said, "but you two have got to go."

Text

D: Are you in your office?

N: Yes.

D: Describe what you are wearing.

N: Red corset, nipples on the ridges, bursting over the bustier. No panties, for easy insertion.

D: Really???

N: Sure.

D: Oh fuck.

N: You like?

D: You know, if that's real, I may cum without even touching myself.

N: I have done that twice with you, so catch up.

D: Promise it's real?

N: I promise. No reason to lie.

D: Mother fucker. I will have a hard-on tomorrow every time I visualize this.

N: Red in red. Nipples erect, pussy dying for you.

D: That might get me through the weekend.

N: Now I am leaning over the chair, wiggling my ass at you.

Declarations

Dylan got to work early and sat out by the garden, reflecting on his plan to make the restaurant more of a wine and food resort. Because they were in the heart of wine country, he wanted to make it a destination spot for wine tasters. The warmth of their wisteria-covered patio welcomed the weary, purple-toothed visitors. The connection between great wine and impeccable food was immediately apparent as you entered the restaurant. Along the wall was an impressive selection of Santa Barbara County and Paso Robles wines, with a massive concrete fireplace and bar connecting the café to the garden. Diners could eat indoors with a view of the outdoors. He was proud of his contribution to this beautiful venue and never wanted to leave.

Today was a big meeting with the whole staff, led by Nadailia. As the chef, Dylan was seated next to her, and they taught everyone about the new menu. He was happy to have a crew that embraced his changes. Dylan and Nadailia worked well as a team, their passion for the success of this restaurant was apparent.

Nadailia found that every time they even lightly touched each other, both blushed. She was afraid their affair was apparent to everyone and it was. She had the lunacy of a love struck woman, believing she could not let that happen.

Jeffrey started the meeting by announcing a new policy that employees are not allowed to date each other or to be married. This statement earned a groan from the whole staff. Since they all worked so many hours; it was hard to date anyone from outside the restaurant. A lively discussion ensued, Nadailia brought it to a close by saying she would take it to upper management and get back to them. A busboy in the back blurted out, "Yah, you'd hate to give up your boy toy." There was a collective gasp by the group, and everyone knew that his busing days had ended. They moved on, tasting and learning the new menu with Chef Dylan leading the group.

They sampled the tasting with a 2010 Flying Goat Cellars Pinot Noir from Dierberg Vineyard. Then it was time to get the stomach juices flowing. The first dish was Pulled Beef Sliders, an East Coast delicacy made with savory pulled beef in a light jus, smeared with creamed horseradish, topped with baby arugula and served on a fresh brioche bun. The beef was melt-in-your-mouth, and the spicy tang of the horseradish made this an interesting and delicious dish.

The next dish was a salad of roasted butternut squash, sun-dried cranberries, toasted pumpkin seeds and gorgonzola, served on field greens with a sweet and wonderful molasses vinaigrette. It was refreshing and full of flavor. They also tried the rolled spinach gnocchi with oven-dried tomato, fagioli beans and spinach, drizzled with black truffle butter and parmesan. Any food that was enhanced with truffles lent a richness and delicacy to the menu. They paired this with a rare Lane Tanner Pinot Noir, and the elegance of the wine brought forth the interesting flavor combinations.

The next dish was delicious, free-range lamb shanks braised with red wine, tomato, sweet onion and herbs and complemented by couscous, asparagus and a natural jus. Nadailia got up during the meal and went to her office. When she returned five minutes later, she whispered in Dylan's ear, "I finished with my vibrator in my office. This dish was that good. Thank you, Chef."

The last new dish was the Café Scream. This warm, flourless, chocolate torte served with vanilla ice cream and caramel sauce was so splendid that the whole crew moaned in delight. Ideas were exchanged, and everyone was happy to start service tomorrow afternoon.

As they tasted more wines, with Maman bringing out her new finds from the local garagiste winemakers, Dylan reached his hand up under the table and felt Nadailia's bare leg. Even though the weather had turned cold, Nadailia liked to keep open access to his touch, so she seldom wore tights or pants around him. The touch of his fingertips on her thigh was still one of her greatest pleasures. It was intimate and daring. It represented the sweet beginning of a love affair she considered the most miraculous gift she had received.

He grasped her knee and pulled her leg open to him while he moved his hand up her inner thigh. This made her pant. She pretended it was a sneeze, and covered her mouth with her napkin. Their dining companions kept on talking and tasting the food, the real explorations were happening under the table.

They claimed they had to go inspect a delivery of fish that had arrived and left the employees. They held hands as they left the restaurant, loving a moment alone of touching. They approached his big truck, and he opened the bed liner top and gestured for her to look in. The back of the truck had been transformed into a small nest of feather beds and silk sheets. She looked back, smiled, then climbed in. He joined her and closed the top.

With only minutes to be gone before suspicion was aroused, they began to kiss. Soft and full, exploring each other's mouths as he removed her panties and unzipped his pants.

He traveled his fingertips up her thigh and found her pussy, which was soft as satin. He masterfully strummed the folds of her pussy, making her moan with pleasure. She worked his golden cock, which always seemed to be at attention when she touched it.

He climbed on top of her and slid his cock into her dripping pussy. The power and fit of their docking always surprised and delighted. They stayed like that for a few seconds as they deepened their kiss. Because of the limited space, all they could do was rock together, their harmony was enough to take Dylan over the edge.

They kissed again and dressed lying down, giggling while they squirmed back into their clothes in the confined space. They ventured back to the restaurant, spinning a story of street musicians delaying them.

Text

N: What a crazy day!

D: What can I do to help?

N: Relax me.

D: How shall I do that when you are there and I am here?

N: With your words. Write our next sex scene.

D: Ok, I will give it a try.

I like your writing style. Much smoother than mine.

N: I like yours. It is more hot and too the point. I am too wordy.

I am thinking about you day and night.

D: How many times did you cum?

It was SO HOT knowing you got yourself off during the luncheon.

N: Every spare second I am thinking of sex with you.

I had a vibrator in my purse I was about to send around the table and drop it in your lap. But the opportunity didn't present itself.

D: I was hard the whole time during the presentation. Did you feel it when you reached back?

N: Yes. I am such a bad girl.

D: You're perfect! I will dream about you.

The Monkey Springs

They opened the restaurant the next night to a full house, which led to many respectable reviews. The new menu was well received. It went flawlessly, and that was a testament to both the chef and the owner.

The hit of the night was the Garden Party. The chef selected a menu of five courses, creating an excellent way to try many of the new dishes. To start, he made a tomato and flowering basil tea with lemon verbena. Then came baby Swiss and sarvecchio gougères. Tasting these simple puffs brought on ecstasy. Next course was a garden salad with crispy beets and whimsical carrots that were cooked under pressure with flowers and herbs. The raw oyster was served simple with tomato juice and a garden radish. Its inebriating lusciousness was apparent to everyone.

Chef Dylan concocted a sweet, fiery gazpacho with local olive oil and sherry vinegar. The balance of flavors was impeccably paired with a 2007 Foxen Sea Smoke Vineyard Pinot Noir. Smoked white quinoa with shaved melon, cucumber, apple and nasturtium flowers were a surprised and delight to all who enjoyed this amazing garden delicacy.

The main courses were savored. Grilled Local Snapper featured saffron poached potatoes with a hint of honey. The favorite of the night was Hand-cut Tagliatelle pasta with sweet baby corn, cippolini onions and squash blossoms. This buttery pleasure was comforting and enchanting. The Prime Beef Sirloin Cap with a mustard béarnaise sauce mesmerized everyone, and the huge portions of Drake Duck Breast with roasted carrot, baby eggplant and cippolini onions combined the savory of duck with the sweetness of the vegetables.

For dessert it was a chocolate pot de crème with Chavez strawberries and a raspberry polenta cake with buttermilk ice cream. Thinking one thin wafer would make them explode, all found room for the tomato and Happy Acres goat cheese cannoli.

Chef Dylan was dubbed a culinary genius and a gift to the region. Patrons loved his Mediterranean flair with garden-fresh produce and local proteins. People raved that he was creative, humble and someone to be worshipped. All the patrons treasured the fact that the menu would change as the chef became inspired from the garden and always changing offerings from the sea.

After the last dish was done, and all employees were gone, Dylan walked into the dining room to find Nadailia. He wrapped his arms around her as she backed against him. She could feel his burning hardness pressing against her ass. He leisurely slid his hand down the front of her blouse and gently touched her nipple. His touch was like a branding iron. Scorching against her skin. Her nipple instantly became erect against his fingers.

She reached around and grabbed his cock through his pants, feeling his rigid cock. She could also feel how wet he already was. Her desire to have him in her mouth was overpowering. She deliberately turned and reached for his belt. She knelt before him, gazing up into his eyes. Losing herself in the depth of them. As she unzipped his pants, she reached in and freed him from his clothes.

His stiff cock was dripping. She touched her tongue to the tip and tasted him. It was pleasing and warm. She encircled his manhood with her warm moist lips and took all of him in her mouth. She was skilled at her task.

Dylan moaned, "Lord, you're good at this."

Nadailia worked her tongue around the head of his dick. Pulling her mouth almost off the tip and then sliding back down the shaft, taking almost all eight inches into her throat. She gently caressed his balls with one hand and held tight to his hard ass with the other.

Using her experience, she watched his breathing closely to make sure she didn't make him cum too soon. She had plans for that later. As he would get close, she would pause and hold the base of his cock tightly. He finally squeaked out, "Please let me."

She knew he would be able to go again in a few minutes.

So she pulled her blouse down, exposing her beautiful tits, and rapidly started to work him.

Using a combination of her hand and her mouth, she built him up to a pressure boiling point he couldn't return from.

He exploded and she swallowed every drop.

Nadailia sat back on her heals and looked up at Dylan, who was trying to recover. He whispered, "I'm not sure what's so intoxicating about this. I'm in new territory. But, Lord, I feel like an addict."

"It is new to me too."

"I'm hotter and more turned on than I've been in years."

They deliberately disrobed not taking their eyes of the other. Then they lay on the couch by the fireplace, draped around each other. Dylan was gently stroking her sex and feeling her wetness on his fingers.

He moved off the couch and knelt on the floor and maneuvered her so her legs draped over his shoulders. Nuzzling her pussy, first with his nose, then slowly started to use his tongue to explore her clit.

He rolled her clit gently with his tongue and compressed it with his lips, sending a white bolt of lightning through her core.

He flicked upward with the tip of his tongue and teased her clit.

He gently sucked on it, pulling it into his lips and nibbling gently, so lightly, with his teeth.

Each nibble brought a full-body shudder to her.

As he sucked her, he inserted two fingers into her pussy, which was now flooded with moisture.

He slowly rotated his fingers upward and used the tips to find the ridges at the top of her vagina.

Steadily keeping pressure on the ridges, he continued to lick, suck and nip at her clit.

As he slowly started moving his two fingers across those ridges, he used some of her copious wetness to lubricate his thumb.

He gradually maneuvered his slippery, wet thumb into her ass, a fraction of an inch at a time, letting her rectum slowly acclimate to the size.

Once fully inserted, he moved his whole hand in a gentle thrusting motion.

He pumped harder and harder, keeping pressure on her G spot as well.

He could see her concentration and feel her pushing against his hand.

She pushed him away and moved to lean over the arm of the couch.

"Fuck me. Fuck me in the ass."

She was completely flooded by now, and he needed no further lubrication.

He put the head of his steel-firm rod against her ass, and it slid in with almost no effort. She pushed her ass against him, seating his dick fully in her.

"Dylan."

She moved slightly forward and then backed against him, beginning the rhythm.

Together they worked as one, she pushing at exactly the right time and he driving his hard dick into her. He grabbed her hips with both hands and, after minutes of mutual pleasure, convulsed his cum into her. His spasms triggering an explosion of senses and light in her brain. Exposing naked raw pleasure.

Nadailia was floored. All she could say was, "She who talks too much has no words."

He smiled and sat her down.

"Glad I could be of assistance."

They sipped on the last of the wine, and she was much inside her head as she gazed into the fire. He was happy. A perfect new menu and a perfect sexcapade.

Suddenly the door flew open and in blazed Jeffrey with a camera, taking pictures of them naked. He was screaming hysterically, "I knew it! You bitch. You fucking whore! You can't do this to my father. Both of you are fired. Get the fuck out of my restaurant."

The Reveal

Nadailia went home with trepidation and saw Jeffrey's car in her driveway. It was so late at night that she knew her husband was sleeping, as was his caregiver. She walked into the house, hoping there would not be another outburst of screaming. Jeffrey was sitting in the living room, drinking a scotch and looking quite pleased with himself.

"Jeffrey, how did you get in here? Why are you here?"

"The nurse let me in. I hadn't seen father in a long time. He had no idea who I was."

"I am sorry. I told you it was bad."

"Bad enough for you to take a lover? To betray him?"

"Jeffrey, what I do with Dylan has nothing to do with your father. You know we never had that kind of marriage."

"But Dylan is your employee. When the board finds out, you are going to get tossed out on your tight ass."

Jeffrey was clearly drunk; so she proceeded carefully and kept her purse with the pepper spray close, ready to stop him if necessary.

"I agree that it is not the best of situations, the restaurant is successful."

Jeffrey stood up and came toward her in a menacing style.

"You think you can have everything? I will destroy both of you. Your little chef will never work in this town again. I am calling an emergency board meeting tomorrow and calling for your resignation."

He slammed down the empty glass and stormed out.

Dylan went straight to Pedro's house to seek his advice. Pedro had been a waiter his whole life, and there was no situation he hadn't witnessed. Dylan trusted him and vowed to do whatever he suggested. Pedro brought out a bottle of Haka Tempranillo for them to share.

"Pedro, I fucked up."

"You got caught."

Pedro had a wise way of explaining complicated issues.

"Dylan, you two clearly care for each other. This is so much more than an affair. I know she is married, I know that Jeffrey wants the restaurant. What do you want?"

"I think I love her, it is impossible if she is married and my boss."

"Impossible is stapling water to a tree, not loving. Loving seems to always work out in the end."

Dylan looked at his friend and almost started to cry. He was lost. He loved his job and wanted the restaurant to succeed, his lust for Nadailia would not subside. He knew it was wrong, his heart and body still longed for her.

"What do I do?"

"Take the rest of the week off; your kitchen staff can handle it. Nadailia is a capable woman; she will make sure everything turns out the way it should for you, the restaurant and – most importantly – her."

Dylan went home drunk but feeling a bit more balanced. Nadailia called him as he was getting into bed.

"How are you doing?"

Just the sound of her voice made him feel at peace. And then horny.

"I am OK. Do we still have jobs? Do you still have a marriage? I am so sorry, Nadailia. I should have known better."

"Dylan, everything is fine. Jeffrey has been trying to throw me out for years. I am undeterred by his threats. That is why I have a board of directors, so I have a safety net. They will not care about our affair. Trust me."

"I do, and I don't trust easily, and I know you don't either. But when we do, it's real and forever."

"I know that. Down to my bones."

"Each time we step closer to each other, fear jumps into the mix. I guess it is the formula for this."

Dylan was still afraid and she wanted to go comfort him, she knew it would be dangerous.

"So know this: I love what we have. We are both growing in this, and we will both protect this with everything we have. Do not live in fear."

Dylan was once again astounded by her strength.

"Thank you. I needed that. You mean more to me than I can ever remember feeling. It's a precarious place for me. It's not physical; you live in my brain. You hold my heart. That incident with Jeffrey made it apparent to me that I need to protect this from me and my damn libido."

"Dylan, we learned tonight how close this whole thing is to destruction. It doubles my resolve to protect it, even over the objections of my desire. I think we both agree that from now on at the restaurant, nothing more than secret touches."

"I agree. We are both learning how to manage and nurture what we have. No more sex?"

"I think it might be a good idea to back off for a day or two. Why don't you take the weekend off? Anyway, I get as much from stroking your hand as I do your cock."

"That is probably why I am aroused the whole time I am around you."

"Me too. It's like walking through fire."

"Good night, my redheaded fury."

The Board

Nadailia awoke the next day as conflicted as ever. She was resolved to keeping it hands-off while at the restaurant. She met with each of the board members privately and talked with her lawyer to make sure she was not in danger of losing her place in the company or her home because of the affair. As it turned out, her husband's guilt was so crushing to him that he had written into his living trust a provision that she was entitled to a lover. He had also inserted a clause that Jeffrey could never touch what was hers. Nadailia was amazed that he could have been so intuitive and such a bad husband at the same time.

Text

D: What's the Boss doing for lunch?

N: Shareholders meeting.

D: Want some inspiration?

N: I'm frightened.

D: You got this?

N: I hope so.

D: What can I do to help?

N: I'm not sure how to reconcile this.

D: Jeffrey is a douche. The board won't get rid of both of us.

N: I hope not, because I am not giving you up.

D: You want more?

N: Yes.

D: Tonight.

The Horses Shaking Hooves

The meeting with the board of directors went well and in Nadailia's favor, she was told not to have sex in the restaurant again. They were considering Jeffrey's proposal to ban co-workers from being in relationships, but that was ludicrous. The restaurant business demanded so many hours; most employees only had time to date each other. The meeting ended on a happy note with reports about soaring profits and reservations set six months out.

The night that Dylan returned to work, the restaurant had an acoustic concert, so the bar area was darkened with a semi-circle of light focusing on the stage. Nadailia was at the back, watching the show and enjoying being in the dark, unseen by her staff and customers. For her, it was a rare moment of solitude and pride. She was happily swaying back and forth when Dylan approached in the blackness. Their hands grazed each other, and the blazing energy from their last set of texts flooded both of them with desire. He moved behind her, encircling her with his arms. She started to protest, he responded by thrusting his hand up her skirt and grabbing her pussy. The shock of this daring moved made her inhale loudly and begin to get moist. She looked around to see if anyone noticed or heard them. He continued to stroke her and pinch her clit. She leaned against him, dropping her head back into the nook of his neck. She whispered, "Be careful."

He slipped his fingers into her pussy, rubbing it back and forth and grazing her clit. She reached around and felt his hard cock. She stroked it through his pants. He murmured and ripped her G-string off. She quaffed at the violence of this act that now had her completely dripping with anticipation. She unzipped his pants and freed his throbbing rod. Still standing, he entered her from behind with a hard thrust that scared and delighted her. She looked to make sure no one had spotted them. All eyes were pointed toward the stage, so she pushed back. With his raging hard cock inside her, they swayed to the music. It was extremely erotic doing something so private in public. She knew this was the worst idea, but passion clouded her judgment. They fell into a rhythm that matched the band. While the climax was quiet, panting sounds, the explosion between the two was nuclear in its energy.

As he exited her, the separation felt shocking and cold. She could feel their combined juices drip down her leg. Weak in the knees, she leaned against him, not wanting any more separation between them.

He whispered, "I have to go back to the kitchen. Thank you."

This declaration of gratitude infuriated her. She stood there, conflicted and furious with a muddled brain.

Once she straightened her skirt, she marched into the kitchen. He looked up from his prep table, and his smile nearly knocked her back. With a sly smirk he said,

"Do you need something?"

She wanted to scream out, but the kitchen was full of staff all waiting to see what she did indeed want in their kitchen.

"I need to see you in my office, Dylan, immediately."

He followed her into her office, and as the door shut, he reached for her. She slapped his hand back.

"How dare you!" She was shaking with fury and passion. "That stunt was dangerous and out of line."

"You seemed to like it."

"That's beside the point. This is my restaurant, and if anyone caught us again, I'd never live it down."

"We didn't get caught."

"Never touch me again!"

The power of her words struck him as hard as the message.

"Your call. Are you done?"

He turned and left, not waiting for her answer.

Text

N: I'm sorry.

D: What have you been doing?

N: Beating off.

D: Holy shit, love it. Are you still pissed at me?

N: I am over it.

D: Have you used the toys?

N: All fucking night.

D: That is incredibly hot. I love anticipation.

N: So keep going.

D: I admire your lust and desire.

N: Come over.

D: I thought I was never to touch you again.

N: Get over here.

Cicada Affixed

This passion for him never let up. She was still surprised that afterward waves of lust were still hitting her. It was like a fever. Feeling her whole body affected by this heat pleasure. This coming undone with a simple touch from him. It was all in secret, so every touch was stolen. She had begun to run her fingers over everything, trying to displace the energy. Towels in the kitchen, the grass, a rose petal, even the metal hood of her car felt sensuous. Everything was heightened. The smell of food was stronger, more gratifying. She began to feel erogenous zones on her body that she didn't know existed. This was something quite extraordinary, something different. Grown people understanding the appetite for each other. She knew that the possibility for it to end poorly was real. This new restaurant business had to be foremost in her mind. She reconciled herself to that, she was forever looking forward to his texts or being in the same room with him and lightly grazing against him. This kind of hunger was wonderful and something she wanted to carry with her forever. She worried that she hadn't yet achieved an orgasm and maybe that was the only reason he took over her brain. She was pretty sure she had climaxed, but not certain.

The next morning they took a day-trip and spent the hours at the beach, alone and unnoticed. Dylan wanted to surprise her with something different. He took her out into the dunes to experience the ocean and the sand in its raw, most powerful form. The chef knew mixing food cooked over an open fire with the pounding ocean would be a powerful aphrodisiac.

The beach was full of people and bonfires. They were singing, drinking and telling stories. Nadailia and Dylan went back deeper in to the dunes to have some privacy and shelter from the wind.

He built a fire, placed a small grill over it and put a pot of water on to boil. He took out the live California king crab and positioned it in the pot. As the crab cooked, they enjoyed the appetizers; bacon-wrapped dates stuffed with blue cheese, prosciutto-wrapped mozzarella, and strawberries and crème, all of diverse flavor and structure to completely opened up the palate. Dylan knew seduction was better when it included food. While the crab cooked, they spread out the blanket and he pulled her close. Dylan had positioned them so they could view the sunset over the Pacific Ocean. They feasted on the crab using their hands.

Afterward, they moved up against a sand dune, using the natural landscape as a backrest. Nadailia smiled as she rolled over and dipped her head between Dylan's legs. Sucking him off had become her favorite way to get hot. It actually was the only way to get her started. They tried other things, her favorite to get ready was to take him in her mouth.

In this comfortable position, she could take him deep into her throat. He loved the way she knew every button that would fill him with pleasure.

Before she let him cum, she straddled him. Face to face, she slid his throbbing cock inside her. He pushed her head back and began to nuzzle her neck. Dylan nibbled on her earlobe and bit her neck. He started to suck, and she jumped from the threat of a hickey. It was more than she could stand. They began to rock and kiss deeply. The rocking, the deep kissing, was opening up something in her she hadn't felt before. The top of his cock was rubbing back and forth inside her, stroking her G spot. His pelvis was thoroughly massaging her clit. Usually a sensational like this took a hand, but there was no hand, only his body, and this was twice as stimulating. She rocked and rocked, losing all sense of time or common sense. The fire that was about to explode in her was like nothing she had ever felt before. He was braced against the sand dune, and let her do all the work. He hung on for the ride, watching with delight. It was an absolute turn on to see such pleasure rise up from her. Nadailia was amazed that with her rocking she completely controlled the stimulus. He felt her tight muscles tightly squeeze his cock until he came. She dropped her head onto his chest and purred.

Text

D: Hey, Boss lady! Thanks for the beach ball.

N: Haha.

D: How are you feeling now?

N: It was everything I dreamed of and more.

The best part of the afternoon was having the freedom to talk, touch and kiss at will.

I will always recall the feeling with the simple taste of a strawberry. I find myself shuttering today when a memory slips into my conscience. That beach dune became the most erotic place I can go to.

D: I knew it would be comfortable.

N: I was still surprised at the ease with which I became totally yours.

D: This is a special tryst. If treated with the right respect and reverence, it will never betray us.

N: I was as excited to openly touch your hands.

It was so nice to stare into your eyes, watch your mouth and then take it.

Ridiculously hot.

D: Yes it was, and so are you.

Once in his life, a man is entitled to fall madly in love with a gorgeous redhead.

N: I am fueled with what we had today.

It was magic, perfect, sensual and so comfortable.

The comfort surprised me.

I've been "out of my body" for a most my life.

I didn't think I had the courage to share.

But it seemed natural with you.

D: I love the strength, the rawness of you.

The desire pumping through my veins was so exhilarating.

That feeling, alone, will power me for weeks.

N: It was easy and natural, like we had been lovers for years.

D: I love your lips, soft and yielding yet hungry.

N: The ebb and flow was pleasurable.

Not expended but regulated.

Passion simmering beneath the surface.

D: We must be careful not to be cavalier. We don't want to squander this opportunity.

N: Yes!

D: I am still finding sand in parts of me I did not know I had.

The White Tiger Jumps

Nadailia received a call from the nurse, telling her that her husband had died. She was shaken and sad, but knew that he had actually died many years ago when his mind slipped away. She called Lauren, who came over to help her start the funeral planning.

While they were in her office writing the obituary, Jeffrey came bouncing in.

"Now that he is dead, I will get you out of this company," he said. His red face looked like that of a toddler who had his favorite toy taken away.

"Your father just died, and your first thought is to get rid of me? What is wrong with you?"

"I am tired of you fucking your way to the top. I will throw you out of here."

"You are a sad little man, Jeffrey. You have always have been a shit. I am not going anywhere. In fact it is you who may be looking for a new job. I have noticed your "creative" financing tricks. Out of respect to your father, I left you alone, but now the gloves are off. Get out of my office, you viper!"

Jeffrey slammed the door, and Lauren shook her head.

"He is going to cause you and Dylan trouble. Better warn the chef."

Nadailia made an announcement to the staff about her husband's passing, and they decided to hold a glorious feast in his honor. The service was held at a bistro overlooking the sea and the docks. It was Nadailia's deceased husband's favorite wine bar, owned by a fisherman. He said he loved this fisherman-gone-businessman concept, so pragmatic and smart, they always succeed. The group sat among some of his favorite friends: Sea Smoke, Turley and Sinor-LaVallee, his dark drinkable companions whom he loved to spend time with over a plate of cheese and freshly baked bread. All in attendance told funny and poignant stories about the deceased.

They toasted him with a Graham Beck Brut Rose paired with a sweet potato blini with crème fraîche and Tsar Nicoulai Classic Caviar. Nadailia nearly exploded with pleasure from this delectable gift. Chef Dylan outdid himself with a mixture of sophisticated tastes, which paired perfectly with the wines.

Next was a Graham Beck Blanc de Blancs paired with Smoked Salmon Roulade. These outstanding treats included a homemade potato chip, called a potato gaufrette, with lox-style smoked salmon rolled with cream cheese and sprinkled with capers, crushed garlic, red pepper flakes and a sprig of baby dill. It was inspired and so delicate in it flavors and textures. The following course featured the Brut NV paired with an Oregon raw oyster washed in champagne and tossed with a mignonette sauce.

The last course was the Brut Zero with a Maine lobster BLT. These tiny sandwiches, filled with the glory of the sea, featured apple wood bacon, lobster, baby heirloom tomatoes and butter lettuce on a brioche toast.

They passed out Vosges Haut-Chocolate, which was an outstanding combination of peanut butter, bourbon, pink Himalayan salt, Maldon sea salt and deep milk chocolate. Next was the chef's chocolate truffle. Chunks of cocoa and cinnamon all dusted in a dry chocolate powder made this treat one that would bring back the Mayans.

It was a perfect event with the right balance of panache and homage. Nadailia was so proud of the amazing job Dylan did to honor her now late husband, but grew tired of the whole funeral/will/mourning processes. She was excited to get some alone time with her favorite chef.

Text

N: Come over, I need to hold you.

D: Are you kidding? You are in mourning.

N: No, I am not. He died years ago in my mind. This was a formality.

D: How can you be so cold-hearted?

N: Are you fucking kidding me?

D: No, there is a proper mourning period.

N: Please tell me this is a joke? We have been fucking for months now, and here is where you take the moral high ground? Un-fucking-believable.

Get your ass over here NOW. I need a proper fuck!

D: Don't you order me around like I am your slave.

N: Get over here or else!

D: Or else what? You gonna fire me if I don't fuck you on command?

N: Fuck you, Dylan. Just fuck you.

Dark Affixed Cicada

Nadailia was pissed and exhausted. She vowed to get him back into his right mind tomorrow. She took a shower and declared to make herself cum, seeking the much needed release he was now denying her.

She warmed up the stainless steel butt plug, then lubed herself up and inserted it hard like she knew Dylan would. She turned the water wand to pulsating and started on her nipples, working them until they were as hard as erasers. Then she moved down to her clit and braised the folds of her pussy with the hot water, then put it so close to her insides that it was like being fucked by water. In her mind, the carousel of sexual scenarios swirled and played like a passion film.

She turned down the pressure and moved back to her clit, making wide circles. Changing the distance; then altering the pressure. Her ass was pressed on the cold tile, forcing the plug in deeper. The front was all hot water and pressure. She soaped up her other hand and ran it over her nipples.

The best part was thinking about Dylan.

His words.

His food.

His touch.

His cock.

She imagined his dick in her ass. With her knees weak and her skin dripping water, she went to her phone to see if he had texted.

He had not.

The next morning there was a note from Dylan:

To: Nadailia

From: Dylan

Regarding: I am an ass

Nadailia,

This is my attempt to apologize for being an ass. I am not sure how to proceed or how you want to proceed. I don't want to ruin things with us, and Jeffrey is still talking about firing us. I thought some time apart would be the smart thing to do.

Dylan

Deciding to take the high road, she wrote him back:

To: Dylan

From: Nadailia

Regarding: IYF

Dylan,

I am fueled by your trust in me, and it keeps intensifying. I will never doubt or undermine your morals again, as they are a delightful gift to me.

IYF (and I will wait),

Nadailia

They avoided each other at work almost successfully, when they passed in the hall, their hands always met, if only for a second. It was this slight touching that twisted Nadailia, and she backed off from suggesting that he come and fuck her. This was not easy for her, she found a delightful side to him while being hands-off. She wrote to him about what she would do to him when they are together. The act of writing sexual prose to him ignited her mind as well as her loins.

Text

N: I can still taste you.

See your glorious cock.

I can still feel you in the back of my throat.

Your hands holding my hair like reins.

Sucking you after you came to make sure I did not miss a drop.

D: That was wonderful.

N: You honestly surprised me.

D: I'm so glad you came over.

N: For over 4 months you have invaded my mind, body and soul.

I literally can't think about anything but fucking you.

It does not let up.

Each interaction results in more desire.

D: I love hearing about you being hot and getting yourself off.

N: I took a shower at work.

I improvised and stuck the vibrating razor up in me.

Using my shower gel for lubricant.

I inserted it and turned it on.

D: I am so fucking hard right now it is crazy.

Fuck.

N: I rocked and thought of your eyes, your food, your electric touch.

It was all there, every hot molecule of you.

With my memory on full recall.

D: I am so fucking hard right now.

N: I would die to feel every inch.

D: Real or not, I love that kind of storytelling.

N: It is real.

Mountain Goat Facing a Tree

Nadailia was closing up for the night and decided to rob her wine cellar and take something luscious home to enjoy. She was strangely at peace with the hands-off rule, as it powered their imagination and their writing. It was also making it easier to focus on securing her future, getting Jeffrey out of her life and her business, and cleaning up her late husband's estate. She unlocked the door, already having decided on a 1997 Foxen Cuvee. When the light flickered on she saw Jeffrey's bare ass pumping into Maman. Jeffrey jumped, turned and started screaming. His tiny cock amused Nadailia, and a slow smirk populated her face.

"What the fuck are you doing down here?" he roared.

"It's my wine cellar."

Maman smiled as she pulled her panties up and smoothed out her skirt.

Jeffrey was seething as he pulled up his pants.

"Why are you still here? What are you looking at?"

"The last straw."

Nadailia turned and left without the wine. The wonder of this discovery began sinking in, and she knew she finally had a way to get Jeffrey out of her life.

As Nadailia climbed the stairs, she heard Maman run up behind her. Maman was holding a bottle of 1997 Foxen, the same bottle that Nadailia was going for.

"Here you go, my sweet. Now you and my son should be left alone to fall in love like proper adults."

Maman smiled and rushed back to the cellar where Jeffrey was still cussing.

Later at home Nadailia sipped the delicious wine and planned for independence.

Text

D: Hey, what are you doing right now?

N: Planning? You?

D: Almost dozing off. You about finished for the night?

N: I think your Maman and I have come to an understanding.

D: That's good, right?

N: Yes, I hope.

My body is aching for you today. I am so distracted.

Give me a Truth or Dare.

D: Ok.

Get one of the carrots from my garden, the ones you told me you practice on.

Wash it, put a little lube on it and use it like a fat dildo till you cum, wash it again and eat it.

N: OMG!

D: :-)

N: And proof?

D: Pic of you taking a bite of the carrot.

Comments?

N: I'm getting my carrot.

D: Hahaha.

N: OMG. It's cold.

D: Not for long!

N: It's big.

D: Perfect.

Just short, right?

N: Yes.

Still cold.

I wish you could see this.

D: Me too! You amaze me with what you will try.

N: Holy fuck.

D: Does it feel exciting?

N: Strangely, yes.

D: Beautiful. Did you cum?

N: I did, and here is your proof.

Thank you. Maybe now I can focus.

D: You will definitely have better night vision.

N: Hahaha

D: And "Eat your vegetables" has a whole new meaning now.

Hey, a new concept for your restaurant. In addition to "Garden to Table," you can use "Garden to Labia"

N: Oh my, Mr. Dylan. You are bad.

D: Yes. But fun!

N: The best fun.

D: And carrots are not the only possibility.

N: If anyone knew what you get me to do, they'd never believe it.

I want the real thing before any more vegetables.

I guess I need you in my mind more than I need you actually touching me, that's hard to believe.

Part of it is that you're so damn creative.

I never know where you're going.

It's a huge turn on.

D: I never know where that stuff comes from either.

N: It's the magic realm.

I could say you're my magical mystery ride.

The Tortoise Mounts

Nadailia invited Dylan over to her house for appetizers and to strategize. She had not told him about the night in the wine cellar, he did know that Maman was somehow involved. Every time Jeffrey came to yell or insult Dylan, Maman gave him a look and he backed off.

Dylan brought a plate of delectable food, mostly made with harvested items from his garden. He was proud of the bountiful yield this little garden had produced. They started with an almond gazpacho paired with a Justin Chardonnay. Dylan explained that gazpacho is now usually made with tomatoes, it was originally made with whatever was available. The almonds from Olea Farm were pulverized with garlic into a stout soup, then sprinkled with olive oil and herbs. This cold soup was an explosion of restrained flavor.

Next were oysters Rockefeller, made with Tomalas Bay oysters. The oysters were layered with bacon, onion, cream cheese, spinach and Romano cheese, broiled and served on their shells. They toasted using the empty oysters shells, and as their hands met, electricity flew through them both.

The salad was a work of art with arugula leaves wrapped at the base with thinly sliced cucumber (it made a tree) with a thyme emulsion sprinkled in the leaves like snow. On the plate was a poached pair, candied pecans and Blue Paradise cheese. After so much time apart, the simple act of feeding each other made them hot.

The main dish was a mustard-crusted lamb chop with mashed potatoes, baby summer squash and lamb sauce. Dessert was as beautiful as it was succulent: fresh market berries with a sweet chèvre and a crispy lace cookie.

After the meal they moved to Nadailia's office to work on their plan to get rid of Jeffrey once and for all. They had proof that he had stolen money and wine, was sleeping with at least one employee. The wine and the fraternization is not something they can point fingers at, as they were doing the same, the stealing of cash, the molesting of tickets? That would be an unforgivable sin to the board of directors.

They laid out their evidence for the presentation and toasted to the better restaurant that will be "douche-less."

Nadailia pecked Dylan on the cheek and walked him to the door.

"See you tomorrow. I have more work to do."

"Wait! I am leaving? We are not going to fuck, or at least neck?"

"Nope, on your way. Use your extra energy to create a Sunday brunch menu."

Text

D: I can't believe I can't have you. How long is this going to last?

N: Until the will is settled and I know for sure the restaurant is mine.

D: I am sure I will explode.

N: You will be fine. Talk dirty to me.

D: I want to tell you a story.

N: Goody.

D: I'm standing in front of you in the foyer by the couch. The restaurant is closed, only the kitchen and cleaning staff remain.

I'm wearing jeans, no underwear, shirt, no undershirt, shirttail out, no shoes or socks.

N: Beach casual.

D: I put my finger to my lips to make sure you don't say anything, because the staff is in the next room. We sit on the couch. You are naked.

I pull you toward me by your ankles.

And put your feet on my chest.

Your pussy is exposed and wet.

I unzip my jeans and push them down.

N: Yes, this is good.

D: Freeing my hard cock.

I step in toward you and I slide easily all the way into your pussy.

I stop and look in your eyes.

I begin to move slowly in and out, never looking away.

You never blink.

I'm holding your ankles pinned to me.

As I push against you.

You feel my hardness meld into your softness.

N: My hand is on my clit.

D: And your other hand on my balls.

You move your hands to hold my ass as I begin to grind on you.

N: This is so good.

D: No strokes now, grinding against you.

You lightly stroking my balls.

We are so wet we barely have friction.

N: Yes.

D: I make sure I lean right to keep my hard rod rubbing your nub.

N: Perfect.

D: I lean closer, and your legs slide over my shoulders.

I lean in and kiss you.

Now arching my back to withdraw and stroke in you.

I pull your legs down and push them wide open.

N: So hot.

D: And lean even harder on you.

My chest is against your glorious nipples now.

They are rubbing against mine.

I put one hand behind your head, on your neck.

I pull your lips to suck my hard nipple.

You flick it with your tongue.

I pull your hair as you do.

Still humping you.

Trying not to make noises with our mouths.

But can't help the slapping sound my balls make against your wet pussy lips.

N: This is beyond good.

D: You feel your juices run between your legs and down toward your ass.

It tickles and feels cold as it crosses your asshole.

You want another cock in your ass at the same time I'm fucking you.

I sense this and move my hand there.

N: OMG!

D: I use your natural lubrication on my finger and shove it deep into your hole.

I alternate in and out with my dick and my finger.

N: I want you so fucking bad. You know me.

D: You can't stand this and start pushing hard against my cock.

I put my other hand over your mouth.

N: I'd be squeaking by now.

D: It makes you a little dizzy, and you begin to cum HARD like on a drug.

Your cumming makes me squirt my hot load into you.

You can feel my balls contract as they pump my cum out.

I keep fucking at the same pace.

The only way you know I came was my spasm and I had closed my eyes.

N: Perfect.

D: Determined not to make a sound.

I fuck until I'm soft.

Then I keep moving my soft, wet dick around the outside of your cum-soaked pussy.

N: Please let me suck it.

D: Teasing your lips and keeping you on edge.

You reach down and gently pull my soft now smaller dick to your mouth.

Tasting both you and me on it.

You slowly lick and suck it.

N: This is beyond amazing.

D: You have it fully in your mouth, as I get hard again.

It feels different as my cock grows to its full size completely in your mouth.

You slowly lick and suck me and caress my balls.

N: Round 2?

D: Yes! Tomorrow?

What Lies Beneath

They dined together in their restaurant, sitting side by side at the table. Dylan liked to evaluate the wait staff and empower his kitchen staff to create without his hovering. Beneath the tablecloth, he had his hands on her thighs. She whispered in his ear, "I'm not wearing any panties, and I am as wet as fuck."

He slowly and secretly slid his hand under her long, flowing dress.

The amuse-bouche, a hard-boiled quail egg deviled with white truffle, was utterly amazing. The second appetizer was a Washington raw oyster with black caviar and citron gelatin. She was in heaven. They ordered wine pairings, and the Manzanilla sherry from Spain was a spectacular accompaniment to the oxtail consommé with braised oxtail, sesame oil, satsumas and caramelized onions. The Flying Goat Bubbles paired perfectly with the sylvetta-beet salad with butternut squash fritters, chèvre and sherry vinaigrette.

They shared a cheese plate. All were American artisan cheeses, and her favorite was from Santa Margarita, a Pozo Tomme served with sliced pear and flatbread. The Truffle Tremor goat cheese on gingerbread with honey was an eruption of flavors. The Rogue River Blue, served with Marcona almonds and guava, was a delight. But the seared Sonoma foie gras was the best she had tried. Served on brioche with quince paste, peanuts and a bourbon-barrel-aged maple syrup. Words failed her. That's how perfect this was. It was paired with Château d'Yquem Sauternes from France. Impeccable, wonderful, orgasmic.

Maman was circling around suggesting wine and keeping an eye of them, Dylan felt like everyone was watching them. He told himself to keep his hands to himself, his body seemed to not function unless touching her. When Maman suggested the wine for their meal, they both took only sips hoping that a lack of wine would keep their wits about them.

The touch of Dylan's fingers on her naked flesh burned her skin. It felt power-driven. At first she couldn't believe he was working his way down her leg, after all they had been through. He held his hand on her thigh. Her mind was blanking. She realized the waiter had asked her twice about her selection.

He quietly said yes to more water and gave her thigh a squeeze.

After the waiter left the table, he pulled a small package from his pocket. Dylan decided to give her his recent gift now, but the next dish arrived.

The palate cleanser was hibiscus soda served in a shot glass. The essence of hibiscus is boiled down to a tea, simple syrup is added and it's stirred with Pellegrino. The main courses were even more amazing. The butter-poached Maine lobster was flawlessly prepared with the soul of the crustacean shining through the butternut squash purée, chanterelle-beet demi-glace, and fennel pollen. The bone marrow fritters were a first for Nadailia, and she vowed to pay this chef more.

The package was wrapped in light blue paper with no bow. He handed it to her and whispered, "Take this to the bathroom. You'll know what to do."

She slowly walked to the bathroom, feeling as if everyone's eyes were on her and they all could see that she was so hot she was ready to fuck the chef on top of the fancy white tablecloth.

In the bathroom stall, she opened the package. It was two small egg-shaped items connected by a small wire. She deduced that one was for her pussy and the other was for her ass.

She inserted the larger one and used her wetness to lubricate the smaller one for her ass. She took slow deep breaths and forced herself not to finger herself.

She walked back to the table, hoping they would not fall out because of her liquid.

Sitting down, she was afraid to make eye contact with him. He placed his hand on top of hers and squeezed.

More food arrived. The presentation was amazing, she could not muster any desire for it. Just as she reached for her fork she felt a slight tingle. Her head snapped to him, and they locked eyes. He smiled and opened his palm, revealing his phone with an app open that was called WeVibe.

He would touch a button, and the vibration would alternate from front to back, pussy to ass. It took all her concentration not to scream. She called for Maman and ordered the most expensive bottle of wine they had on the menu.

The Kobe beef with sweat breads and a tamarind glazed zabuton short rib with pomme purée, truffle butter and shallot rings sang through their taste buds with L'Aventure Optimus as the liquid. This chef should be cloned, dipped in gold, she thought as he zapped her again.

One dessert was a flourless chocolate cake with passion fruit caramel mousse and passion fruit sorbet. The flavor was equal to the passion building inside her. The other was a lemon meringue tart with an amaretto crust and candied kumquats. Pure magic. Time passed. The food, the pleasure. The loss of control was making her crazy. Somehow she made it to the car.

As soon as she sat down, he set it to the full vibration. She threw her head back and screamed, "Oh My Fucking God!"

Text

D: Well. How did I do, Boss?

Did I fulfill my promise to make you cum with my food?

N: I'm beyond inspired.

D: Would you change anything?

N: Not one crumb.

D: Magnificent!

Getting you off is a great mental exercise and motivator for my cooking efforts.

N: I appreciate your efforts.

D: Now put your wet self to bed.

N: Sweet naughty dreams.

The Phoenix Flutters

They took a ride through the wine country to choose a heritage pig for the restaurant. Dylan had plans to use every inch of the animal to honor French peasant customs. First, he would provide a special feed for the sow, as he wanted the meat sweetened by walnuts and fattened by avocados. He was also planning to give the happy pig a bottle of wine every day.

It was a long drive to the middle of nowhere, with nothing to do but count the lines on the road.

Then Nadailia thought, "We are alone!" She moved beside him and crawled to his lap. He tousled her curls and slapped her ass. She undid his pants and brought his huge cock out. He protested about safety and driving, but she took him in her mouth anyway.

"Yes!"

Circling his head with her tongue. Licking the sweet most sensitive of spots. Then she took him farther into her mouth. Imbibing. Twirling. Trouncing.

"Keep going."

He worried about traffic, trying to keep his eyes and focus on the road. She took him deep into her throat. Bobbing up and down for maximum pleasure. She placed her hand at the bottom of his cock and squeezed as she swallowed. The friction was making him weak. She doubled her effort as a headlight appeared, coming toward the car. He exploded, and she sucked in every drop. Licking, slurping every bit while he shuddered with pleasure. "Yeeeesss. Perfect."

She rolled over and smiled at him.

"Damn, girl! How about you?"

She smiled, still worried about her climax issue and happy he did not have a problem. She never wanted him to know she was frigid.

Text

N: You sleeping or awake?

D: I'm ready to make you cum. Smarty pants.

What are you wearing?

N: Snowflake jammies.

I got cold.

D: Hahaha. That's a first!

N: I know! I can take them off.

D: No...It's ok.

N: I needed more of your heat.

D: Are you a little wet?

N: Very.

The field trip was my fave.

Been juicy all night.

D: Ready for a story?

N: Yes.

D: You were headed to a business meeting and already in the building to meet the client.

You were wearing a navy blue business skirt, white blouse and navy blue suit jacket

N: I'm blue. And hot for you.

D: You were going to stop by the bathroom on the way up.

As you passed the men's room door, it opened and I stepped out.

I looked in your blue eyes and reached for your wrist.

I pulled you into the men's room and spun you around as I locked the door.

I pressed up against you, and you could feel my hardness against your ass as I leaned in and whispered in your ear.

"Shhhhhhhh, don't say a word."

N: No squeaking.

D: You nodded your head vigorously, "Yes."

I grasped both your wrists and pulled them above your head as I kept you pinned face-first against the door.

I used my other hand to reach under the edge of your tight skirt.

I grasped the top of your panties and yanked them down to your thighs.

N: So hot.

D: I pulled your skirt up on your back and used my hand to feel your wet pussy.

N: It's always wet for you.

D: I inserted my fingers in you and began to finger-fuck you from behind.

You pushed your ass against my hand to force me deeper into you.

You heard my belt jingle and my zipper slide as I freed my stiff cock.

N: Fuck yes.

D: I used my hand that was not pinning your wrists to guide myself into you.

I slid into you, fitting like a glove.

N: Perfect fit.

D: As I pushed into you, I could feel your juices flow down the insides of your thighs.

It was a slippery mess, but hot and electric.

I began to pump into you.

Our rhythms matched perfectly as you arched your back into me.

N: Damn, you're getting good at this.

D: I then turned you around and let you slide to your knees.

You greedily took me in your mouth.

My cock was shiny with your pussy juice as it slid between your lips and down your throat. Your hands and your mouth to massage my cock and sent shock waves through me. You used your nails to gently rake my balls and made me moan.

N: So fucking good.

D: I pulled your hair into a ponytail and used it like the reins on a horse.

Guiding your mouth and using my hips to fuck your mouth.

N: I like that a lot.

D: I guided you up and over to a sink.

I had you lean on the sink with your ass and dripping pussy exposed to me.

N: Holy shit.

D: I spread your ass cheeks, spat in my hand and used that as lube to allow my rock-hard cock to penetrate your ass.

I pushed until I was all the way in.

I spit on your ass, and it ran down to my cock and further lubed it.

I began to fuck your ass, slowly at first.

N: Perfect.

D: I was so wet that it glided in and out with little friction.

Just the tightness of your sphincter gripping my dick.

The fullness of my cock filling you made your eyes water.

I reached around and pinched your nipple.

N: I'm dying here.

D: Making it harden and lengthen.

My strokes became faster.

And harder as I bounced off your ass.

You had to push back hard against my thrusts to keep from hitting your head on the mirror.

N: I'd match you with each stroke.

D: I was sure the slap of our naked wet skin slamming together could be heard in the hall.

My balls were bouncing off your wet pussy with each thrust.

N: I'm rubbing my clit.

D: I gripped your shoulders and, with a final thrust, pumped my hot load into your ass.

As you felt me explode into you, you came and your knees almost buckled.

I continued stroking in and out until my cum began to leak out.

N: So fucking amazing.

D: After a few minutes, I began to soften and pulled out.

I pushed your panties the rest of the way down and off.

And used them to dish up my cum leaking out of your ass.

N: Nice.

D: I turned you to face me and kissed you hard on the lips.

I then wadded up your panties and put them in your briefcase for a reminder during your business meeting.

N: Nice!

D: Wish I were there.

Are your jammies soaked now?

N: Yes!

D: My mission is complete.

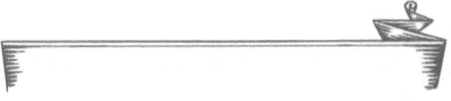

The Best of The Best

Dylan showed up as uninvited to Nadailia's house. She answered the door, still in her work suit; hair pulled back, glasses on her head and talking on her cell phone. She waved him in and went to her office, assuming he would follow. He did, and sat like a kid in the principal's office as she finished her call.

"Well, this is a nice surprise. What brings the chef to my neighborhood?'

"I thought I would offer to make you an intimate dinner."

"Sure, a girl's got to eat. Today was five days worth of work in one in terms of workload. I focused and got three-quarters of it done. I have six hours of work to do, but I have to eat. So you cook, I'll type."

"How is it going with Jeffery?"

"I believe I have sealed his dismissal. But I am starting to think I will move him to another restaurant instead of completely letting him go."

"Keep your enemies closer tactic?"

"You are as smart as you are sexy."

They moved to the kitchen and he began pulling out random ingredients. He was a master of taking chaos and turning it into deliciousness. She watched him with a far away look, not typing, staring.

"What are you thinking about?"

"I'm thinking of your touch. Electric, vibrant, strong and sure. The touch of a real man. A man who knows how to bring pleasure through softness and pain."

"Oh, I like this. Tell me more." He turned toward her as he stirred the risotto.

"The way you go to work on my breasts is perfection. At first soft and exploring, and then with a hard desire, a lustful exuberance that is still making me shutter."

"I love kissing you."

"I close my eyes and taste your mouth, feel your lips and your tongue taking over my mouth. The feel of your hand on my ass and releasing my nipples from my bra."

She noticed that his chef pants were getting tight, and she enjoyed toying with him.

"It was such a gift of time together. The passion we shared and felt has renewed my vibrant energy. I feel sated and yet want you more than ever.

I can't wait to see where this goes, what we try next, how it makes me feel." He was floored by this honest and unsolicited praise.

"I feel a bit less dependent on the physical because I have another way to express my craving for you. I always felt my passion was not translated correctly with my kisses."

"No, your kisses are perfect." He crossed the kitchen to get a kiss, and she moved to the pantry. Like a cat, she was toying with him. "Close your eyes and feel my longing for you. See me hopping on your lap and taking your mouth with mine. See yourself taking my hand, drawing me into my office, removing my shirt, pulling down the straps of my bra and taking my breasts into your hot, molten mouth."

He moved to the other side of the kitchen island, in pursuit, but she held him off and kept reciting the hottest things he had ever heard.

"I recall feeling my hand on your crotch, exploring the length and girth of your tremendous cock under your pants."

He lunged for her and she twirled away. He finally realized that he was being played with and stood still, not cooperating with her game. Yet he was, his body's reaction to her words was more than obvious.

"All these memories and more are seared in my brain, firing neurons of joy and pleasure all day through mundane meetings and marketing tasks. Next time we are together, here is what I am going to do to you."

"Wait! We are together now. Just show me!"

The pleading in his eyes amused her, and she knew she should take him, but she was having as much fun telling the tale as he was hearing it. If she learned anything with Dylan, it was that passion comes in many forms and it is not always good to convert it into the physical.

Nadailia backed up to the wall letting him approach as she talked. He stalked her slowly, moving in rhythm with her words.

"I am going to drive our pleasure. I am going to take you up against a wall. Kiss you deeply and explore your mouth. Then I am going to drop to my knees and rub my face in your crotch. I'm going to release your cock from your pants and take it in mouth. I'm going to explore every inch of it with my tongue. Then take the tip into my lips, imbibe and lick. Then I will slowly take you in my mouth, a bit at a time. Extracting, trouncing and engulfing. Then I will swallow you whole and pulse in and out.

You don't get to cum like this. I will stop before you do.

I must keep you wanting me."

He made it to her on the last line and grabbed her like a starving man. They made love right there in her kitchen. Slow and deliberate with each move, exploring each other as if they were blind.

Afterward, he made catfish, grilled and served over sautéed vegetables, all basking in a sweet-hot Thai sauce. One of the side dishes was sushi balls, which consisted of rice, rolled in sesame seeds and flash-fried in the catfish pan – great finger food that matched their sultry mood perfectly.

Dylan also made a Mediterranean salad medley. It was a savory combination of delights, including baba ghanouj, Italian white bean and tuna salad, cucumber tzatziki, Adriatic beer and potato salad, beets with a crème sauce and hummus, all served with grilled flatbread. Nadailia was amazed at the meal he had pulled together with what was in her fridge and pantry.

The main dish was Caribbean pork roast with yam risotto and peach chutney. Nadailia loved it and commented that it was as if she were back on the island of Grenada and listening to a steel drum band. He also threw together a Cabernet-braised lamb shank, a recipe from Buenos Aires, that included simmered parsnips, onions, dried apricots, garlic, serrano chiles, tomatoes, cumin and other wonderful Latin spices. It was served over potato-zucchini latkes. The food matched their lustful evening. She knew they had turned a corner.

Text

N: I was longing for a dark theater.

I was imagining you had a big carton of popcorn on your lap

D: I like where you are going.

N: You put a hole in the bottom, and your dick was up inside it and I could stroke you while feeling for my popcorn.

D: Hahaha. The salt may be tricky.

I was thinking about you having a coat in your lap.

And your dress pulled up and my finger in your pussy.

N: Fuck. I soaked my chair.

D: That's what I would use for popcorn seasoning.

N: Damn you.

D: Turnabout is fair play?
N: Yes.
I need relief. Fucker.
D: And I would lick the "butter" off my fingers.

Fast Stepping Steed

Needing more ideas on what to plant for the second harvest, they went to an event that paired six of the area's best chefs with a mixologist. Served in a chef's garden, this family-style meal had each course paired with a specialty garden cocktail. The mixologist deserved an Academy Award for these original creations. Each drink was so unusual and although at first surprising to the taste, harmonized flawlessly. The greeting beverage was a spicy Sriracha-infused vodka concoction with herbs and a salted rim. Hot, but not overly so, this burned the taste buds clean to better receive the first course. The impeccable wait staff swirled around, serving each dish, which was garnished with edible flowers for both beauty and flavor.

Dylan was impressed that each chef brought passion to every creation. The chefs had obviously stalked the garden for each impeccable element, picked it and prepared it as if cooking for sultans and kings.

The table was prepped with a basket of bread, including smoked tomato focaccia and rolls. The second drink was Mojito-esque with muddled basil, honeydew juice and limes. It was served with the tom yum soup that started with a bowl of tiny-cut cherry tomatoes, sliced cucumber, flowering coriander, pork belly, shishito peppers, Thai basil and a lemon verbena. This savory roasted-vegetable base that brought all the flavors to life.

The next plate was as charming as it was delicious. Mixed melon and tomato salad with emulsified cantaloupe and dry-farmed watermelon, eight kinds of tomatoes, a sprinkle of sea salt, olive oil, Tellicherry pepper and cinnamon basil buds. Refreshing and different enough to make your taste buds sit up and pay attention, it came with a Midori sour cocktail that featured pickled watermelon rind and a sugared rim.

The following offering came from an unlikely source, Nadailia loved this delicacy called skate wing. Skate is a ray-like sea creature that usually gets thrown back by fisherman, this chef knew that the wing part was delicate and had the consistency and flavor of crab, only better. Because of its short shelf life, it is rarely served. This chef used the fresh-from-the-sea skate wing, dipped it in brown butter and breaded. Then he pan-fried it and served it with a Meyer lemon sauce, parsley blooms, sweet cherry tomatoes and flowering thyme. To say this was outstanding was an understatement. It was soft and rich, with a buttery texture. Served with a martini glass containing egg white foam, cucumber juice and thyme sprigs, it blew their minds.

The next drink was a surprise to the nose, but appealing once the second sip went down. It was mescal with kale and celery juice. It was by far the strangest drink Nadailia had tried, but it balanced impeccably with the roasted suckling pig. The chef also prepared a whole pork confit and pork belly to go with the main course. In the hands of this extraordinary chef, this delicacy was in a class by itself. Tender, succulent and resting on a bed of chopped hand massaged kale, it was served with pickled radish and infused melon cubes. When their dishes were empty, they were presented with a palate-cleansing drink. This included a basil sorbet surrounded by sparkling water and cucumber extract. They sipped and then gave into the icy sorbet, which opened the palate and made way for dessert.

The dessert was an upside-down green tomato tart with a caramel pecan piecrust and sea salt caramel ice cream. Dylan was shocked, this absolutely worked. It was enchanting. This extraordinary concoction defied all the rules.

As the last course came, a huge blue moon rose over the garden and the crowd applauded the show as if it were happening for their magical dinner. Last not least, a brown-sugared bourbon with candied cherry tomatoes and Vietnamese cinnamon, it accompanied basil beignets stuffed with tomato curd with a basil-sugar base. Pop one in your mouth and it was paradise; pop another and you experienced bliss. The garden party was a hit, and Dylan had a renewed passion for his garden and future menu.

Nadailia dropped Dylan off at home, explaining that they still had to lie low until Jeffrey was gone. He protested, but was excited to funnel his passions into his new garden. She knew that in 10 minutes he would text her. They had become quite addicted to this method of passion play.

Text

D: Watcha doing?

N: Working. You?

D: Creating. Thinking of you.

N: You know what I want? Us lying on the lawn, wrapped in a wool blanket that is scratchy but warm. We are listening to the crickets and watching a meteor shower.

We are naked and surveying each other.

D: Oh fuck. You need to stop sending me mixed messages.

N: I am ignoring what I want. That is what we do. And texting.

D: It is torture.

N: You love it.

Finding the zones that thrill, startle and throb.

We are taking our time, getting to know what makes our breath quicken, our hearts soar.

I decide to take a tour of your neck.

D: Love it.

N: I am kissing, sucking and biting it.

Your head is thrown back, your eyes are wide open.

You moan, squirm and relax into it.

I move my hot breath down to your chest.

D: Mmmmm. Hard and wet.

N: I find your nipples and tease them with my tongue.

When they are wet, I blow on them.

The cold air makes them harder.

D: Fuck, this is pure evil.

If you are going to write to me like this, you need to let me touch you.

N: No.

I move down your stomach with my tongue.

Kissing and caressing.

It is hot under the blanket, so I throw it back.

Now you have the sensation of the breeze and the hotness of my mouth.

Your body is reacting out of your control.

D: Delicious.

N: I move down to your crotch and kiss your pubic bone.

I kiss your inner thighs.

I kiss your balls.

I take the tip of your hard cock and place it on my lips.

D: God. I am coming over.

N: NO. I gently kiss the top, down the shaft and back up again.

You are now pulling my hair.

Begging for me to take your dick in my mouth.

I tell you to watch the stars and let me do the driving.

You relax back, and as you do, I take your whole cock in my mouth.

D: Ahhhhhh.

N: I suck and licked while the whole thing is in there.

A wild moan escapes from me, and you can feel the vibration on your dick.

I open my mouth and throat and swallow you whole.

You can feel the back of my throat on the head of your cock.

D: Mmmmmm.

N: I move my head up and down on your lap.

Slowly with precision.

Swallowing you with every stroke.

Your eyes are open, staring at the meteor shower.

I place my fingers on the base of your cock and lock them on.

I alternate the pressure of my fingers with the stroking of my mouth.

D: My God. You're torturing me.

N: I have not been able to breathe because you are so deep in my throat.

I come up and take a breath.

I take your cock in my hand and begin to stroke.

D: Hot.

N: With the other hand, I am slapping it.

When you are ready to cum.

I take you in my mouth again.

D: Oh fuck.

N: I release you as you cum, loving the feeling of your cum on my mouth and tits.

D: Oh God.

That is fucking amazing!

So hot!

I am coming over.

N: No Dylan, good night.

Recumbent Covered Pine

Nadailia agreed to meet him at a public park. She figured it would be safe to discuss the topic of Jeffrey and note instantly jump into bed together. He was bringing some of the items from his new Sunday brunch menu.

The blanket was laid out by the river at the huge park. The picnic was made up of erotic finger foods, all arranged on a board. The huge amount of food included one of the best baguettes she had ever tasted. Warm, soft and supple. On the board was a mother lode of accouterments: thin cracker bread, almonds, honey, house-made pickles, fresh raspberries, Granny Smith apple slices, apricot jam, white raisins, purple pickled onions and a huge clove of roasted garlic. Each of the trimmings delighted and complemented the meat or cheese it was paired with. Honestly, this was a party in her mouth.

The cheeses included: Purple Haze goat cheese from Cypress Grove Chevre, infused with lavender and wild fennel pollen. This unusual marriage made it completely addictive, and was highlighted with the apricot jam and almonds.

Seascape, a cheddar-style cheese from Central Coast Creamery. The delicate blend of cow and goat milk creates a semi-soft cheese with a sleek, creamy texture and noticeable tanginess.

San Joaquin Gold from Fiscalini Farmstead in Modesto, California. It has been described as a cross between cheddar and Parmigiano-Reggiano. It has a sweet, salty, buttery taste that becomes nuttier as it ages. The cheese was flavorful, still mellow.

Point Reyes Farmstead Toma finished off with the subtlety of an opera singer. This cheese is made in round-edged, Gouda-style molds. A technique known as curd washing brings out a flavor that is sweet and buttery with a cultured-milk tang. They found they were slicing another piece of this cheese long after they were no longer hungry. With a dab of honey and an apple slice, this was pure ecstasy.

The spectacular meats were next. The candied bacon lying across the country pork sausage was perfection in every way. When she started to eat the sausage, Dylan brought out pretzel bread and some house-made hot mustard. It kept getting better. Nadailia's favorite was the wild boar sausage. She twisted the board around so it was closer to her. The prosciutto and pepperoni both dazzled with flavor. The bresaola, an air-dried, salted beef that is aged for three months until it becomes hard and turns a dark red, almost purple.

They had been fighting often lately at work, the smallest details sent them into a raging match. Neither wanted to win or start the fight, so conversation was at a minimum. Nadailia was wearing a twirling skirt, and Dylan considered that she was more than likely naked underneath it. She liked access and liked allowing her lady parts to breathe. This made him instantly hard.

He was lost in thought about her commando habits when she fed him. Snapped back to the present, he looked into her bright blue eyes and concentrated on the lushness of the food.

After the meal, Dylan was lying back on the blanket, looking up at the clouds. A shadow passed over him, and he realized Nadailia had maneuvered her skirt over his face. She hovered over him, slick pussy pulsing with desire. He grabbed her ass to let her know the invasion was welcome. She positioned her pussy on his lips. Her strong legs held her aloft, and he heard a squeal from a child on a nearby swing. He licked the outer ring of her, stroked her asshole with his thumb. She maneuvered her clit into his mouth, never one to wait for her pleasure. This is one trick he knew, and one he could control. He gave her enough, not as much as she wanted. At one point the balance of power switched, and she gave herself to him. He held her hips as she undulated under his masterful tongue. She kept whispering, "This is so fucking hot. All the mommies are watching."

He pulled her clit in like a small cock and sucked it hard. His finger slid into her hot, wet cave, and he found her pleasure center. She was writhing in pleasure, and he could hear slightly hedonistic librettos escaping from her mouth. Both were surprised by the action of their bodies, but not by their lust for each other, which had only scratched the surface.

Text

D: You know what's weird is that I'm not running out of steamy situations to experience with you. Scary, huh?

N: This could go on forever. You are such a perfect muse.

D: I'm not sure what the world record is for continuous erections, I'm pretty sure I'm getting close. This is fun.

N: I have never had so much sex in one week. I should be exhausted, I want more.

D: Who knew you could have a hard-on for almost a week? I'm never more than about two of your words away from the next one.

N: I love that. You juiced me up again.

D: Ok. I'm headed back into the kitchen. User-friendly texts only for now.

N: Yes Sir!!

The Greeks Have It

M ore R&D took them to a Greek and Slovenian wine-tasting harmonizing with the chef's small plates, also known as meze. They had asked Maman to come along, as Nadailia was still trying to repair or build some kind of relationship with this small woman who ruled Dylan's life, she said she had "other business." They started with a Kupljen Winery Sivi Pinot from Slovenia that was paired with a plate of hot olives with a rosemary olive oil dusting. The flavorful olives with the crisp fruit notes told them they were off to an excellent pairing. Next they tried the spanakopita, a fluffy phyllo dough stuffed with market spinach, green onion, garlic, dill and delectable feta cheese. It was matched with a Domaine Porto Carras Malagouzia. This indigenous Greek white wine from the Sithonia region is so ancient that it was thought to be extinct until some vines were found in a monastery in 1975. The wine was not Old World; it was Ancient World, and Dylan approved.

The next offering was a board of cheese and charcuterie that was able to stand up to a wine that was mentioned in the writings of Homer and Aristotle. The Domaine Porto Carras Limnio, a delicious red, is a 6,000-year-old indigenous Greek varietal. The board had luscious meats, such as jamon serrano, chorizo autentico and duck salami. The cheeses were equally flavorful, including idiazabal, a semi-hard sheep cheese; and Caprichio de Cabra, a soft goat cheese. Marcona almonds, quince paste and olives with a sliced baguette accompanied all this. Nadailia observed that she could eat like this every night. Dylan commented that most French people do eat like this every night.

They moved on to the Medjool dates that were stuffed with fromage blanc, a Spanish goat cheese, then wrapped in Speck (smoked cured ham). This was one of Dylan's favorite items, and it was perfection with the Erzetic Winery Cabernet Amphora. This award-winning Cabernet is aged in an amphora, a traditional clay jar that's buried in the forest. For dessert it was bourbon bread pudding with stone fruits. They left happy and filled with an ancient lust.

They stopped by their restaurant to check on the night and locked up. When they walked in the front door, Nadailia heard a strange "bleating" coming from the bar. Making their way through the closed bar they were astounded to see a live goat standing on the bar. Maman seemed to be running a photo shoot of the goat, as there were photographers and photo equipment laid out. On the bar 20 shot glasses had been placed under the goat, and Maman was milking the goat into the shot glasses. Nadailia could not wrap her head around why there was a live farm animal in her bar, on her bar and being milked into her shot glasses.

"What the fuck?" was all that escaped from her mouth.

Dylan and Maman yelled at each other in French, and the photographers were smart enough to take their things and scatter.

All Nadailia could think about was the colossal clean up this would require, and she feared that the Health Department would get word of this prank, or whatever it is.

Dylan and Maman were still having words when Maman pulled the goat by its lead off the bar and approached Nadailia.

"You said to do whatever it takes to replace the wine. This was one of those things. I am sorry if I screwed up. I take my leave now."

Maman dramatically left the bar with the goat in tow, and Nadailia turned to Dylan for an explanation.

"She said it was a TV commercial for a wine maker who also sells goat milk. She sold him on the concept and told them you wouldn't mind the goat in the bar."

"Do you realize the kind of trouble we could get into if the Health Department ever found out that a barn animal was on my bar?"

"Yes I do, and I told her that. She said you said to do whatever it took, and this little photo session earned her two cases of vintage reserve."

"Dylan, this is a business. A serious business. I can't have your Maman running amok, drinking wine, and fucking my staff. For fuck's sake."

"Nadailia, this is your fault too. I did not want her to work here. I told you she was impossible. This is not all my doing."

"Dylan, I don't give a fuck whose fault it is. Fix this fucking mess. Strip this bar and clean every crevice. I'm going home."

She stormed out, and Dylan was pissed at both of the woman in his life.

The next day, Dylan put his Maman on a plane with a one-way ticket back to Marseille. She was bubbling over with anger and promised to rain hell down upon him. He looked as if she already had.

Nadailia accepted his apology after he cleaned up the bar and sent Maman back to France. She knew it was not the end of her troubles with Maman, at least she had a respite from her every disappointing comments and crazy behavior. That night, she had several members of the board of directors as guests at the restaurant. She was buttering them up for her next move.

They started with a plate of stuffed Peppadews, small sweet-hot red peppers stuffed with Alcea Rosea Farm goat cheese (the irony was not lost on anyone), and Provençal olives on a bed of micro greens and mint oil. They were off to a good start with everyone's sweet, hot and savory taste buds tantalized. Nadailia had to try the chicken wing confit, as this simple food done with a flare can bring bliss. The chicken wings were boiled in olive oil, then seared with a Sriracha glaze and sprinkled with sesame seeds. To say these where the best wings she had tried would be an understatement.

The salads were equally impressive and tasted as fresh as Dylan's garden. The roasted stone fruit salad was a hit with Fairview Farms white peaches, nectarines and pickled summer berries all resting atop succulent butter lettuce with smidgeons of sesame brittle. The Farmgirl Creamery honey and sea salt fromage blanc brought the savory, and the apricot vinaigrette brought the tangy. The braised duck salad was as complicated as it was impressive. It was filled with luscious duck breast, squash noodles, shiso leaves, pickled plums, peanuts, snap peas and their tendrils, mint, basil, cilantro, green onion, ginger relish, fried ginger and chile vinaigrette.

For her main course, Nadailia had the ahi tuna tataki style. Large pieces of seared ahi served with avocado, sesame, cucumbers, sunflower sprouts, wakame, green onion, pickled apricots and drizzles of ponzu sauce, all sitting upon a ginger relish. It was tasty and did two loops around the table letting everyone taste this dish. The board members each ordered the grilled filet mignon, a perfectly cut and cooked piece of meat served with Spanish chorizo and potato hash, asparagus, heirloom cherry tomatoes, Italian frying peppers and a red-pepper coulis. It was topped with a fried egg, which makes everything taste better, they all agreed.

Dylan made an olive oil cake that blew everyone's mind. It was spectacular in its simplicity, with a dash of orange zest in the frosting. Each large slice of cake was absolutely moist and tender, and its cream-cheese frosting was topped with fresh strawberry slices.

They finished with chocolate mousse and then decided it was time to head home, having been thoroughly impressed by the eclectic and eccentric organic treats. They were awestruck and confirmed

Nadailia's insistence on the significance of organic, regionally grown food. It was nice to have them affirm that this chef was bringing pure magic to the table.

After work, she drove to his house and let herself in. He stood at the top of the stairs, amazed at the beauty that had walked into his house. Amazed that she was his, even if only for this one night.

Nadailia looked up and smiled. "I see you seeing me. Standing at the top of the stairs surveying and striking the flint between us."

She made her way up, as time stood still for a split-second, moment during which caught the faint tune of an elusive song only they could hear, a symphony of passion. There were feelings they each wished they could say, touches to discover.

Then they kissed, floored by the desire, the unrelenting yearning that makes two people throw their bodies at each other, trying to absorb each touch. There was a trust now and a distinct knowledge that this was more than a physical affair. It could not be fucked away.

Nadailia loved how he took her, despite her weak protests. The power of his hands, guiding her, she trembled. This was a new sensation. No one had ever made her tremble. All she wanted was to taste him. All she wanted was to fuck him for hours.

She felt his strong hand on her clit, his mouth on her hard nipple, a feeling that resonated. Unbuckling his pants. Feeling a hard, silky-smooth cock. Tasting him again.

They rolled and tasted and touched for hours.

The Boy

D ylan was cooking lunch at the restaurant for Nadailia and Lauren. Nadailia had the Rosemary Chicken Beet Salad, since she recently had discovered that she loved roasted beets. The chicken was marinated with rosemary and white balsamic vinegar. Thin slices of breast meat were layered on a bed of arugula greens. White and red roasted beets were tiered on the side, accompanied by toasted hazelnuts and a balsamic sauce. It was topped with fried goat cheese that was lightly breaded and added to the heft of this perfect salad. Lauren had the Chipotle Pulled Pork Sandwich. The braised pulled pork, which had been marinated in a spicy chipotle sauce, was served on a ciabatta roll with pickled red onions, coleslaw and Dylan's unsurpassed sweet potato fries. A smattering of house-made barbecue sauce made this sandwich devour ready.

"Damn, this boy toy of yours can cook," Lauren said, licking her fingers.

"Yes he can, and I am starting to think he is more than a toy."

Dylan came and sat with them after the last dish was placed. They were eating fish and chips made with beer-battered Alaskan cod, crispy hand-cut fries, coleslaw and a house-made tartar sauce. A Roasted Chicken Apple Walnut Salad accompanied. The salad was crisp and light with fresh greens, candied walnuts, Granny Smith apples, roasted chicken, shaved Manchego cheese and dried-cranberry vinaigrette.

"What do you think ladies?" His smile showed his insecurity over satisfying these developed palates.

"It is all wonderful, Dylan," Lauren declared.

"The pork was a bit too spicy," Nadailia said honestly after sampling a bite, not realizing this would hurt his feelings. "Back off a bit on the chipotle, and it will be fine."

Dylan was taken aback. She had never criticized him, and now, to make it worse, it was in front of her best friend.

"Well, that is your opinion," he said.

"And the only one that matters, since I sign your paychecks."

The public slap down was more than his ego could take, so he turned and stomped back into the kitchen. He had the waitress bring out the dessert.

They finished by sharing the most original dessert they had ever had the pleasure of eating. It was called Pink Peppercorn Pavlova. This meringue-like substance was littered with pepper and served like an igloo. Resting inside were port soaked cranberries and vanilla crème with candied walnuts dusting the roof. Each bite was a combination of sweet, hot, sour and creamy. It was absolutely divine.

"Holy shit, this is amazing," Lauren said, inhaling the dessert while Nadailia picked at it.

"I think I might have hurt his feelings," Nadailia said.

"You are a bitch."

"He is so easily overexcited. I like that in bed, not so much in my dining room."

"Then maybe you should stop fucking him and treat him like all your other employees."

Nadailia wished the constant desire for him would subside, but it never did.

After lunch Lauren left and Nadailia joined Dylan in the kitchen. He was slamming pots around and the sous chefs scattered when they saw her. She crossed to him and lightly stroked his arm.

"What is wrong with you?" she whispered in his ear.

"Are you fucking kidding me? You criticize me in front of your friend. You tell me my food sucks."

"Calm down. I made a comment about the spice. It wasn't criticism. And you are acting like a boy."

Infuriated, he threw a spatula. "Get the fuck out of my kitchen."

"This is my fucking kitchen!"

"Fine. Fuck you." He pulled off his apron, threw it on the floor, grabbed his knives and stormed out the door.

As she stared at the swinging door, her first thought was, "Who is going to cook tonight?"

Luckily the Sous Chef was well trained and kept the restaurant on track while Dylan pouted at home. Even though he was glad Maman was back in France, he missed her and knew that the key to a successful relationship with Nadailia included his Maman's approval and acceptance. Previously, Nadailia had offered to fly them to France to convince her that their love was real and meant to be.

The Monkey With Six Legs

Nadailia was glad Dylan agreed to go to Marseille to see his Maman she felt it was an appropriate apology for being such a bitch. She wanted to make him comfortable using her private jet. All attempts so far to spend money on him had been disastrous. This was something he needed, something she could provide, and she wanted to help. She had an in-flight plan to relax him, so maybe he would not be too awkward with the gesture. She told him to wear something sexy and accessible, as she was doing the same.

To get ready for this trip and gift to him, Nadailia drew a hot bath and added scented bath salts. As she stripped off her clothes, she took a look at her tanned body. No tan lines and as brown as a roofing contractor. Of course, she could only see the flaws in her body, completely missing the raw sexiness she exuded.

She tested the water with her toe, then eased her whole body down into the steamy water, letting the heat radiate upward from her tingling ass all the way to her nipples, which were at the water line. The heat sent a tremble to her brain that ricocheted straight between her legs. She immediately thought of him.

She poured body wash into her palm. She had not used a washcloth in years. This was part of the Practice. Learning to touch, to awaken the senses. She liked the sensuous velvet feel that her hand imparted to her skin as she rubbed each part of her body.

As she cleaned, she thought of him. His touch, the smell of his skin, his tongue in her mouth and on her clit echoed. A powerful desire began to build. She moved her hand between her legs and cupped her pussy. She let her middle finger begin a sideways motion on her clit. Slowly increasing speed.

As she was nearing relief, she made a deliberate decision to stop. Knowing from experience that anticipation and delay of gratification would make for an explosive ending to what she had planned for them later that tonight. "Sexy" and "accessible" were two hot and predictive words of delight.

Nadailia was waiting on the street, her town car and driver ready to whisk them away. Dylan parked down the street, so she walked to greet him. Walking down the sidewalk, he noticed her and was captivated. She had on an amazing dark blue wrap dress, revealing her deep cleavage and was cut above her knees. Her high heels had a touch of bling on the straps to draw attention to her sexy calves. A single string of pearls flowed down her neck and into the cleft of her dress. She hoped him seeing that necklace would encourage his personal pearl necklace later that evening. As he opened the car door for her, his scent was already intoxicating her. Nadailia braless nipples hardened and pushed against the flimsy material of her dress. She had second thoughts about her decision not to wear panties as she felt a warm flow start to moisten her labia. Dylan was equally hot and found it hard to deal with his already-stimulated lap.

He leaned over to her and brushed his lips against hers. He pulled back and with an appraising eye looked her over. "Amazing! You look absolutely stunning! I'm ready for a fun flight."

Nadailia answered with a whisper, "I have surprise, I guarantee you'll like it."

She would have been content to lean over and pull his cock from his pants and take him in her mouth, then fuck in the back of the car like teenagers. Every time she thought of him, it was like a flashing neon sign blinking, "Sex." She did not understand it and could not help herself. She wanted to share with him her surprise, she stroked the back of his hand.

He felt the car stop, and she barked orders at unseen men. This bossy side of her drove him wild with hedonism. They were standing on an airport ramp before a large private jet, with two gorgeous, young pilots flanking the folding stairs. Their chiseled physiques nicely filled out their navy blue uniforms.

Dylan was flabbergasted and looked to her in surprise. Nadailia explained, "This is a Gulfstream G550. It belongs to me. I use this airplane to get you those fresh, rare ingredients you are always ordering. We will fly almost 6,000 miles, so I have plans for the trip."

If the exterior of the large business jet was impressive, the interior was absolutely extravagant. It looked like it could seat 30 people if it had airline seats. It had four huge cream-colored leather seats with gold seatbelt hardware. They were facing each other across a huge glossy walnut table set with fine china, silver, crystal glasses and white linen napkins.

Along the sidewall of the jet was a long leather couch. Standing beside the couch was a uniformed flight attendant. She was as beautiful as a super model with exotic features and a knockout body. She motioned toward the rear of the plane, and he followed this gesture. He opened a beautiful walnut door, and she took a step inside. Luxurious would not begin to describe the room. The main feature of the room was a round king-size bed surrounded by mirrors. The room was glowing softly with indirect lighting. Beautiful fresh-cut flower arrangements surrounded the room. In a gold ice bucket beside the bed was a magnum of their favorite Cristal Champagne. To the side of the bed he saw an erotic sex couch complete with red silk ties. On the opposite wall was a huge flat-screen monitor. Laid out on a folded crisp white towel was an impressive arrangement of sex toys. Watching him take it all in, she became weak in the knees and was sure the flush in her face revealed the sexual explosion that flooded her brain.

Nadailia heard the stairs being retracted, and the pilot's voice came over the intercom welcoming them and asking them to take a seat for takeoff. She took his hand and led him to one of the forward-facing seats, and she settled in beside him. They both buckled in, and the plane began to taxi. He reached over and placed his hand on her bare arm. She was already so sexed that his touch sent a tremor through her.

He felt the throbbing of the engines through the firm leather and into his core. He closed his eyes she said, "Look out the window." The sun was setting and the sky was beginning to turn pink on the horizon.

An attendant approached with a tray holding two covered plates. He set the plates before them and removed the silver covers. The sushi chef from their favorite Raku had outdone himself with the dishes before them. Succulent, beautiful and passionate were the six different dishes. The first was pink and red and called a Love Love. They fed each other each morsel, licking any lingering bits of sauce off each other's fingers. This sashimi roll consisted of spicy diced tuna and avocado slices wrapped with tuna sashimi, spicy small scallop pieces and drizzled with a chili sesame sauce. It was hot, sweet and delectable. Next they tried the Pink Lady with real crab claw meat and avocado wrapped in big salmon sashimi and a tasty creamy lemon sauce. Their favorite was the Cucumber Special, which had cubed pieces of salmon, tuna, albacore and gobo wrapped in a cucumber skin and drizzled with a garlic ponzu sauce.

"One of the things I like best about these rolls is that you don't fill up on rice; there is room for more raw fish." He moaned at the pleasure of the meal.

As she ate, he placed his hand in her lap. He parted her wrap dress easily and slid his hand up her thigh. Nadailia thought he must have been a woman in a former life because he touched her exactly like she touched herself. Not clumsily or greedily but gently and with purpose. She flooded his hand with moisture and began losing focus on her meal. She placed her left hand on his lap and was rewarded with the feeling of his hard erect cock. She squeezed it and moved her hand lightly up and down the length of him through his trousers. She was certain he was not wearing underwear. They finished their meal and the bottle of Champagne and then moved to the bedroom.

The oblique lighting warmly lit the stateroom. He untied her wrap dress and let it slide from her shoulders. She stood naked before him, wearing only her pearl necklace. She unbuttoned his shirt and pushed it over his shoulders to the floor. She reached for his belt, undid the buckle, slid his zipper down and freed his throbbing cock. She knelt before him and insatiably took him in her mouth.

He withdrew his dick from her mouth before he came and pulled her to her feet. He kissed her hard on the mouth, tasting his sex on her lips. He maneuvered her to the bed and had her lie on her back. He gently stroked the insides of her thighs with the back of his fingertips. He was still hard, his cock now dripping clear pearls of his passions.

She leaned over to the phone on the nightstand and pushed a button. Within a minute the door to the suite opened and the female flight attendant entered wearing a red silk bra and G-string. Dylan was scorching at this point; he didn't think he could take this kind of stimulus. The living doll sat down on the bed and began to kiss them both, but mostly focusing on Nadailia.

He sat back against the headboard and watched the ladies appetite build. Nadailia had a skilled hand as a pleasure giver, this he had experienced, watching it was almost as erotic. The women kissed each other, deeply caressing each other while they did. Nadailia moved her hand down and lifted the attendant's breast out of the bra cup so she could have her nipple in between her thumb and forefinger. The sound that escaped out of her mouth as she snapped her head back was like an animal. Nadailia moved her mouth to take the nipple with her tongue and teeth. When the attendant was about to cum, Nadailia pushed her back onto the bed and slipped her G-string off. She spread her legs and started kissing and lightly nipping the inside of her thighs. Nadailia looked over to make sure Dylan was watching. He was rapt with attention and flushed with desire. She smiled with an evil grin. She made sure he could see every detail.

She began to lick the attendant's pussy. Her tongue passing slow circles around her labia, gently grazing the clit as she passed by it. She conquered and sucked every inch of her while one hand still rubbed her nipple. Nadailia moved on to her clit and sucked it like a small cock. Alternating nipping, sucking, thrashing and finally consuming. Nadailia moved her finger inside her and found her G spot, ridged and ready to be stimulated. She removed her index finger and brought it to her mouth, tasting the juices from deep inside. Again, the attendant was about to explode when Nadailia moved her thumb into her ass. She pulsed back and forth, all the while consuming her clit. The attendant couldn't take it anymore and began to scream with her orgasmic delight. Female ejaculate squirted out in a spray, as Nadailia continued to work her until the five-minute orgasm ceased. Dylan was delighted and a bit surprised. Without realizing it, he had taken his dick in his hand and was stroking it as he watched.

Nadailia crossed the room to him, took him by the hand and whispered, "She is ready for you now."

Gamecock and Fowl Approach

Dylan walked into the house they had rented by the ocean in Marseille, ready to cook Nadailia an amazing meal. Two heavy bags of groceries weighed down his arms. She stood by the couch wearing a black silk robe. Nadailia was a timeless beauty, barefoot and her hair loose, bouncing with curls. The informality of her look struck him right in the groin. She smiled, and he got hard. It was amazing the effect this woman had on his body.

She took the groceries from him and told him to sit on the couch. A glass of red wine was already poured. The couch was draped with a satin sheet. He ran his fingers over it, loving the tactile feeling of the softness. Nadailia walked into the room, took a drink of his wine and straddled his lap, facing him. Before she kissed him, her robe opened and he saw the black corset beneath. Her kiss was different. Slow, practiced and sensual.

While kissing him she removed his clothes. She kissed his neck. After he was completely naked, she untied her wide sash and removed her robe. She wore only the black corset with her breasts resting on top of the boning. Like a demi bra but better. She wore no panties.

She took her sash and made a blindfold for him. He started to protest, she whispered, "Trust me." He knew he did, so he let his inhibitions drop and knew to his bones he was going to enjoy what she had planned.

She pulled his legs down and laid him out on the silk blanket. Marveling at the beauty of his body, she turned to her tray of tantalization. First she selected a goat-hair whip. The long hair stung and tickled. At first he was startled by the whip, and then he began to welcome it. She started at his chest, then his neck, torso, hands, thighs and then his cock. Slowly she flicked it, so it was not painful, intense. Like getting in a warm shower when you have been out in the freezing rain. The purpose was to bring his nerve endings to the surface of his skin. She worked him up and down, and he moaned with pleasure. After she hit every spot on his body, she took his magnificent cock in her mouth. She sucked him for a bit, bringing more blood and nerve endings to the surface. When she pulled back, she blew on the shaft, creating a cold sensation. She was pleased to see goose bumps on his stomach. The nerves were reacting just as she had wanted them to.

Next she took two large, flat obsidian rocks that she had warmed in a crock pot to a few degrees above body temperature. She put one on his chest, the other on his belly. She moved them around in small circles. Then she placed one on his neck and one on his pubic bone above his hard cock. The last she placed between his legs, underneath his scrotum. These were his chakra points, and with the warmth of the rocks, they were ignited. She left his head chakras alone, as he needed to be out of his head and into his body for what was about to happen. She rubbed two more rocks up and down the insides of his thighs and his arms. The largest one she placed in his hand and closed his fingers around it while kissing the back of his hand. He was lost in the feelings, and she could tell he was enjoying every touch. Massaging him with a phallic obsidian wand brought his nerve endings to the surface.

She left a rock in each palm, facing up. She whispered in his ear, "Enjoying the warmth?" He responded with a smile. She went to her tray to find a wine glass. It was filled with round ice cubes. She put one in her mouth and began to kiss him. The cold surprised him, as she took the ice cube into her hand and ran it over his lips. Then she moved down to his nipples. She could tell he was on sensory overload with the cold and hot ambiences. He had started to writhe and his breath was labored. Before he could protest, she put the ice cube in her mouth and enveloped his cock. He gasped and began to plead, repeating her name over and over. She sucked him until the ice cube melted and he was about to cum. She pulled her head off his cock with a suction that popped when she released it. He was worked up, so she took off the blindfold, removed the rocks and straddled him, kissing him and pushing his cock into her belly. He tried to penetrate her, she held him at bay.

"Next I am going to bind your hands lightly with my sash. You can escape at any time. It is a reminder that this next part is hands off. The only stimuli you are allowed to use are your eyes and your mind. Agreed?"

Dylan looked crazed with desire and could barely form words. He shook his head, and she bound his hands in front of him.

"I am going to show you something. You cannot touch me or yourself until I tell you that it is okay. I will not tolerate you breaking this rule. Know that if you do, even a little bit, your punishment will be not cumming. Got it?" He nodded and knew that he must cum soon or he might implode.

Nadailia lay back on the couch. Her legs on his thighs, her pussy exposed for him to see. It was flushed, as she was as hot as he. She had a silver plug in her mouth. She opened her legs and put the stainless steel plug with the handle into her ass. She produced a glass wand that was precisely angled and placed it inside her pussy. Then she took out her favorite vibrator and pressed it against her clit.

"You are going to watch my intensification. It may take a while, as performance anxiety may slow me down. I will be thinking about you fucking me. First in my pussy and then in my ass. Do not touch me or I will stop the show. You will obey me." He nodded, fascinated by this intimate theater.

She turned on the vibrator and arched her back at the first jump of electricity. She worked her inner lips with one hand and with the other hand moved the wand in and out. Her eyes were closed, but a serenely sexy smile on her lips. She put the plug all the way in and moved her hand to her nipples. Dylan was captivated by how she handled them, trying to lock the memory in and keep his promise not to touch her. She arched her back more and moved the setting on the vibrator to a faster speed. Her pussy blushed red, while her legs moved in and out, dancing to unheard music. She began to pant and breath heavily. When she was done she used her Kung Fu vaginal muscle training with such force that both the plug and the dildo leaped out of her. It took all the willpower Dylan had not to take her, he was afraid of the punishment. When her breathing returned to normal, she sat up and smiled.

"Ready for more?"

His cock remained hard, so hard it hurt. She took it with her mouth to lube it and then placed one hand on the base, circling it holding it firm. With the other hand she stroked up and down. She used her mouth every other stroke, licking the pre-cum. She looked up at him and ordered, "Cum on my tits." He followed her order and came quickly and loudly. She took him in her mouth after and sucked off all the remaining cum.

Afterward they lay together on the silk sheet, and she teased, "Ready to make me a meal now?"

He went to the kitchen and appeared 30 minutes later with a feast. He had prepared Snow Crab Chinois, a delectable treat of three crab claws stuffed with crispy crab swimming in a cream sauce flavored with ginger, garlic and cilantro.

They shared the hoisin-marinated-chicken lettuce wrap. Fresh leaves of butter lettuce were stuffed with sautéed chicken, toasted peanuts, soy sauce and wasabi. They licked the juice from running down each other's arms while enjoying this messy but amazing treat.

Next was the petrole sole done picatta-style with lemon cream sauce and capers, baby broccoli and fingerling potatoes. It was like swimming in a warm sea of pleasure for their taste buds. Last was the sautéed duck breast and confit of duck with spring vegetable and Yukon Gold hash with apple wood-smoked bacon, goat cheese, rainbow chard and a port-blackberry sauce.

The next morning she had to leave. The restaurant needed her, and she had a pivotal board meeting scheduled where she would finally get rid of Jeffrey. Dylan stayed to get his Maman settled and promised to be back in 10 days. As he dropped Nadailia off at the private airport, he saw the flight attendant welcoming her, and he wished he were going to be on that plane.

Text

N: Do you want one true sentence?

D: Yes, here is mine.

"No one or nothing has ever been able to get to me as fast as you can. It's like you've got Pavlov's buzzer wired to my dick."

N: Nice. My turn. "Because she couldn't see him, she had resolved herself that this was a temporary feeling. The feeling had remained in her heart, her loins and most poignantly, in her brain."

D: Did you write that?

N: Yes, just now.

D: That is stunning!

N: "She knew a love affair that leaked into the brain was dangerous. She didn't want to damage or destroy the status quo. The thoughts, the feelings, the pure desire for him was real."

D: Whatever literary oasis you got that from, go back and get the rest of it.

N: I am.

D: That is a whole new level!

That is real!

That is stuff people memorize like poetry!

N: "She had suffered three days without his touch, and passionate suffering was the nicest term for the torture her body and mind were going through."

D: That turned some kind of magic corner.

N: "She had tried to alleviate the tension with toys, multiple shower episodes, even rubbing herself."

D: I may not know how to write, I know heavy duty prose when I see it. That is book-selling quality right there!

N: You are my muse.

This has never happened before. I give you 50% credit.

D: I smile when you say that. I like it.

Glad to be of service.

N: "But the satisfaction, the release was not there. Each mental episode was not enough. She knew that this had to be turned into a magical realm. The one of words.

He obliged and was as hot on the keyboard as he was in the kitchen.

She had found the holy grail of a man.

This was the treasure of a lifetime. Something to be honored and revered.

D: Mmmmmmm

Thank you, Nadailia.

N: No, thank you, Dylan.

D: I've got to sleep now. Mind if I dream about you?

N: Please do. I dream of you nightly.

When I sleep, which doesn't happen much in this temperament I am in. Welcome to the state of desire.

D: Cause I promise you I will be fucking that black corset right off you.

N: Promise?

D: Abso- fucking- lutely!

N: Lord, what I wouldn't do to see you.

D: Same here. I have a raging hard-on for you right now.

N: Please cum and think of me.

D: My heart beats for you until I see you again.

A Great Bird Soars Over

Seven long and lonely days later, Dylan was still not back. He was difficult to talk to or text. His Maman was sick with an unknown condition, and he was spending most of his time at the hospital with her. Nadailia knew that if he didn't return soon she would have to replace him as the executive chef. She was not sure which would be worse, getting a new chef or losing the love of her life. They had never had this much silence. Each time the text tone went off on her phone, she'd pray it was him and that he was coming back.

She sent Dylan a note:

To: Dylan

From: Nadailia

Subject: Rain

Hey Chef,

I'm sitting on my front porch in the rain. Light drops pelt the earth as I snuggle under the wool blanket, my skin bare and alive.

My fingers find my pedals as my mind recalls your flower exploration. The divine sense of you knowing where to touch, press, pause and pet.

The memory of our exploration from the first touch, kiss, contact – each one—swirls like a carousel in my mind.

No one stands out as most delectable, since even the lightest touch of your hand holds a pound of desire within my memory.

You fuel me with absent pleasures and sweet words expressed in between pleasantries via text. It's as if I can feel your smile and your heart swell when you type a word, no matter how innocent or abashed the word is. I feel the strength of your soul behind each letter.

I am now comforted by our alliance. It is a warm place my mind goes to, filled with unspoken truths and beautiful tapestries of fantasy, yet rooted in something real, concrete, eternal.

I live with a compulsion to succeed in this restaurant for you. Thank you for responding to my ideas with absolute honesty and encouragement. I no longer question if I can. I'm destined to create something that will reach up under your armor and show you love.

My only distraction from the restaurant is necessities, which I find little of today, the rain and the memories drew me out, to relive our passions.

Nadailia

IYF- (but please come home soon!).

His response was short and curt. She knew she was losing him to the drama of his Maman, his duty to his family. That was an unacceptable outcome for her, so she tried a different approach. She appealed to his lust.

She made a video of her consuming a missile popsicle. Just her loving up the icy treat in a way that would make his hair stand on end. About five minutes after she sent the video her text tone sang out.

Text

D: Oh you fucker :-).

A little small though, wouldn't you say?

N: You weren't supposed to see that until tomorrow.

Bottom line: I'm practicing.

D: You don't need any practice. You could teach that.

N: Yes, it was too small, I was trying to make a point.

Why aren't you asleep?

D: Only been home 20 minutes. Hell of a day with Maman. Fixed something to eat, and I'm headed to bed now.

N: You like?

D: I got your point.

N: I'll sneak in quietly and crawl in bed and spoon.

D: Ahhhhhhhhh. If only.

N: I'd be on you like a lion in heat.

D: Is it still spooning if I have a massive hard on, I mean, technically speaking?

N: It becomes forking.

D: Hahaha.

N: Your lips, tongue and strong arms are on my mind.

Watch that again before you go to sleep.

D: Good night, gorgeous.

A Phoenix Frolics

Dylan was conflicted and stuck in France. Though his Maman was better, she still resisted coming back to the States.

Nadailia sent him a note that said Jeffrey was trying to take her down. The board had been reluctant to fire him because of his heritage. Jeffery's case against Dylan was growing with his absence. He was furious Dylan had taken Maria Away. Nadailia knew if he didn't come back soon, she would have to find another chef.

Dylan texted her in the middle of the day.

N: Hang on.

Fuck.

D: You ok?

N: Totally busted. I was sitting at my desk, skirt hiked up around my waist, fingering myself, when your sous chef walked in with the whole kitchen staff.

D: OMG, what did he say?

N: He said, "Clearly you miss him too. Get him back."

D: Hahahahaha.

N: Not funny. I am sending the plane for you and your Maman tonight.

I have had enough of this long-distance bullshit.

D: Maman won't come, and I can't leave her.

N: She will come. I have a proposition for her.

D: Like what?

N: Like I hire her back as my sommelier.

D: Are you fucking out of your mind? That was a disaster.
You want her working in MY kitchen?

N: So you do admit to it being YOUR kitchen?

D: That was sneaky.

N: Ask her, she can live in the cottage behind the restaurant, paint and buy wine.

D: No.

N: Why not?
Don't you want to get back to your life?
To me?
To us?
Dylan, I promise not to be such a bitch.
I am begging you, and I have never begged anyone.
Please come back to me.

D: I will ask her.

N: Please come home soon, or we may lose everything.

Wailing Monkey Embracing a Tree

The longing for him was more than she could stand. His kitchen staff was doing an excellent job covering for him, they needed a leader. Not sure what to do, and trusting Lauren more than anyone, she took her on a chocolate-tasting expedition.

The chocolatier presented them with five disks of chocolate on a golden tray, each about the size of a quarter, each dusted with a different color cocoa powder in order to distinguish the the difference between each chocolate without affecting its flavor. They were told to take a sip of the wine, a bite of chocolate, and then more wine to mix and allow the flavors to bloom on the palate.

The first coupling was a true cocoa butter with a rich creamy flavor and a buttery texture accompanied by Scharffenberger Brut Cuvée. The bubbling wine was dry, which complemented the sweet velvety flavor of the chocolate. They were off and running and having a ball getting a chocolate education. The next flight was a 38% milk chocolate from Hawaii paired with a Calcareous Pinot Noir. The chocolate was fruity, rich and creamy, while the wine opened up vivaciously with each sip.

They tried a bittersweet 65% cocoa from Ecuador with a Sebastiani Cabernet Sauvignon. The chocolate had accents of green forest and tea, followed by subtle flavors of nut and banana with a cake-like finish. The next chocolate was from Madagascar. It had the tart and fruity flavor of a rare cocoa bean called Criollo, and a deep rich chocolate flavor. This paired perfectly with a Maloy O'Neill

Zinfandel. Thus began a conversation about big bold Zins, and a bottle of Turley Dusi Zinfandel was promptly ordered for them to share.

The last pairing was a bittersweet 70% cacao from Hawaii served with a Saucelito Canyon Zinfandel Late Harvest dessert wine. The chocolate was rich and velvety with a hint of berry and some serious dark chocolate flavors. This chocolate company was full of premium exotic chocolates.

High on chocolate and wine, they went back to Nadailia's house to get some protein and figure out the Dylan problem. There was nothing more resolute than two drunken woman high on chocolate.

"This existence needs more passion, less bullshit," was Lauren's opening statement.

Nadailia agreed and took the dialog the way all conversations went since she had met Dylan.

"He has permanently changed me into a more sexual being.

The feel of my hair falling down my back, the small vibrations of the car, the smell of jasmine all makes me wet. Because I can't have his touch, I'm having to find my pleasure elsewhere."

Lauren needed to remind her friend who she was.

"I think it's always been there; you needed a catalyst."

Nadailia ignored her and kept on with her drunken soliloquy.

"And while the toys are excellent for fantasy, I'm finding this constant state of arousal beneficial. It's a powerful state."

"Use your super powers wisely."

"I've always had that thought, to a fault sometimes. And I think it's so funny that I'm so strong and powerful. Until I see him, or don't see him. Or hear from him. Then I am swooning like a fucking teenager."

Lauren knew her friend was in deep. She also knew she was a freight train once she wanted something, so for now she humored her.

"Caution, men can sense the power they have over you and use it to their advantage."

"I honestly have never, nor will I ever, care what anybody thinks about me. So they can resent me all day. I learned that people either love me or hate me; there is no middle ground when it comes to me."

"We all say that. But deep down we care. It's our nature."

"I think it's that I'm sexed up. Honestly, I am looking for him and wanting him and I'm drowning in this state of desire."

She sent him a drunken story, still appealing to his lust to bring him back. Afterward she felt like a stupid teenager and wanted to retract every word.

To: Dylan

From: Nadailia

Regarding: Torture

Dear Dylan:

Today at the restaurant, I saw a couple holding hands and I realized we'll never do that. Never anything like it. No picnics or unguarded smiles. Just stolen moments that leave too quickly.

I live in torture, thinking of these moments. There's a burning in me, I feel on fire and have a guilt I can't codify. Does it make you happy to know that?

Know that I love you. Wherever you go, whatever you see, I will always be with you.

You were right. I don't know if life is greater than death. But this love, this exchange of words, was more than either.

IYF,

Nadailia

Text

N: So you want my sexcapades today?

D: Yes please!!!!

N: Since I'm so sexed up, cuming with a vibrator is useless. It makes me more horny.

D: What are you doing to get release?

N: Never have I had this situation. Big Easy Reach and a nice pulsating shower always sated me.

D: Ok.Is that working?

N: No.

D: What are you going to do?

N: I am not sure, since you are on the other side of the planet and it seems you are the only thing my body wants.

D: I cannot tell you how HOT it was for me when you said my texts make you cum.

N: So this afternoon, I went for the big vibrator. I remembered your texts and put myself mentally with you.

D: And?

Did you get there?

N: So, I pictured you sucking my clit, your fingers in my pussy.

D: Mmmmmm yessss.

I can feel the wetness.

N: I came, but like the last 100 times, it made me hornier.

D: Are you sure you are cumming? Really Orgasming?

N: I think so. It feels good, then I want more.

D: Sorry.

N: So, I went for the toy box.

D: What did you find?

N: I got the nipple clamps, the glass wand and the butt plug.

D: Oh Fuccccck.

N: I clamped, inserted and penetrated. Then I thought of you.

D: Blue Steel Hard. I need to get home.

The Dog of Early Autumn

It was not a good day for Nadailia. Things out of her control disturbed her thoughts, and the desire did not let up. She missed him terribly and knew she could not keep flying back there every time she was horny. She had to figure out a way to get his prideful Maman back to the States, so he would come back to her.

To: Dylan
From: Nadailia
Regarding: Sailing
Hello Dylan, my chef,
This is my story for you, with a bit of truth.

I had a moment to genuineness. Since I'm unable to see you, touch you, I went sailing this weekend on my beautiful catamaran, Tunnel Vision. My spirit is buoyed by the freedom I've longed for but haven't tasted in a while. The elements behave differently on the sea. The wind becomes our friend, our power and our lover. At night the breeze comes in through the port like a hand caressing me. I feel in come in tender puffs, each awakening my pleasure.

I feel the touch of your hand in the wind. The rocking of the ocean is sensual, erotic. Mother Ocean doesn't let up; she never stops bringing pleasure.

My hearing is more in tune. The slap of the water on the hull. The musical sound of the sails when they fill with air. Full of promise, peace and freedom. Food tastes better and you need less of it, although you are constantly in action. The flavors spring fourth, seasoned by the salt in the air.

It is here, filled with beauty and passion with no distractions, I think of you most. Each touch and sensation, like a predator, I stalk it.

Once again, you are invading my waking and sleeping. There is power between us. This desire is overwhelming. I feel your energy in me constantly. A fleeting memory of a touch, or when I made you laugh, sets my loins on fire. Your prose has a visceral effect on my pussy. This power is palpable to me. It is the fuel running my imagination, my writing.

This is not a fleeting feeling; it's sustainable. Like a crop that becomes bigger each season, this is growing.

This lust is tangible and would probably register on a volt meter. And it doesn't wane. It grows exponentially and becomes more clever and sure. I'm so trusting in this, so sure that it is divine, I do not worry. With our life experience, our strength of character and our ability to keep the status quo while having unfettered access to each other – if only in our words – is beyond inspiring.

I can't wait to touch you, look into your eyes, kiss you. I have imagined scenario after sexy scenario when we finally taste and let the sparks fly. Be sure this is what you want, because once this passion freight train gets started, there is no stopping it.

IYF

Nadailia

The next night her presence was requested at a charity dinner. She was pissed that Dylan was not going to be her arm candy. She only agreed to go because he suggested it would be fun to dance the Flamenco. Not sure if she was torturing herself or defying him, she inserted the vibrating eggs into her pussy and placed a clip on her clit. She texted him and vowed to keep the eggs vibrating through the night, not turning them off once. She thought this was a way to get him out of her loins.

Text

D: You home?

How was the benefit?

Did you insert those eggs?

I am worried about you.

You seem to be unraveling.

N: I am alone.

Finally. The vibrating infidels have been put to bed. That would be the horrible little womb invaders. I placed them inside me to punish you tonight. It ended up pleasing the doctors, as the blush on my face was apparent to men. And envied by woman.

D: Oh man, sorry!

N: If you want to "capture a room" get all sexed up on a man whom you can't talk to or touch. Insert vibrating balls, a seriously tight clit clip, and the world is your oyster.

D: I'll bet you were the star! I am smiling so big right now!

N: Fucker.

D: Remote or always on?

N: Always on.

I made a promise, and I keep them.

I was trying to out run this desire for you.

Trying to make it stop.

No luck.

D: That is so fucking HOT!

N: It has been an eternity since I touched you. I am dying here. No lie.

D: You are the most liberated woman I have ever met.

N: I have rubbed myself raw thinking of one taste of you.

I have desired before, but nothing like this.

D: Nadailia, trust me, if it weren't for the ocean between us,

I would be on you tonight.

N: We will figure it out.

As smart, passionate people, we will make this work.

You are the smartest, kindest, most resourceful man I have ever met.

Let's not think in traditional terms.

D: Funny, clever and creative is how I would describe you, too.

N: So we sit at a desk or an ocean apart.

Status quo with a bunch of pleasure (very private pleasure) inserted.

D: Well, you've got my undivided attention.

N: I must see your face soon.

D: So your text early tonight called this an affair.

N: You see it that way?

D: It certainly is an affair of the heart.

N: I will never do anything to hurt your life.

But I am a realist. I see our passion.

I am also a selfish, horny bitch who needs some Dylan time.

You spoiled me with unfettered access, and now you are gone.

D: I am sorry.

N: I need time with you. I can graze your hand, look deep into your eyes. I really miss you.

D: Remember our first night?

That horrible interview?

How I wanted to molest you among the cabbages?

Were you thinking of me in those terms even then?

N: Kind of.

I thought there was no way you would ever want me.

I am so different from what you have had before.

D: I tried to explain why.

Your desire.

N: What is happening between us is not a cliché. This is different. You can trust that opinion from someone who has chased every untraditional lifestyle.

D: I'm afraid I could turn it into a cliché.

I am not that experienced.

N: I need to have access to you.

D: I do not trust easily.

I've clearly given my trust to you.

N: That is something I admire and treasure.

If I could fly right now.

I would meet you in Marseille for this conversation.

Maybe trying to cum in public, thinking about you, was hot, but not a good idea.

I'm dying for you now.

D: If I could get at you, it would be a pretty short conversation.

It's not polite to talk with your mouth full.

N: Love it!

I would be gazing into your eyes while swallowing you.

D: And that is exactly where our meeting would head in about 39 seconds.

No person or porn has kept me in a constant state of arousal like you do.

N: Me neither.

What ever this is, it's real.

The literal term for it has not been defined.

Maybe that is our purpose. New term. New word.

D: Ok. I've got to shower and climb into bed.

Thanks for sharing.

Get some rest.

N: NOOOOOOOO!

D: Sorry.

N: Damn

Sad Nadailia
D: Sweet Nadailia
N: Bad Nadailia wants more Dylan.

The Master of the Cave

D ylan was spending every minute trying to convince his Maman to come back to the States. It was not going well. This woman embodied the art of entitlement, thinking that the world owed her, after doing literally nothing deserving of luck or even dispensation. Dylan knew that if he didn't leave in the next week he would lose everything he had worked for and everything he loved. To make up for his time away, he combed the restaurants, looking for a perfect dish to take back and dazzle all in Consumed.

Marseille's modern food scene was one of the most exciting in France. The bistros served a diverse range of cuisines from around the Mediterranean. You could grab a table in the tiny garden for a light supper of Spanish ham, poutargue, grilled aubergine with chopped mint, raw artichoke salad and a tortilla. His favorite bistro posted changes daily on a chalkboard menu. Grilled turbot with a purée of escalivada (a Catalan dish of aubergines, peppers, garlic, onions and olive oil) and slow-roasted free-range pork with girolles and butternut squash purée show off a cooking style that was consistently precise, generous and inventive.

While he was waiting for his dinner, Dylan received a text from Nadailia. She was passive-aggressively begging him to come back. This did not suit her personality.

Text

N: Are you in bed?

D: No, at dinner, why?

N: Just getting my visual.

When you are in bed, what is the sheet color?

D: White.

N: Blanket?

D: White.

Comforter, white.

N: You in a convent?

D: Funny lady.

N: On your back or front?

D: Stomach.

N: So I'm going to slide up from the bottom of the bed.

Under the sheet.

D: I went to the beach today. I'd love to go with you to a nude beach.

N: Me too. Field trip!

First I rub your feet.

N: Pressing hard. Using my ancient Chinese secrets to stimulate all the right parts.

Then I spread your legs

I come up your legs.

Hot breath on your skin.

N: Rubbing.

Loving your taut muscles.

Pressure, then lightly touching you.

Butterfly touches.

N: I work up to your perfect gluts.

I lick with my hot tongue.

D: Nice.

I'd be turning over by now :-)

N: Then trace it with my hands.

That is where my hot mouth goes next.

Hands on your thighs.

D: Yes.

N: Mouth on your amazing cock.

N: Bobbing. Sucking. Swirling.
Swallowing.

D: My hands in your hair.

N: Loving the head of your cock on the back of my throat.
Right before you cum.
I mount you.

D: Yes.

N: Quickly.
Every inch of you inside me.
I milk your cock with my pussy muscles as I ride.

D: I'd explode inside you.

N: And I have my hands on your chest.

D: Pulsing my hot cum into you.

N: Milking the last few drops.

D: Mine would be running down my cock and out of you.

N: Then I collapse on you and say, "Let's do it again."

Strengthening the Bones

Nadailia asked Stu out for dinner. She knew he was probably starving with his brother gone, and she was trying to understand why Dylan would not come back. They went to a family-style farm-to-table pizza restaurant that was the new rage.

Stu started with rose sorbet with candied rose petals and kumquats. The sorbet was rich and creamy with the scent and taste of an English rose garden shining through. This dessert-first idea was intriguing to Nadailia as she watched him inhale it.

Every item on the menu was so fresh and rare that diners needed to get there early as the menu sold out every night. Nadailia was delighted with the salad. It was a little gem with vegetables from Roots Organic Farm, green goddess dressing and roasted beets. She proclaimed it all tasted as if it were pulled out of the earth that morning. She made a note to have Dylan add it to the menu. Then she remembered. He may never be back.

"Stu, can you answer something for me?"

Stu was busy enjoying a black truffle flatbread, which was priced at $45. It had a garlic-brown butter sauce with spring onions, grana cheese, serena cheese, and a semi-poached farm egg from Lily (which is the name of the chicken). As they served it, they shaved big, fresh slices of truffle onto the flatbread.

"I have never had truffles so large, and it was brilliant," he said. "Full of flavor and rare, it was a treat for the senses. I swear I have never had anything that rich before."

"Sure, what do you need to know? Why my brother is crazy, or why my Maman is insane?"

"I don't think you believe either statement. Do you think Dylan is coming back?"

"I know he loves you and the restaurant, so yes, eventually."

Nadailia had ordered the seafood sausage, a combination of black cod, squid, rock shrimp and leeks all stuffed in a casing. Black olives were puréed and the oil used to fry the sausage.

"I don't understand the hold your Maman has on him."

"Neither do I, but it is something you must learn to deal with if you want a lasting relationship with Dylan. If Maman is happy, Dylan allows himself to be happy."

Dessert was a chocolate-blood orange cake that was magical. They also had a bowl of mandarin oranges served with a quince salted caramel sauce. She took Stu home and hurried to text Dylan.

Text

D: You there?

N: I am. Can you talk?

D: Yeah. Tricky. I've got a few minutes.

Mom's reading

N: Ok.

Don't compromise. I'm ok.

Using our forced separation as a character building experience.

Body not happy, but character needs it.

D: Can I share some thoughts with you?

N: Yes! I'm missing your words terribly.

D: Ok.

N: You're safe with me.

D: I am still trying to make sense of whatever this is between us. It may be lust. I've had lots of opportunities, but never saw the upside of an affair without potential for permanency.

N: I agree.

D: It may be flattery.

You flatter my fledgling career and my lovemaking, me.

I like that.

But again, I've seen that card played many times in my professional arena with agendas by the flatterers.

I think I'm immune to that by now.

Although I do love it when something I create moves you!

But that's not the reason either.

So I had a revelation tonight.

N: Tell me?

D: It's desire.

N: Yes, it is.

D: You desire me, and I have never in my life been desired.

I've been needed.

Wanted.

Required.

But not desired.

N: It all started with a night of us communing over food.

Us getting to know each other.

Me falling in lust.

D: I know.

So I don't have an answer for when we will be together again.

But I can tell you I like working with you.

Creating with no limits.

I have never in my life had the freedom to do that.

I've always been someone else's support system.

N: You are free with me.

I don't need you for anything.

D: I like having a confidante.

A friend.

Maybe a potential life partner, but most of all, someone I can relax with and share raw feelings. Yes, a lot of them are sexy for now, built on a solid friendship.

N: I agree

D: So there.

Way over-sharing.

A lifetime first for me.

N: I'm loyal to a fault.

D: Me too. Why do you think I am sitting in Marseille?

N: I was wondering that myself. I had dinner with Stu tonight.

D: Did he ring up a $500 tab?

N: Just about; that boy can eat.

N: First, I need to tell you that you and your job are safe.

D: Thank you for holding it for me; I can't imagine it is easy going.

I am here out of duty. I love my family, even though they are crazy. My heart, my desire, rests with you.

N: Second, the lust/desire thing is human and good.

I promise to never compromise your life or family.

D: Mmmmmmm that may be the sexiest thing you have ever said to me.

N: I care way too much for you to do that.

You are in a special place in my head and heart.

D: Nadailia, thank you for that.

N: No, thank you, Dylan.

It is a mutual admiration society.

D: It feels good to me.

N: I am smart enough to know this is special, unique, and not to be tampered with.

It will bob and weave like all good friendships.

Right now it is about the desire, the lust.

But someday it will be companionship.

Because we can trust each other.

D: Can you imagine what we can have on the other side of this?

N: I adore you.

D: And I you!

N: I am not ever letting you go.

D: Thank you for that.

N: You have brought out a part of me that I have been longing for for an eternity. As I've said before, you are my greatest gift.

D: I love your unconditional love for me.

You know I have the same for you.

N: I have not been able to bridle and rein in this passion.

I have second-guessed myself on every front.

Now I love freely.

It is the best gift ever.

As I've said before, I will never be able to thank you enough.

D: Thank you. I needed to be able to say what I did tonight.

Blending the Conduits

Nadailia had run out of ways to keep Dylan's job safe for him. Even Dylan's own staff was starting to rebel and break down, as any group without a leader is likely to do. On Monday when she showed up at Consumed, there was a strange woman in the kitchen, dressed in executive chef garb and taking inventory of the spices.

"Excuse me, can I help you?" Nadailia said, trying to not sound like a bitch who had caught her man with her best friend.

"Hello! I am Candy, new executive chef of Consumed, and you are?"

"I am the owner. Just who appointed you EC?" There was a snarl to her words that made Candy step back.

"There must be some confusion, I was hired by the owner, Jeffery."

A black cloud passed over Nadailia's face and her eyes turned dark as the fury spread through her. She didn't want to take it out on this chef, so she turned quickly and stormed out of the kitchen.

She found Jeffery in the wine locker. He was sipping wine, and it was only 9 a.m.

"Just what the fuck did you do?" Her blazing eyes were like laser beams, her face was twisted in vehemence. Jeffrey looked up from his glass of rosé, "Care for some breakfast wine?" His casual demeanor infuriated her more.

"Are you fucking kidding me?"

"I have the board's backing. They agreed that we can't wait for your boy toy to decide to come back. And I hired a woman in the hopes that you will not try to sleep with her."

With a thousands retorts in her head, she knew it was better to back away than to have an altercation at the restaurant. As she turned to leave, Jeffrey raised his glass to her and smiled a weasel smirk of satisfaction.

She found words, "There is nothing more consistent than the acts of cowardly men."

She left the restaurant in a hurry and called the pilot. "Prepare to leave in two hours. Marseille is our destination. Next she called her restaurant broker and made a plan that would either sink or save her. She didn't care which; she knew that she had to do something.

In route she texted a picture of her in a red corset to Dylan. She had a plan and hoped he would go along with it.

Text

N: Hello!

D: A picture of a red fucking corset?

N: I blurred out my girl bits.

D: Tell the truth. Were you laughing when you pushed send? Going hehehe. Watch his dick blow up?

Because it did, instantly.

N: Nope. I want to make you smile (from the inside out).

D: Girl. You completely have my number.

N: I'm a strange one.

D: It makes me smile!

I love it!!

I love your diversity. Your experiences.

Your stories.

N: And I love our secrets. We have both lived a full life. Filled with experiences, deaths, disappointments and loyalty.

This makes us see each other.

D: Yes, true. But still we have hope, love, desire and dreams.

N: Yes, we do. I never give up. I always know it will be better. I will have what I want. I will get what I desire.

Damn, I miss your face.

D: Mmmmmm, sounds like my line.

N: Not a line, my mantra.

I have never wanted anything I have not gotten.

My life is a constant stream of getting what I want. Until now......

D: What do you want now?

N: You, back in my kitchen and in my bed.

D: Wish that was doable, as in right now.

N: What if I told you it could be?

Guess Who's Here for Dinner

There was a knock at the door, and Dylan got up from the computer to answer it. There stood Nadailia with a briefcase in hand. He was shocked at first, and then grabbed her face in his hands and attacked her mouth. She dropped her purse and briefcase and assaulted his mouth back. Lost in their lust for each other, they forgot about Maman. She came in the room and started coughing to let them know she was witnessing their hunger.

"Excuse me, I will go out and leave you two for your avoir la passion."

Nadailia collected herself, picked up the briefcase and looked seriously at Maman.

"No, do not go anywhere. I am here to meet with you. I have a proposal."

Maman and Dylan exchanged glances and led Nadailia to the kitchen table. She took out plans, a proposal and pictures.

"Maman, I have purchased a wine bistro in Napa Valley. I am going to make you the owner with Jeffery. I have found an over-the-top chef named Candy, who will be properly trained by Dylan. This will be yours and Jeffery's to run as you see fit, as long as it breaks even, you will have no interference from me. What do you think?"

"Mon Dieu! Are you serious? After all the harm I caused? You are kidding, no?"

"I am serious; you have a talent and need your own palate to ascend."

Maman looked at Dylan, who was smiling at Nadailia like a crazed schoolboy in heat. Maman understood that Nadailia was doing this for Dylan, and that was all she needed to know.

"I accept your offer."

The Stone Room

D ylan and Nadailia spent one last day in Marseille picnicking at the beach. They stopped at a Spanish bistro to pick up tapas. First were Spanish potatoes, a simple dish of diced potatoes fried with paprika and served with red pepper sauce. Nadailia commented that this was an upper-class version of country potatoes, delicious with a European flair. Then came the almond meatballs with white wine sauce and slivered almonds. The garlic calamari was flawlessly cooked and full of flavor. They also snacked on breaded calamari, fried ravioli and garlic shrimp. The sun was hot, so they took a dip in the ocean to cool off. The rocks on the beach hid them from view, so they could sneak a kiss as the sea rocked them. They ran to a cave to continue satisfying each other. Dylan took her up against the rocks, pounding her into sweet oblivion. They rolled in the waves, connected and made love, not worrying about sand or people on the beach who could possibly see them.

Then the three of them flew home in Nadailia's jet, dropping Nadailia and Dylan in Los Angeles to pick up supplies for the restaurants. She rented a Jaguar convertible for them to drive home, languishing in each other's presence. They were dressed in beach casual, Nadailia wanted him prepared for a romp in the outdoors.

Dylan was driving with the music turned up loud. He sang along to every classic rock tune, one of the features she found completely enduring. Traffic came to a halt on the 405 freeway. It was bumper to bumper, they had the top down. The radio was playing Berlin, good old erotic music about being a slut. Nadailia reached over and rubbed Dylan's knee, excited about having access to his bare skin. She began with light circles on the insides of his thighs. He was concentrating on the car in front creeping forward, but as always, he was stirred by her touch. He glanced at her and saw that she had a mischievous twinkle in her eye. He loved that look; it always led to erotic adventures.

Her hand worked up his leg and found the tip of his dick. She scratched it with her fingernails. He hardened almost immediately, squirming in the leather seat. She released him by unbuttoning his shorts. She placed her head in his lap. He was alarmed; he was sure this was not safe. He had learned not to say no to her desire.

She took him completely, dropping her face to his pelvic bone. This trick drove him crazy and could often make him cum instantly. He observed the car next to him, and a gorgeous blonde looked over and winked.

With the music and her head bobbing up and down on him, he had lost the consciousness that he was in a car. The traffic started to move, and bellowing horns snapped him to his senses. He grabbed a handful of her thick red hair and pulled her mouth off his cock. It disengaged with a sound like a cork. She licked her lips, now swollen from riding his engorged cock. It was her sexiest look. Face flushed with desire, lips engorged and red.

The traffic again slowed to a standstill. A semi truck had pulled up on her side of the car. She saw the portly driver looking at her. She took Dylan's cock in her left hand and started to peel down her shirt with the other.

Now she had everyone's attention. She slipped the red silk shirt off her shoulders and exposed her black lacey demi bra. The bra's sole function was to highlight her nipples. It lifted and exposed them, and now all could see the right one. She checked to make sure she had each voyeur's attention. Neither man could look away.

She took her tit in her hand and lifted it to her mouth. She licked and bit the nipple.

Then she moved her hand to her skirt and lifted it up, showing her matching black lace panties. She fondled the outside of the lace a few strokes, then raised her hand to her mouth to wet her fingers.

Meanwhile, she was continuing to whack Dylan's cock, slowly, to keep him on the edge.

She traced her dampened fingers down to her crotch and moved the lace aside, inserting them deeply into her pussy. Her head rolled back as the exhibitionism took her. As she finished, the truck driver blasted his air horn, startling drivers all around.

Dylan was taken and yet unsure. She looked at him and said, "Never leave me again. I'm breathing passion, exhaling desire and swallowing lust. This is what happens when you leave me to my own devices."

Barely able to speak, he mumbled, "I promise I am never going anywhere."

The Dragon Turns Over

S he rolled over and felt his strong body at rest next to hers. He'd been away too long, and she had been worried that the flame which had drove them might somehow be damped down by time and space apart. The evening before, when they had cooked together, he had maneuvered her body next to his and cornered her by the sink. The contact had made a lightening bolt rocket through her body. A deep longing sprang alive, and she knew the eternal flame still melted them both.

He was sleeping on his back, a look of peace on his chiseled features. She went beneath the covers and spread his legs gently apart, softly rubbing his inner thighs. She took him in her mouth, and his cock responded instantly. Taking the whole of him as he hardened, her head bobbed on his cock, while her tongue made circles around its head, and her long hair gently brushed back and forth on his belly. He was awake now, and moaning, but letting her lead the dance. As her strokes became bolder, she swallowed him. This deepness ignited her almost as much as him. She caressed his balls, tickling and then applying a bit of pressure below his scrotum.

As she fucked him with her face, he felt her protruding rock-hard nipples grazing the insides of his thighs. He almost came from the sensual way her tits felt on his legs.

He was always surprised how much giving head turned her on, and he loved how her body responded with such unabashed passion.

She moved on top of him like a panther and inserted his hard cock into her dripping soft pussy. Placing her hands on his chest, she rode him. Her muscles milked his cock as she gyrated and pumped. He was fully inside her and could feel her clit on his pubic bone. Letting her do the work, he opened his eyes to see the smoldering passion on her face. The force of his orgasm almost took her over the edge, and he let the energy bolt through them as they melded together.

Afterward she lay on top of him and whispered, "Did I tell you how much I missed you?"

The Tigers Tread

Dylan moved in with Nadailia. Maman and Jeffery were in Napa, fighting and fucking like cats in heat, both happier than they could have ever guessed. Dylan's long hours sometimes left Nadailia home at night alone. He had devised a game to keep her interested called Truth or Dare. Via text, he made her do things. Sexy things. Public things that both thrilled and terrified her. He knew this was the key to keeping her interested, as her brain was as big a sexual organ as her pussy.

Text

D: You ready for Truth or Dare?

N: I am busy!

D: Not too busy.

Sneak your left hand under your shirt and pinch your right nipple.

Squeeze it slowly, harder and harder, until it HURTS.

N: Ok, I am.

D: Tell me when it hurts.

N: Ok, it hurts and is hard.

D: Good girl.

N: Next?

D: I thought you were busy?

N: Never too busy for pleasure.

D: Now do the other one until it hurts.

N: Ok, wet now.

D: Good girl.

Ready?

N: I'm reclined in my chair ready to explode.

D: Take that same hand and slowly slide it down and get your finger wet.

N: Ok.

D: Put that wet finger in your mouth and quietly suck your juice off of it like I would.

Tell me when it's in your mouth.

N: Fuck.

D: Do not cum.

N: Now?

D: Good girl.

Now put your finger in your wet pussy again.

Get your finger really wet; keep it there.

Do not touch your clit.

Do not cum.

N: Ok.

D: Is it in there?

N: Yes.

D: Is it slippery?

N: Yes.

D: Slide your hand around your hip and insert your slippery finger in your ass like it was my wet hard cock.

Do it.

Do not cum.

N: Fuck.

D: Is it there?

N: Hang on; repositioning required.

D: Mmmmm.

N: I'm in.

D: Good girl.

N: Fuck, you better make me climax.

D: Remove your finger.

N: No.

D: Your final assignment for the night:

With the same hand that's been in your pussy, your mouth and your ass, push down into your pants and grab your clit with your thumb and forefinger.

Squeeze until you are there.

DO NOT MAKE A SOUND! Do it.

N: Yes, sir.

Mission accomplished.

Fucking hot.

D: You're a good girl!

The Jade Stock

Following hours of love making the night before, they slept later than either had planned. Both were in the habit of springing from bed as the sun rose and attacking the day. This particular morning he rolled over and brought her into a spoon position and caressed her back. She snuggled in nicely, marveling at his morning wood and trying to stay calm. He ran his hand up and down her side admiring her curvaceous, soft body. She lay still so as not to interrupt this intimate act. He kissed the back of her neck and her melon breasts in his hands.

Her sharp intake of air notified him she not asleep, but letting him lead. He slipped his cock into her easily, staying in the spoon position. She marveled that this simple act of filling her with his cock made her feel visible, even whole. They rocked gently, both of them wanting to keep the suppleness and splendor of this act going as long as possible. She tried to keep her passion down, the energy was rising. Even though he was stroking slow and easy, it was right on her spot, and she marveled at how completely they fit together. He whispered in her ear, "You consume me." He could feel her tight muscles milking, so taut he felt she might break his cock. His pleasure began to build. He kept the same slow and lovely pace, it overcame him and he began to cum. Afterward, when he softened and slipped out, she felt immediately empty, and her desire began to rise again.

Text

N: I want to re-live this morning every day.

D: Is that a proposal?

N: Yes.

I have never been so affected by someone's touch.

I felt like I was 12 and had kissed a boy. You had me shaking when you tried to touch my hand.

D: I enjoyed our breakfast.

N: I was so tickled to have a morning alone with you.

D: I liked holding your hand, if only for a minute.

N: I was trembling.

D: You were great.

D: This is getting serious.

N: I know.

Fish with Scales Joined

They went wine tasting, picking out the finest selections to pair with Dylan's new menu. They tried an organic farm-to-table restaurant they had heard rivaled theirs. They started with roasted beets with Humboldt Fog Cheese, vanilla bean vinaigrette and candied walnuts. It was refreshing and opened up their tannin-filled taste buds. Next they tried the seared ahi tuna salad with field greens, cucumber, feta cheese, kalamata olives and oranges. Both agreed that this chef's talents reached the table with a flourish. He paid attention to detail, and the subtle flavors tantalized their taste buds. Yet while they ate, they never lost contact. They were skin to skin, whether it was hands, feet or lips. The Laetitia Brut Rosé paired with the appetizers brilliantly.

They ordered a pizza cooked in the brick oven, and it was delectable. The cracker-bread crust was topped with pesto sauce, gorgonzola cheese, onions sautéed until they were sweet and drizzled with balsamic vinegar and olive oil. This was too good to be called something as ordinary as pizza. Next was the pork tenderloin with apple and a Gouda-assaggio potato gratin. A root and a swine never tasted so delightful together. They shared a bottle of 2006 Justin Savant that was spicy and had a lush finish of cocoa. Dylan ordered two scoops of the lavender infused, house-made vanilla ice cream. She about fainted with pleasure as he spoon-fed her.

Dylan was impressed by the meal and slightly jealous of the chef and his talent. When the chef approached the table, it was clear that

Nadailia was taken with him. He was full of energy and laughter, powerful aphrodisiacs for women. Dylan planned to make her know later that she belonged to only him.

After dinner they walked to the end of the pier. They could hear the curling and crashing of the waves, and the full moon shone like a beacon on the water. She leaned over the pier, looking at the moonlight reflecting in the sea. From behind her, he wrapped her in his arms. Her short skirt had been arousing him all night, as each time she twirled hinted at the promise of seeing her bare bottom. He put his hand under her skirt and started to rub her ass cheeks. She swayed back and forth with the pleasure of his touch. He knelt down on the pier and put his face up to her clit. She was surprised how he had taken to public displays.

He licked her clit and then moved his tongue inside her. His thumb moved into her ass with ease, and she began to moan. With the rush of the next crashing wave, she finished, but still felt a strong desire. Knees weak, and breath taken, she dropped to her knees next to him.

He looked deeply into her eyes and saw a glimmer of something he had never experienced before. He had to have her, possess her and take her to heights she had never experienced.

She unzipped his pants, and his hard cock leapt toward her. She shifted to a crawling position and wiggled her ass toward him, inviting him. He accepted her offer with a rigid thrust of lust and craziness, as if he had been undone.

When he emanated, he actually howled. The animal in him was unleashed. And they had begun.

Text

N: Hey.

D: Hey back.

N: What are you doing?

D: Prepping lunch. What do you need?

N: Remember that vegetable scrubber you bought me?

D: Yes.

N: I used it in the shower to pleasure myself while thinking about sucking your cock.

D: Holy Fuck.

N: Have a nice prep :-)

Unicorn Horn

D ylan took Nadailia to a pastry shop to sample their goods for possible inclusion on their menu. He had met the owner at a café, and she had agreed to stay late that night for a private tasting. They arrived at 9 o'clock and could see a light on in the back through the glass front door. They walked in and were enveloped by the warm, creamy scent of fresh baked goods.

The bakery chef, Brenda invited them to the tasting room in the back. The room was softly lit with lamps and had a chopping-block table in the middle and two couches along the wall. A tray of beautiful pastries was arranged on the table, along with three glasses of red wine.

Brenda explained, "There is something spiritual about a properly made cinnamon roll. Although most have similar ingredients, a bit of panache can turn the ordinary into extraordinary." It was impressive to see someone so passionate about the art of baking. "Mine are an orange-infused swirl of phyllo dough, dense with cinnamon delight and rolled in sugar." It looked like it might be too sugary, it was the perfect ratio of savory and sweet.

They moved on to other treats. "Not to be confused with the macaroon, a coconut confection, the macaron is a sweet meringue-based confection made with eggs, icing sugar, granulated sugar, ground almonds natural flavoring and coloring. Also called Luxemburgerli, they are bright in color, long on flavor and taste." She had the Moon Pie-looking treats in numerous flavors, including

Chocolate Lavender, Hazelnut, Pistachio, Strawberry, Raspberry Champagne, Rose and Irish Cream. Raspberry Hand Pies, shaped like hearts, were the crowd favorite.

The tiny strawberry cheesecake and the moistest chocolate cupcakes were next, along with scones stuffed with fresh berries. They were all something to worship. The wine flowed, and the conversation was easy.

After sampling the pastries and agreeing to an ongoing order for the restaurant, Brenda put the tray away. She leaned over and whispered something to Nadailia that sounded like ménage à trois. Nadailia smiled and reached out to wipe a dusting of flour from Brenda's lips.

Dylan sat there stunned at this sudden turn of events. As Nadailia and Brenda's lust rose, Dylan warmed to the idea.

"You OK with this?" Nadailia whispered in between nibbling on Brenda's lips.

"I like this."

Brenda slowly unbuttoned her jacket, revealing beautiful full breasts. She then gently led Nadailia toward the table and sat her on one of the high bar stools. She took off her blouse and bra, kissing each piece of exposed skin. After a meandering time undressing her, she led her to the couch. Dylan sat at the table, removing his clothes as Brenda was undressing Nadailia. Brenda bent her over the arm of the couch and slowly rubbed her already wet pussy. Dylan maneuvered in front of Nadailia and let her take his rock-hard cock in her mouth. She was swallowing him in a fit of desire as Brenda fingered her and sucked her glistening pussy.

Brenda walked away and returned with a black strap-on tied around her waist. Nadailia was shocked when she shoved the black silicone dick into her wet cunt. She now had a cock fucking her pussy and one in her mouth. Almost more that she could bare, she stopped before it ended to soon.

Brenda sat on the couch with the dildo pointed at the ceiling. Nadailia mounted her, facing her and ramming the dildo into her wet cunt. Dylan watched in delight. Then Brenda laid back on the couch with Nadailia on top, fucking her.

They left with a bag of pastries. Nadailia was happy, Dylan seemed distracted.

"Pastry for your thoughts?"

Exposed Fish Gills

Her goal was to give him his every desire, every fantasy he had ever imagined or was in the process of conjuring up. In his sexy writings, he always described her pussy as completely shaved. In reality, her body was in its most natural state. Her curly red hair was often unruly, she wore little makeup, and she did not have any false adornments.

To give him this imagined state in reality, she drew a hot bath in the big round tub and filled it with lavender scented bubbles. She sat on the edge of the recessed tub with razors and a mirror. She lathered up her pussy with expensive conditioner and brought the mirror down between her legs.

They had a no-door policy in their love nest, complete access to each other at all times. Here they fucked day and night, never tiring of new places to make love or techniques to try on each other.

He walked in on her and smiled at the strong concentration on her face. "What are you doing there?" She smiled, always so happy to be able to gaze at him with the deep lust that was constant. "Working on a surprise for you."

He knelt down besides her, laying out a towel.

"Would you like some help?"

"Sure."

He laid her back on the towel and lathered her up. With strong and sure strokes, he put the blade to flesh. He loved seeing every inch of her and the sublime position she offered him. He ebbed with the razor and flowed with the conditioner, rubbing her more than required in this barber task.

She was blown away by the intimacy of this act.

He dried her with a towel and carried her to the fainting couch, a favorite piece of fuck furniture. The length of the couch and the ridged side provided comfort for a variety of positions.

This time he chose to take her on her back. He placed her right leg on the back cushion, opening her entire sex to him. He admired his work as he drove his hard cock into the newly shaved fresh cunt.

She adored the sensation. After they went back to the tub to scrub up for the next adventure.

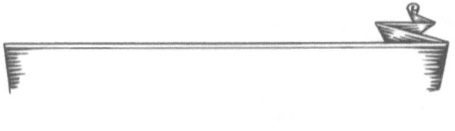

The Buffet

Dylan told her he had a new experience for her to try. She listened intently. Nadailia trusted him completely. He said she would not be in control of the experience but it would be liberating for her. He described what he had in mind. At first it frightened her. Then it titillated her. He gave her the day to think about it. She did. She considered it a little scary, usually the most intense sexual experiences are infused with an element of fear. She said she would do it. Dylan hugged her tightly and whispered softly in her ear, "That's a good girl."

"I'll have a key waiting at the front desk of that opulent hotel you love. Go there and relax. I will have someone come to the house tonight at 7 o'clock to help prepare you." Nadailia spent the day in delicious anticipation. She let her mind race. She alternated between wanting to call this off and wanting to get it started immediately. She stayed wet all day. She was desperate to touch herself and relieve some of the tension, Dylan had given her explicit orders not to cum.

She took a shower. She paced. She tried to listen to music and read. Nothing could clear her mind of what he had planned for her. Her nipples stayed hard all day to the point they were aching. She gave up on wearing panties; she was soaking them through in minutes. Her labia stayed constantly engorged, and her clit was super sensitive even to the air. She had never had this type of reaction. Anticipation was truly the greatest aphrodisiac.

At 7:00 pm sharp, she heard a knock on her door. She opened the door to two beautiful, six-foot-tall twin blond women, one holding a black roller suitcase. They both had perfect bodies, wearing matching outfits. Black, short, stretch cocktail dresses. Their tanned legs tapered down to six-inch heels that had straps wrapping up their ankles. They each wore wide rhinestone collars. Their hair was swept back into high ponytails. They said "Hi!" at exactly the same time and smiled.

Blonde Number One said, "My name is Andi." Blonde Number Two said, "My name is Brandi." Nadailia beckoned them in. "We are here to prepare you," said Andi.

"Come in. I'm all yours," Nadailia closed the door behind them.

"OK, first of all, take your clothes off," said Brandi. Nadailia opened her robe and dropped it on the bed. She was wearing a see-through black negligee. She pulled it over her head and put it on top of the robe. She stood naked in front of the two strangers. They ran their eyes over every inch of her body, looked at each other and smiled approvingly.

Andi headed to the bathroom and started the water in the whirlpool tub. Brandi led Nadailia into the bathroom where Andi had filled the tub with hot water and lavender bubble bath. They both helped Nadailia up the marble steps and down into the whirlpool. Once she was seated, they had Nadailia lean her head back on a rolled up towel, and they placed another towel over her eyes. Soft music played in the bathroom speakers. After a few minutes of sitting with her eyes covered, Nadailia felt the water move. She reached up and lifted the towel from her eyes. Both twins had undressed and were entering the tub. They had identical bodies. Every private place was like a clone image of the other. Both shaved, both had exactly the same shaped vulva and labia.

One sat in the soapy water between her legs and the other worked her way behind her. They scooted as close to her as possible.

The one between her legs was touching her pussy against Nadailia's. The one behind pressed her breasts to Nadailia's back and reached around her to pull her sister into Nadailia until her sister's nipples were touching Nadailia's. If this was "preparation," Nadailia was 100 % for it.

The sister in front kissed Nadailia on the mouth. Nadailia melted. She tasted like oranges. They held Nadailia like this for five minutes. Then as if on cue, they both disengaged. They were all business as they used the body wash over every inch of Nadailia. Their fingers were strong and probing as they cleaned her vagina and her anus.

Satisfied with their work, they stood and pulled Nadailia to her feet. She was glad they were holding on to her, because she did not trust her legs to hold her up. They used the gentle spray of the detachable showerhead to rinse all the soap from their bodies and from Nadailia's.

Once rinsed off, they helped her step out of the tub. They removed a huge white fluffy bath towel from the towel heater and wrapped it around her. The heat on her nipples almost pushed her over the edge. They dried her off and walked her out of the bathroom.

The twins, still naked, sat her in front of the huge lighted mirror and carefully and professionally applied her makeup. They styled her hair similar to theirs in a swept back ponytail. The girls were experts at hair and makeup, and in no time Nadailia could barely recognize herself. She was movie-star beautiful.

One of the naked blondes, Nadailia had lost track of which was which by now, opened the black roller bag and removed several items.

The first was a stretch smooth black dress. They had Nadailia hold her arms up over her head, and they pulled the tight dress over her naked body. It took several minutes of adjusting, once in position the dress fit her like a glove.

The dress was cut to expose her breasts and had extra elastic panels that pushed them up and together from the sides. Her tits seemed to be floating, sticking straight out. The dress flowed tightly down her thighs but was cut above her pubic bone in the front and above her ass in the back.

The matching four black leather bands from the case. They installed one on each wrist and one on each ankle. Each leather band had a chrome steel ring attached with rivets.

The matching leather collar with a chrome ring was fastened around her neck. She lifted her feet, one at a time, on to a chair and put on black Coco Chanel heels. As she stood with one heel on the ground and the other the foot in the in the chair, one of the blondes noticed at her soaking wet pussy. She looked up at Nadailia then back to her pussy and swiped the moisture from it with her two fingers. She looked Nadailia in the eye and smiled as she sucked the wetness from her fingers.

The girls stood back, crossed their arms, and nodded approvingly. The twins had both somehow dressed and reapplied their own makeup while preparing Nadailia.

"Are you ready?" they asked in unison.

Nadailia, not sure of her voice, nodded her head.

They walked her to the door, stopping before opening it.

They leaned in from opposite sides and gently kissed Nadailia at the same time, one on each cheek.

One of the blondes held the last item from the suitcase in front of Nadailia and raised her eyebrows in a question.

Nadailia nodded, and the blonde put the blindfold over Nadailia's eyes.

They opened the door and walked her down a long hallway to a private elevator. She could hear people in the hall and knew they could see every inch of her. Her tits out and up, her exposed pussy bare in front and her round ass exposed in the back. At this point, she didn't care. All day waiting, the astounding last hour with these two beautiful loving creatures, and the anticipation of what was to come made her bulletproof. She was in another realm. She was a goddesses. Beautiful, strong, invincible.

They led her to the main dining room. They were alone. They removed her blindfold and she saw the opulent surroundings.

A long buffet table with every type of food known. Tables of wine and Champagne all waiting for consumption. There was a six-foot space in the middle of the buffet table. It had a horizontal x-shaped fixture like a St. Andrew's Cross. The legs of the cross had snap links attached to them. The cross was padded with foam and covered in black leather.

The girls helped Nadailia up a set of stairs and onto the cross. She laid down, stretched her arms above her head, and they snapped each wrist cuff into the links. They did the same for each leg.

Nadailia was now spread eagle in the middle of the table.

She was the centerpiece for the buffet.

The girls adjusted her dress to best display her tits and show off her bare pussy.

They attached a circular fixture over each breast. The fixtures circled low on her breasts and had sides that were the same height as her nipples, making a bowl out of each breast with her tit and nipple in the center. They took a tray with short legs on it and centered it over her stomach. The legs reached the table under her, so the tray was positioned barely above her stomach. The tray stopped at the top of her pubic bone, leaving her wet pussy exposed. The two final trays were placed, one over each thigh. The trays' short legs allowed the trays to balance on the table and clear the tops of her thighs.

After removing the steps, the twins brought food items to place on the three trays on her stomach tray they place small smoked sausages. On her thighs, a variety of cheeses.

They poured warm dip into each of her breast bowls, covering the ends of her rock-hard nipples. The feeling was exquisite. The girls moved to her head, kissed her on the cheeks again, and asked, "Ready?" This time Nadailia found her voice and answered in a sex-stoked throaty tone,

"Siempre."

The girls reattached her blindfold and placed a black stretch gag over her mouth.

Nadailia drifted blissfully.

She heard the main doors open, and the crowd began to enter. They all headed straight to the centerpiece. She heard comments like "She's amazing!" and "How beautiful!" and "The best ever!" Soon they began to eat from the buffet.

She could feel the movement of the trays of food on her as the diners removed pieces of cheese. The feeling of the food being drug through the dip on her breasts was indescribable, every dip raking her hardened nipple.

The diners began to take the delicate, small sausages from her stomach tray. She felt the heat from their hands. Without warning they began to dip the small sausages into her soaking wet pussy and place the dripping meat in their mouths. Nadailia, suffering from sensory overload, road this cosmic pleasure-train to oblivion.

Entanglement Revealed

N adailia sat cross-legged in her overstuffed chair on the porch and watched the rainfall. Low gray clouds overflowed and spilt their cool liquid on the earth. A soft blanket, worn but thick and smelling of him, was wrapped around her shoulders, keeping the damp chill at bay. She liked the rain. It walled out the rest of the world. It encapsulated her, partitioned her and gave her a sense of control in the small cocoon she created with her blanket. She sipped her red wine and allowed the smooth buzz to wash over her. The alcohol flooded her brain, allowing her to release thoughts she would normally repress. Some good, some not. The rain beat a cacophony of drumbeats on the tin roof of her porch. The water flooded off the gutter-less roof in a sheet and splashed to the ground, making a narrow divot line in the mud outlining the edge of the roof.

Occasionally there was thunder in the distance. She couldn't see the lightening associated with the deep rumble. It seldom rained here, much less produced a thunderstorm. Whenever she was home and a thunderstorm was forecast, she turned off her phone, stripped off her clothes, wrapped herself in her warm blanket and sat on the porch in anticipation of witnessing nature display her release of tension. She floated and drifted, searching the corners of her consciousness for fun contemplations, new ideas or pleasing memories. Occasionally she smiled to herself and recalled a pleasant memory. Dylan. That is the only place her mind went. Dylan. She felt a tingle of desire and a sexy thought. It always made her grin.

They say that an association can be triggered by any of the five senses. Tonight it was the fruity smell of this particular red wine. As she lifted the glass to her nose, she flashed back on the amazing night she had spent as the buffet centerpiece. She rested her head on the back of the soft chair and let the memory of that night take her. Just like he did.

The replay in her mind unfolded like she was watching a movie, in color. She could almost feel his touch. His hot breath on her neck, his hard body pressing against her. She loved having the ability to relive such moments. The storm crashed around her while she drifted into his arms. Her line of consciousness blurred. She wasn't even aware that her hand had found its way downward and that she had her middle finger inside her. Rubbing in a slow circle. Her wetness provided lubrication, allowing her fingers to glide over her most sensitive parts. The memory of him now overpowering and occupying most of her brain. She slowly dissolved back into human form again and drifted off to sleep – the peaceful sleep that only the truly sated know. She was in love. It knocked her into full consciousness.

Text

N: Dylan, it's raining and thundering.
You know what that does to me.
Get home.
Now.
D: Oh sweet girl, I am on my way.
What is on your passion menu tonight?
N: Ravaging you.
D: No specifics?
N: I have an idea.
Get home.

Under The Cherry Tree

They where dinning out at a white tablecloth restaurant. They got there early and were excited that Stu and Lauren where joining them. Nadailia decided to be bold when the two were late and slipped under the table.

She released Dylan's cock from his pants and listened as he ordered the wine. She took him in her mouth and began to suck hard with a powerful suction meant to bring him to climax fast. Her hand was circled around the base of his cock, pumping in harmony with her mouth. He thanked the waitress for the bread.

Just when he was ready to blow, she applied pressure to the spot between his balls and asshole. It stopped the ejaculate, he had an orgasm. After his electric event, she put him back in his pants and moved up to her seat. She kissed him on the cheek as Stu and Lauren sat down joining then.

"Why are you two grinning like that?" asked Lauren, who was up to speed with their frequent and public escapades.

"Just excited about the meal!"

Lauren explained that this restaurant was born out of a desire to turn an empty space into a gathering spot full of life and the enticing scents of vogue, yet traditional cuisine. They ordered a bottle of Justin 2008 Isosceles and sucked down a dozen Kumamoto oysters. The sauces with the oyster rang divine. Shaved ice sprinkled with red peppers made the taste of the ocean sing, as did the mignonette sauce.

They moved on to the scattered sashimi, assorted wild local fish with a citrus soy sauce plated on kimchi, with pickled ginger to cleanse the palate between bites. Nadailia was falling in love with the wild tuna tartar, with its dab of Dijon mustard sauce, flavorful micro greens, soft avocado and bits of mandarin oranges. This dish surpassed excellence. The next course was red-pepper crab cakes. Three little cakes all bursting with a spicy avocado sauce and grilled corn salsa. A Spanish guitarist playing expertly in the corner only heightened their experience.

The last dish was a foodie's dream. Duck confit crepes, thin pancakes wrapped around delectable duck that had been reduced in olive oil, and served with hoisin sauce. It was decorated with scallions and crispy duck cracklins. This dish defied their expectations and seized their taste buds.

The clever banter of Lauren and Stu were lost on Nadailia and Dylan, who seemed to exist in their own sex-soaked, passion-filled world. They barely spoke to anyone but each other. It was clear they were in love.

After the meal, they couldn't stand to be apart one minute more and drove home fast. She ran to him and held him as if he were her lifeline. They fell to the bed, rolling, touching, exploring.

He mounted her and entered her slowly, gazing into her perfect face that was full of bliss. He could not believe this beauty was his. He said, "No one else will ever touch you again. You belong to me now." He loved her gently, sweetly. They both had their eyes wide open, basking in each other and in the glow of the moon.

Text

D: Thank you for last night.

N: It was more than an appetizer under the table.

D: It was perfect. I found it hard not to fuck you last night at the restaurant.

D: Now THAT would be a whole new level.

N: Yes. Completely on fire here.

D: Wet too?

N: Yes. Completely dripping.

D: I swear that behavior used to scare me.

Now I don't give it a second thought.

I would have rammed my dick in you before you could even think about it.

N: So with all that stimuli, will all that imagination run dry? Do you think we will get bored with each other?

D: Never.

N: My need for you is only heightened each time we are together.

D: Love this.

N: I need your touch, your tongue, your fingers, your cock.

It is the only way I will survive.

D: Sweet.

N: It is like I can't breathe.

I don't eat, I don't sleep. I fuck you and text you about fucking you.

Thank you for that gift.

I will never be able to repay it.

D: I have never allowed myself to trust another human being like this.

It is scary but wildly erotic.

New Plateaus

"**N**adailia, you are only successful lately because I have you so sexed up."

Although his intentions were pure, Dylan had crossed a line by doing his psychobabble on her.

She was telling him how each business venture was succeeding, marveling about how no one said no to her anymore. She was ecstatic that even her business life was full of happiness and joy. He tried to take credit for it.

"It is because I handle your brain and fill you with sex. That is why you are now so powerful. Men sense these things."

"Are you fucking kidding me?" was all she said as she stormed out of the kitchen.

She decided he needed to be punished. Although they were lovers and trusted each other completely with their bodies, he didn't know anything about her past. And she knew little or nothing about his. So for him to tell her that her sexed up state was simply her finally getting confidence was absurd and infuriating. He tried to back-pedal and explain, the damage had been done.

She needed to punish him, so the next time he wanted to push his beliefs on her, he would remember the pain, keep his mouth shut and only whisper sweet nothings.

He couldn't tell that she was mad. She smiled sweetly like she normally did when he arrived home. After the meal, she whispered, "Let's try something new."

Always up for new pleasure, Dylan readily agreed.

She pushed him back on the bed with her foot, her long legs enticing him immediately. With the grace of an athlete, she handcuffed his hands together over his head. These were not leather-lined or fur-lined handcuffs; these were military-grade, high-quality steel handcuffs.

Then she covered his eyes with a heavy mask and put a ball gag in his mouth. He was more excited then scared as his hard-on grew.

Then she took a hard edge and bit him on the neck while whispering, "Don't ever tell me how I am to feel again."

He was startled at the seriousness of her order.

She had a black leather paddle that adorned her bedroom wall, and he thought it was a piece of art. When he felt it slap against his nipples, he let out a cry.

Each time she hit him, he felt a surge of pain, pleasure and fear. It was wildly erotic.

He was bound and blind, so he couldn't tell where she would hit next.

After each strike, she would stroke his cock, keeping him in a constant state of arousal.

She placed something on his cock that encapsulated it, all the way to the base. After it was secured, he heard a snap, and then it tightened around his cock like a blood-pressure cuff. When he thought it would break him in two, it released. He was moaning and begging through the ball in his mouth. She tortured him with the cuff for what seemed like an hour.

She grabbed him and moved his handcuffs to the bed, flipping him onto his stomach and pulling his knees up so he was in a cat's cradle position. The cuff was still on his cock making him dizzy and crazy.

She arrived from behind, she whacked him hard first, and then more gently. The fear/ pain/ pleasure sequence started to flood his brain. As she whacked, the cuff tightened. He was losing all sense of himself and existed for this pleasure. She poured a cold liquid on his ass and rubbed it. It burned as it warmed. Then she coated his asshole with the liquid, lubing and rubbing as he relaxed his tight muscles. He had had some ass play before, in this position it frightened him. She inserted a hard object and whispered, "relax" in his ear. When he did, she rammed it into him, as the cuff on his cock tightened. A flash of pain ripped through his brain, his body loved this. She massaged his prostrate, activating a subterranean feeling at the core of him. This was a new sensation. She rotated the butt plug as the cuff imbibed him. He was about ready to explode, a new orgasm coming from deep inside him, when she suddenly stopped. She withdrew the plug, flipped him on his back, took off the cuff from his cock and removed his blindfold.

She stood over him with the leather paddle in her hand. The seriousness of her passionate lesson shone in her deep blue eyes, as if passion had changed her eye color.

"Look at me. Do not ever analyze me or tell me what I am feeling again, or this will be your punishment."

She turned and left him on the bed, still hard, handcuffed and gagged.

The next day, Dylan woke up pissed, yet yearning. He didn't understand her punishment, at the same time his body hummed for more. His first course of action was to defy her. Like a petulant child he went to Taco Bell and binged on mystery-meat burritos and chemically processed cheese. Even the lettuce tasted like it was made in a test tube. They had a policy of no fast food, as they dined as much on each other as real food. Then he bought a bag of Doritos and a box of Twinkies and sat it at his workstation munching as if it were no big deal. She walked into the kitchen smiling, her eyes turned stormy when she saw the junk food.

"What the fuck is that doing in my kitchen?"

He smiled, happy to have gotten under her skin so quickly.

"First this is MY kitchen, and second, these are my snacks."

"You are kidding, right?" She stood, hands on her hips, poised for a fight. The staff scattered, as they knew this pair's history of loud and passionate fights over nothing.

"I wanted to show you the new dessert menu," Dylan said.

She picked up the menu, glanced down it quickly and threw it at his head. He ducked, and it hit the copper pans, making a cacophony of noise.

"No Fucking Lava Cake on my menu!" storming out the door. The staff had taken to calling her "Stomp, stomp, slam, slam."

They met over wine that night to have a talk. Dylan was pacing.

"Why are we together? It seems all we do is fuck and fight."

Nadailia looked at him incredulously. "Short answer: Because we are alike."

He didn't accept her brush-off as an answer. "As you know, the sex play is fun, it's not just that. We are passionate about each other."

Nadailia looked at him like a child. "Fine, you want the long answer? Because I believe that life is about exploration. That new people and circumstances come into our life to enrich it."

"So I am some project?" Dylan looked hurt, "I am drawn to you. I don't even know if I know what it is? Besides, you make me happy and crazy. I am a little afraid to know what this relationship is."

Nadailia tried to take him seriously, as he was clearly perplexed. He continued,

"I do believe that this will last for the rest of our lives. That we will be friends and confidants forever. I believe that it is important to open your heart to new kinds of love and exploration."

"While that is sexy and sweet."

"And also true."

"I am afraid. I don't understand this. Now you know my fear."

"I do not think that passion ignited is wrong. You and I deserve this. We have been loyal and are passionate souls. To deny this would be torture and stupid. Nothing about this scares me, and it should. I trust you like someone I have known for decades. And I want you. Not your stuff or anything. Just the Island of Dylan."

Dylan seemed placated by this. "Let's continue to play this out."

"Just try and stop me."

Text

D: You are my oasis.

N: I like that. Oasis. It can be our code word.

D: Perfect!

N: Oasis: A beautiful respite from the harsh realities of life. You are so sexy and sweet. I have fallen for you completely.

D: Why?

N: Well, you make me horny.

D: So for you it's sex?

N: No, much more. Friendship, camaraderie, trust and more.

D: And more?

N: And turning you into a sex zombie.

D: We will have to load-test that.

N: I can blow you every hour, for 20 hours, taking you deep into my throat each time.

D: I thought we weren't going there today; I have a party of 60 tonight. (I love it.)

N: Then have you fuck me in every way, hole and position, and then repeat. You will orgasm, but not cum. that will build a power in you like nothing you have experienced.

D: I'm all yours.

N: I swooned.

D: Ok, so I get it. Call me naive. Or in love.

Or both.

N: I like both.

The Climax

She walked over to his writing table. He was immersed in his menu and wine pairing puzzles. He had been scribbling for hours, never even looking up.

She stood by the edge waiting for him to feel her presence. When he looked up- she heard the sharp intake of his breath. She was wearing the black corset; breasts pushed up from the tight boning perched on edge, hard nipples exposed and at attention. And she had on those long pearls. Those pearls that made him hard because he knew she meant to wrap them around his dick as she sucked him.

He shook his head as if to erase her from his mind. She smiled and straddled him. Now he saw she had no panties and was clean-shaven. While the dish he was working on still swirled in his head, his body responded.

She kissed his neck and slid down his trunk like a python unzipping his pants and freeing his hard cock. His brain was beginning to slow down and catch up to what she was doing to his body as she swallowed him.

The sight of her red hair bobbing between his legs- brought him present. And then she wrapped the pearls around the base of his cock. The cold hard beads conflicting with her hot breath and soft tongue.

He threw his head back and abandoned himself to her. She worked him for a long time, taking him to the edge and then backing down so he could ride the high of the pleasure. She was never in a hurry to finish, always thinking about ways to keep him in this erotic desire place.

They moved into the bedroom, his eyes burning with desire. Dylan lay on top of Nadailia and entered her deeply. He couldn't take his eyes off her, his heart felt as if it would burst. For the first time he knew, he would love her forever, and she was his. Nadailia was surprised by the intensity of his look, the electricity coming off him felt like a blanket of light. She relaxed and let the ride envelope her. She could feel his heart beating, see his soul through his eyes, and then feel him deeply inside her. It felt as if this was the first time, so much energy and color but also a new thing; love. The pure love of abandoning herself to him and only him.

And that is when it happened, the bolt of energy, the feeling like she died and went to heaven. A mammoth tsunami of a wave breaking in her soul. Her toes curled, her heart stopped, he spine felt electric. She heard someone screaming. It was her. She couldn't help herself and didn't care. Release was all that mattered. Sweet beautiful relief. She abandoned herself to the sensation. All her senses heightened. Every inch of her skin sensitive, feeling each molecule of air that washed over her. Her surroundings were a blur. Darkness, then light flashed inside her body. Then. Calmness. Peace. A sense of fulfillment. An emotional balance. No worldly problem could pierce this shield of completeness.

It seemed to go on forever, it took her over the edge of sanity to a place of pure bliss. Her first orgasm. She had thought she had had one before, this was what the poets write of, now she had tasted it. She was, for first time in her life, completely consumed.

The Fight

I t started in the kitchen, again. They were screaming at each other
over important issues, such as trash receptacles and tomatoes. The
fight seemed as if it had been going on for three days.

Nadailia had spent the night with Lauren, leaving her own
mansion in a fury. He had driven them home from a dinner out
with some employees who were moving on and opening a wine bar.
During dinner, Dylan drank too much and acted like a dick. She was
pissed. On the drive home, he provoked her.

"You ready to fight now?" he asked, like it was the best thing in
the world to him. She did not answer but seethed in the passenger
seat. As they approached the house, he picked at her some more.
"Did you have to wear that?" When he got no reaction, he bounced
her new car off the trash receptacles in front of their house. Now she
was nuclear pissed.

He jumped out of the car and repeated, "You ready to fight
now?" She knew she could kill him, so she jumped into the driver's
seat and sped off to Lauren's house.

All night he texted and called her. She ignored every one. Lauren
calmed her with wine and girl trash-talk, she was still pissed in the
morning. She had an early meeting, so she borrowed a suit from
Lauren. Even though it was two sizes too big, it was better then
seeing Dylan.

She avoided his kitchen. Midmorning he appeared in her office. He had a rose, a card and a box of chocolates. He placed them on her desk and said, "Do you want to talk?"

He looked scared and hurt. She loved him and did not want to hurt him, this fighting had to stop. In the beginning, they could fuck the fights out of their systems. Now he seemed to want to fight.

"We will talk about it tonight. I have a full day and no time for these high emotions."

He looked even more hurt and, placing his hands on her desk, leaned in and said, "Fuck you and your full day. I am done."

He stormed out of her office, and she followed him to his kitchen.

At the door she picked up a pan and threw it at him.

The staff dispersed quickly.

She threw another.

"What the fuck is wrong with you?" She threw another.

"Why are you picking fights with me?"

He ducked and screamed, "Because I want to marry you!"

She stopped mid-throw.

"That's no way to win a fight!"

"I'm serious." Dylan was now cowering in the corner.

"You're nuts." She threw another pan at his head.

Dylan looked at her seriously. "I want to get married, and I want to do it now!"

Nadailia stopped throwing.

"This is how you propose? You fight with me for weeks? And then mid-fight you say you want to marry me? What the fuck is wrong with you?"

"I know I am screwed up nine times past Sunday, I do want to marry you. Right now."

Nadailia was flabbergasted.

"If I do get married again, it will be forever. We will talk about it. Let's table this ridiculous fight until tonight."

"So you don't love me? You don't want to marry me?"

"That is not at all what I said. Get in there and start cooking. We will finish this tonight."

After the restaurant finished service, they met at the Consumed bar. He brought a plate of Sticks and Stones. The dish was as appetizing to the eyes as it was to the palate. He poured a glass of Kynsi Chardonnay as he took her on a culinary tour of her plate.

"This is a dish to wake up your taste buds to prepare them for the next course. On the bottom are crispy and sweet candied pecans and almonds ground to a dust. Then we have tiers of all the flavor and texture centers. First, creamy burrata cheese, a mozzarella ball stuffed with savory cream for softness. Next, for sweetness, we have Seckel pear and Thai mango. Hot is represented by thinly sliced red, purple and white radishes. This is topped with Bloom microgreens and a champagne vinaigrette."

She loved seeing his passion on the plate, and as she tried the dish, her anger disappeared. For the first time, she realized she completely loved this man, down to her core, and she knew she would forever. This surprised her, as she had never felt this kind of overwhelming love.

She looked deep into his eyes. "Was this an apology meal?"

"I have always felt that cooking for others was a great act of compassion and love, a gift that satisfies and nourishes both the body and the spirit. So, yes, this is me saying I am sorry and I love you."

She took his hands and looked him squarely in the eye, "I love you too. Shall we take this to the next level?"

He smiled, "Let's get married. Right now. Let's hop on your jet to Reno and get married."

She laughed, mocking him. "We can talk about it later. This isn't how it is done."

He was hurt, thinking she would love the idea of getting married when they felt like it. No rules, no audience, just them.

"What are you, afraid? Don't you love me?"

"Of course I love you, this isn't the way you do it."

" Are you chicken?" He began to flap his arms with his palms tuck under his armpits. "Are you chicken? Buck, buck, buck." He continued in a circle, repeating his poultry sounds.

She was both amused and terrified by this man and his current behavior. He kept flapping his arms like a chicken, and she saw the entire staff peeking through the dinning room doors. Thinking she needed to move the fight out of the kitchen or they would be on the headline news tomorrow, she screamed, "Fine. Let's go get married."

He stopped mid-flap and smiled. Dylan took out his phone and dialed. She heard him tell her pilot to get the jet ready; they were leaving for Reno in 20 minutes.

Nadailia thought he would eventually calm down and the wild marriage proposal would be forgotten. They jumped in the car, slammed the doors and drove to the airstrip. She was afraid to talk to him, as another fight was more than she could take. As they boarded the plane, the pilot said, "Hello, what is the destination?"

Dylan answered quickly, "Reno, and we are getting married."

The pilot smiled at this until Nadailia shot him a look. Dylan watched the exchange and asked him, "She should marry me, right?"

The pilot, knowing there was no way to keep both passengers happy, decided to tell the truth. "Absolutely!"

They landed at Reno-Tahoe Airport, and a limousine was waiting on the tarmac. It whisked them to the courthouse. Dylan went up the window, Frisbee-tossed his driver's license to the clerk and declared, "I am going to marry this woman and marry her now!"

The marriage license was issued in less than 15 minutes, and he pulled her across the street to a tacky chapel. Dylan marched in and questioned a balding Elvis, "How much to marry us right now?"

"30 bucks, Dude."

Nadailia had remained silent on the airplane and at the courthouse. She was not going to continue to be silent. She grabbed his arm and took him outside.

"I am not going to get married again unless it is forever. If you are serious about this, we need to talk about it. Since this subject has never even come up in our time together, I think some thoughtful conversation is in order."

Dylan looked at her, and with all seriousness started flapping his arms and bucking like a chicken again. "What are you, scared? Don't you love me? Buck, buck, buck, buck." He continued his display on the sidewalks of the Biggest Little City.

Nadailia bellowed, "Fuck it, let's get this done, I have to go back to work."

The ceremony took five minutes, and they did not have a ring so they used a twist tie from the rolled-up marriage certificate. The chapel staff snapped a photo, in which they both looked astonished.

They jumped back on the plane and went straight to the restaurant, Dylan did make sure they consummated the marriage high over the Sierra Nevada, cementing their Mile High Club membership as man and wife.

Back at the restaurant, Nadailia was sitting in her office, marveling at what had happened when her assistant came in.

"Hey boss, what did you guys do for lunch?"

"I was consumed."

Epilogue

Through their words and an exchange of food, they both found true passion. They created magic, a legacy, a story, and a recipe for love.

Thank you for reading my book! I hope you had as much fun reading it as I did writing it. If you enjoyed Consumed, won't you please take a moment to leave me a review at your favorite retailer? Thank you, and remember: Live Well and Eat Well!

Teri Bayus, Author

Acknowledgments

As the summer of 2014 approached, I searched for my summer read. After weeks of searching, I decided that instead of reading one, I would write a fun summer romp. As a food critic for the last 20 years, I decided that blending my two favorite activities (sex and food) would make a fun novel. I hope you enjoy reading Consumed as much as I enjoyed writing this book.

As with any artistic endeavor, it takes a village. I am beyond lucky to be surrounded by people who love and grasp my words, my gypsy soul. To my writing group (Dove, Janice, Jennie, Steve, T and Tia) who cheered me on and made me read aloud these naughty words. Whose wine soak laughter and love drove me to finish this work, when even after draft 59 I was still unsure, you told me to keep going and follow my gut. I love you all more than I will ever be able to express.

To my family who will forever be embarrassed that I wrote this book, I say remember; Dad and I had a fun summer! To my husband, Gary who put up with a year of me talking about butt plugs, whips and texting, while he tried to behave like a businessman.

To my chefs who shared their dishes and creative influences, I thank you for all the imaginative preparation and love you put into each recipe. To my edit Tiffany Porter, who had the impossible task of checking all my food spelling, (and I am sure there will still be fallout on whether it is chile or chili) you are the best editor with a kind patient heart for crazy writers.

About The Author:

Teri Bayus[1] is a Business Owner, Author, Teacher, Food and Film Columnist, and Keynote Speaker. Selling her first screenplay in 2000[2], she has finished several novels, but Consumed will be the first published. Along with a weekly column in the Tolosa Press[3], which she has been writing for over 12 years, she writes for regional travel magazines and blogs about her culinary adventures[4]. She teaches creative writing classes at the local colleges[5], as guiding new writer's[6] gives her enormous gratification.

She started her adult live by leaving college and joining the circus. She is currently the Host of the TV Travel/Chef show – Taste Buds[7] (which can be seen on Central Coast Now[8]) and is the Director of the Central Coast Writer's Conference[9] (www.centralcoastwritersconference.com).

---

1. http://www.teribayus.com

2. http://www.revelationsent.com

3. http://www.tolosapress.com

4. http://teri-culinarytourism.blogspot.com

5. http://www.cuesta.edu/communityprograms/

6. http://theyearoftheteri.blogspot.com

7.   http://tastebudscc.blogspot.com

8.   http://www.centralcoastnow.tv

9.   http://www.cuesta.edu/communityprograms/writers-conference/

Her greatest joy is spending time with her grandchildren where she learns daily that the mind of a child is an infinite universe of imagination and delight.

More information at teribayus.com[10].

---

10.   http://www.teribayus.com

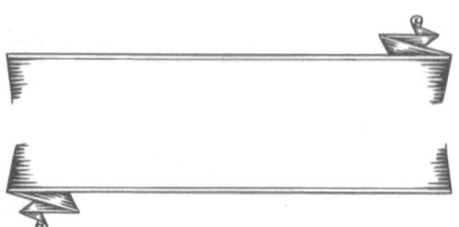

C onnect With Teri
Email: livewell@teribayus.com
Website: http://www.TeriBayus.com
Facebook: Teri Bayus[1]
You Tube: Teribayus[2]

1.   https://www.facebook.com/pages/Teri-Bayus/

2.   https://www.youtube.com/user/Teribayus

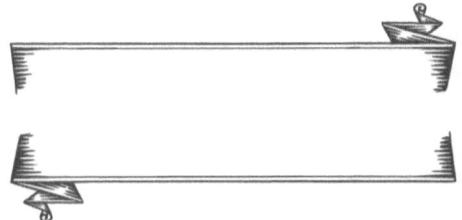

Don't miss out!

Visit the website below and you can sign up to receive emails whenever Teri Bayus publishes a new book. There's no charge and no obligation.

https://books2read.com/r/B-A-EYOV-KZBGC

BOOKS 2 READ

Connecting independent readers to independent writers.

About the Author

Teri Bayus is a writer of words and a builder of worlds.

She has self-published two novels and optioned three screenplays and two teleplays. Her current novel, *The Greatest Of Ease* (www.TheGreatestOfEase.com), is about her time as a trapeze artist in a traveling circus. Her previous novel, *Consumed* (http://www.amzn.to/1jFEeQH), is in the genre of culinary erotica. She has a nonfiction book, *The Universal Conspiracy* (www.theuniversalconspiracy.com), about how the universe collaborates to make everyone's dreams a reality.

Before the plague, she hosted and produced the TV show *Taste Buds* (www.tastebuds.tv), highlighting the chefs' talents and restaurants worldwide. She was a food and film critic for twenty years and the executive director of the Central Coast Writers Conference for six years. She has taught writing and marketing classes at colleges and adult education forums.

Her love for inspiring others has brought her to become a professional speaker. She adores sharing her journeys with others by facilitating workshops, classes, and marketing seminars. She is a serial entrepreneur, owning 28 businesses in the last 30 years.

She lives with her husband, a wild entrepreneur, two terrible dogs, and a wonderful cat in Pismo Beach, California.

Please find more information and contact us at www.teribayus.com.

Read more at https://www.TeriBayus.com.

About the Publisher

Siafu Productions is a small independent publisher and marketing firm focusing on underrepresented artists and authors. We publish with a collective of seasoned professionals. We aim to help new authors find their voices, achieve their dreams, and get their books out to the distinguished reading community.

Siafu offers new authors an innovative approach to help their books achieve the most expansive reach. Siafu seeks to guide authors in finding their audience with a comprehensive marketing plan.

You can find more about Siafu on Linkedin: https://www.linkedin.com/company/teri-bayus-siafu-marketing/
www.SiafuProductions.com

Read more at https://www.siafuproductions.com.